REDEMPTION

WENDY MILLION

Stomill Books

Series Information

Reading Order

Book 1 – Retribution (can be read as a standalone)

Book 2 – Resurrection (first part of a duet)

Book 3 – Redemption (second part of a duet)

Get bonus chapters after you've read the complete series:

https://wendymillion.com/bonus-content/

To my husband for his unwavering belief in me.

Chapter One

Finn

When the guard at the maximum-security federal prison comes to tell me I have a visitor, relief floods my chest. Carys's appearance has the same effect on me every single time. One month, near the start of my prison sentence, I told her not to bother coming anymore. So, she didn't. No note through Brad, the lawyer, or any other way for me to know she was fine. I lost my fucking mind. Didn't take long to realize my mistake. Maybe I shouldn't want her here, but it's better to know she's okay than to sit wondering.

The next visitation, I met with her. We didn't mention how I tried to cut her off. That month of sheer panic was enough to put those thoughts out of my head for good. Is it fair? Probably not. She deserves to find someone else, to start over, to make a life for her and her son, Lucas, without me. Doesn't seem to matter how many times I've said that to her, she won't see our situation for what it is.

Pleading guilty to twelve consecutive life sentences to save her from a bunch of trumped-up charges was the right thing to do. I'm glad she's enjoying her life on the outside, and I shouldn't be part of it anymore. I can't seem to make myself say those words. Selfish. We're trapped in an endless loop of fleeting visits.

As soon as I spot the top of her blond head through the glass in the visitation window, my heart thumps, and the tension from being locked in eases a fraction. Just the sight of her does that to me—makes being here both totally worth it and the worst thing I've ever done.

Her amber eyes scan me, and there's the tiniest furrow in her brow. Must be the lovely shade of blue on my cheekbone. As the new guy, I have to prove myself. My reputation precedes me, and everyone wants their shot. Just how hard is he? There's always a bruise on me somewhere—lots of the hits are cheap. This time, the lucky asshole landed a single decent punch before I got him down. When I was pulled off, the guard told me I should be thankful they weren't putting me in isolation. Any other week and I wouldn't have cared, but leading up to visitation days, I mind my temper. My meetings with her are the only thing I give a shit about, and the guards aren't dumb. Doesn't take long to see a pattern.

Carys wants to ask about my bruise. Concern is etched on her face, but she knows I won't answer. What goes on in here won't make her feel any better about the choice I made. Answering to other people all the time—when to eat, when to sleep, when to shit—is slowly eroding my sanity. By some miracle, I've still got her. I'm not tainting our connection with reality. Neither of us can change where I've ended up.

I slide into the seat across from her with the glass partition separating us, and she picks up the receiver. I grab mine and drink her in. Her blond hair is loose, which is the version of her I like best. Reminds me I get the real her, the woman very few other people see.

I clear my throat of the lump that forms when I realize I'll never touch her again. "How was your flight? Did you bring Lucas?"

"We're all here, holed up in the hotel." She gives me a small smile. "I have news."

News? I brace myself for the worst, but I keep my expression neutral. Has she met someone else? Has she realized flying back to America every month is a waste of her time?

"Brad is securing a transfer for you to another facility. A lower-security prison." Her gaze connects with mine. She's trying to communicate something I can't catch. Those nonverbal cues between us are covered in rust. "All you have to do is stay out of any fights for the next week, and we can push the transfer through. Keep a lid on your temper, okay?"

A chuckle escapes me, and I turn away. Her warning isn't funny, but it kinda is. Does she think I go looking for these fights? These assholes find me, not the other way around. The big guys running this place are worried I'm going to make a power play. At some point, I will, once I've determined who I want on my team. That'll take a while. Right now, I want to survive until Carys's next visit. Not much of a life, but it's the only one I've got.

"Why is that funny?" She squares her shoulders and almost glares.

"No reason," I say. "I'll do what I can."

"You'll have more chances." She gives me another meaningful look I can't read. "More opportunities at a medium- or low-security prison."

"They're not going to move me, Carys. I'm a high risk for being an asshole." Normally, I'd be a tremendous risk for a different maneuver, but I don't have the resources or the clout for that anymore. Then it clicks, and my eyes narrow. Is she trying to position me for a breakout?

Her jaw clenches, and she purses her lips. "Money talks. With enough cash, you can do anything."

This time I'm the one struggling to communicate, and I stare at her, hard. "I'm in here to protect you. You got me? So anything that might get you into trouble shouldn't be happening."

The barest hint of a smile. We've landed on the same page, and that makes her happy, but we're reading a different book. I want out of here, but not if she'll have her fingerprints smeared across the jailbreak.

"Having you moved is no problem." She eases back into her chair and twists the bracelet on her wrist. "There's no need to worry about me. I know what I'm doing."

"Bullshit." My nostrils flare, and I lean forward, the glass blocking me from getting too close. "Leave it be."

"Time's up!" The guard behind me moves closer. Carys and I often linger, needing more reminders to call it quits.

This time, she stands up, the receiver still pressed to her ear. She peers down. "Let's get one thing straight, okay? I'll never leave you *be* as long as you're in this prison. You got *me*?"

Another spark of anger flares between us. There's nothing I can do about her choices from in here, and we both know it. The best I can do is refuse the transfer when it comes. "Yeah, I got you. But I'm not letting you fuck up your life."

"We're already there. Now I'm fixing it." Before I can say another word, she drops the receiver in the cradle and slings her purse over her shoulder.

The determined set of her jaw isn't a good sign. Desperation makes people do stupid things. She's likely to literally bulldoze her way into the lower-security prison if she needs to. Neither she nor Jay has the knowledge to pull off a quiet escape.

I pound on the glass, the receiver still dangling from my hand as she walks away. Her ability to end a conversation whenever she wants is infuriating.

"Not a good visit today?" the guard muses.

Seems to be the way things go with Carys lately—drama dogs us. Either she tells me something I don't like, or we stare at each other, wishing we made different choices. When? Who knows? I've been making bad decisions since I crawled out of the womb.

The guard leads me back to the cell, and I catch a couple of guys giving me the once-over. Something is coming, but I don't know what. I'm glad I didn't make any promises to Carys about staying out of trouble. Until I've established my dominance, or someone kills me, there's no peace in here. The last time I had to stay this alert was when I was fighting in The Cage. So much money rode on those fights, that at any moment, a rival might be looking for an advantage. A quick bout in the streets, a cheap round meant to keep me down, was a possibility wherever I went. Never worked—no one could pin me.

I'm twenty years older, but I'm also wiser. Threats are easier to spot now. The energy vibrates off a guy, as though he needs to psyche himself up. Most people telegraph what they're going to do at least a split second before it happens. More than enough time to react. Step out of the way, hit first, or let them punch me because it'll give me a better angle to hit back harder.

The *something* doesn't strike until we're headed to our cells from the mess hall. We're paused at the door to our unit, waiting for the guard to release the lock, the most volatile stage of the walk. My food hasn't even had a chance to digest before the guy behind me hunches his shoulders and telegraphs his move. I may not be able to see him, but instinct kicks in.

He takes a step and swings, and I duck. His knuckles skim the guy's neck in front of me. I spin and pummel the hulking man. *One. Two. Three.* Each uppercut is aimed at nailing his liver. Steal his breath. Sharp, shooting pains should be migrating across his frame. When he cries out and sinks to his knees, I step back. Those rubber legs coming off the liver punch are a bitch. Done right, no one walks away from that body shot.

Once he's moaning on the ground, I throw out my hands and stare at the rest of the block in my line. "Anyone else?"

"All right, Donaghey," the guard says without a trace of humor. "Back to your cell."

He doesn't mean *my* cell. Another guard will be coming to take me to isolation. I might have gotten away with a self-defense claim or at least having the guard ignore the quick scuffle if my cockiness hadn't spilled out. The prison calls the question I asked *inciting violence*. I call it taking care of business.

Later, when the door to my solitary confinement slams closed and the lock clicks into place, I sink into the mattress and run my hand along the top of my short platinum strands. Perhaps Carys had a point about my inability to stay out of trouble.

Chapter Two

Carys

I draw the door closed on the bedroom. Lucas is napping, and I head for the living room. Sofia is out with her girls and Lena at a friend's pool party, so the house is quiet. They've settled into the Cape Verde community, and Jay wants them away from here when our guest comes later. The less any of his family understand regarding our plans, the better. His wife gets why he's so driven to help me—she realizes the type of man she married. His loyalty runs deep.

From the office, Jay emerges. "You're not going to like this." He tucks his phone into his pocket.

"What else is new? The casino, the hotel, or Finn?" Nothing is going smoothly. The confetti bomb in my Chicago office might as well have been real. Every aspect of my life is in pieces. Every time we think we've found a way to slot them together, a piece ends up being a slightly different shape than we expected.

"Finn. My contacts tell me he's already in solitary."

I snort. "Of course, he is." At least he's not in the infirmary. Whenever Jay briefs me on Finn's fights, I fear he'll end up dead or so injured he'll never recover. Finn is a very capable fighter, but the danger never seems to stop. He's not getting any younger. "He's not happy we're trying to break him out."

Jay's eyes bulge out of his head. "Please tell me you weren't talking about a jailbreak at visitation."

"Not exactly," I hedge. There is a chance we might have raised suspicion. As soon as Finn became annoyed, I wasn't as careful. Not bright. He needed a heads-up for the move and to try to make our job easier.

"Carys." His tone is full of warning. "You want him out, I do, too, but we gotta be smart about this. He doesn't need to be told shit until it's happening. Even then, the less he knows, the better."

I tip my chin in defiance. "You're not there. You don't see him with a new bruise every single time. He's not a twenty-year-old punk fighting in The Cage with his dad's mafia empire at his back. I don't—I don't want anything bad to happen. I needed him to understand we're not sitting around doing nothing."

Jay pinches the bridge of his nose. "Now he knows. You never bring up our plans again. If there's something vital he has to know, I've got ways to get that information to him."

"Fine." I slouch into the couch to watch the ocean from the large picture windows facing the water. "When is Evander arriving?"

"Should be here in ten. Dominic said the plane landed a while ago." He wanders to the couches and takes in the view. We sit in silence for a few moments. "Best part of living here is this."

"I enjoy watching your kids out there in the sand, playing in the waves."

"Yeah, they're adjusting well." He half turns. "Sofia's made some friends. If we could just get Finn out and make our business investments line up, we'd be golden."

"We'll get there." I say it with more conviction than I feel. Can we get Finn out? Will all the problems with the casino and hotel come to a stop?

There's a knock at the door, and Jay goes to the entry with a hand on his gun. Though we've been safe here so far, we're still on edge about the package delivered to my office. The "time's up" message could be linked to the switchover of company control from me to my father, or the note might have been in regard to the FBI raid, or the point could be something we haven't figured out yet. We haven't let our guard down. Security isn't extravagant, but we're not taking chances. No one leaves the house without at least one guard.

I rise from the couch when Jay opens the door. Evander Williams is a tall, bulky Black man who has earned his reputation in certain underground circles. An air of confidence wafts in behind him.

I come forward, and my hand is outstretched. "Mr. Williams, I'm Carys Van de Berg."

His palm slides against mine, and his dark gaze searches my face. "My condolences on your asshole father. Based on what I was able to access, he should have been the person to step up for a plea deal." His lips twist. "Not that Finn Donaghey isn't quite a catch for the FBI and CIA. I see why they didn't hesitate on that exchange."

Since Kimi blindsided me, I'm wary of anyone who knows too much. I narrow my eyes and withdraw my hand. "And how is it you can access government documents?"

He chuckles. "How do you think I'm gonna get your boy out? I've got connections in every government organization in the world. You want information? I get it for you. For a price, of course. I don't take a job unless I'm sure the person I'm working with has both the guts and the resources to do what needs to be done. You passed. Congratulations." His deep rumbling baritone has an edgy amusement to it.

All the inquiries we made trying to find the right guy led us back to Evander Williams. Has your daughter been kidnapped by a warlord? Call Evander. A son accused of espionage in North Korea? Call Evander. Want the love of your life free from a high-security prison? Evander is the man. At every turn, his name was coming out of people's mouths.

"You come highly recommended," I admit.

"'Course I do. If you can afford me, there is no one better." His mouth hints at a smile. "Your photos don't do you justice." His expression turns puzzled. "In person, you remind me of someone else. Can't quite put my finger on it."

I shrug and purse my lips. "People tell me I look like my mother." The resemblance is actually uncanny. In photos of my mother when she was my age, we could be twins.

"Perhaps that's it. I've run into your father a few times over the years when I was dealing with time-sensitive issues and needed materials."

Not surprising since my father never had a problem bending munition and firearms laws to suit the needs of his clients. "Come in. Have a seat. Did you want a drink?"

"No." He waves me off as he crosses to a high-backed armchair. "I can't stay long. I have to fly to Nigeria for an ongoing negotiation."

"That kidnapping case?" This morning the news was buzzing about a diplomat's daughter who was taken for ransom.

"Can't say. Discretion and privacy are two of the biggest keys to my position." He grimaces and places his elbows on his knees. "I wanted to talk Finn's release through in person. I don't like having anything in writing in a job like this."

"Understandable," Jay concedes as he sits on the other end of the couch. "What do we need to do?"

"Right now? Nothing. Keep business as usual. I've set the wheels in motion to get Finn moved to a lower-security prison. Once he's there, we'll get the lay of the land. I have contacts in every single federal prison. The American prison system is incredibly flawed, so finding the routes to an exit are likely. As I said on the phone, there are no guarantees in a situation like this."

"If your network is that big," I say, trying to channel Finn, "how do you know every contact is loyal to you?"

Evander chuckles. "They're not loyal to me. They're loyal to the dollar, and I pay well."

While I took similar risks when I extracted Finn from the FBI raid at the Donaghey warehouse in Boston, taking them now seems foolhardy. Money talks, but when there are other people willing to pay more or have better leverage, circumstances can spiral out of control in a hurry. "You've got nothing else on any of these contacts to keep them on your side?"

His mouth forms a tight line. "Depends on the person, the location. You've hired me because I'm the best. I can't say things don't ever tip sideways unexpectedly. That's part of the risk. Also why I'm here—to manage those *oh shit* moments. As much as we can, we mitigate our exposure through cash payments. Generally, the more money, the less we worry."

I swallow. Money isn't an issue, or at least it isn't yet. Even if I have to bankrupt myself, Finn shoved all his assets into a trust for Lucas before he surrendered, so we'll never be completely poor.

"Step one is in progress right now. We'll have him moved soon. I'm finalizing that process in the next day or two. Once he's at another facility, we'll start looking at plans and schedules and routes to get him out. You want this quiet, right?"

"Well." I glance at Jay. "Yes, as quiet as we possibly can." But if we have to blow a hole in the wall and storm the place, I'm not opposed to that either. As long as we return to Cape Verde, alive, and as a family, I'm not complaining. Dead or still in jail aren't options.

Jay raises his eyebrows. "We're open to whatever strategies you want to employ."

Evander nods his head repeatedly, his brow furrowed.

"Finn's in solitary right now. Does that matter?" What if he's already ruined the plan?

"Won't matter. I'll have paid enough they'll move him no matter what." He stands and offers his hand again. "I'll be back in a couple of weeks with more details and a firmer timeline for his release."

We escort him to the door, and Dominic helps him into the waiting car. With a frown, I turn to Jay. "What d'you think?"

He rubs the back of his neck. "Some of it I liked. Some of it makes me nervous."

"He kept saying *released*. He never once mentioned a jailbreak."

"Covering his ass in case we're recording him, I imagine."

"Maybe. I don't know." I rub my cheeks. "There's this tightness in my chest and clawing sensation in my throat, and I don't know if it's hope or dread." A humorless laugh escapes me. "If Finn were here, he'd think we were stupid."

"Nah." Jay chuckles. "If Finn were here, he'd have asked how much the bulldozer was to remove the wall of the prison. Nothing subtle in that man."

I rotate my shoulders, trying to throw off my unease. "Maybe that's all this feeling is—Evander is too subtle compared to the smash-and-grab jobs I'm used to."

"We talked to a lot of people, Carys. If he wasn't the real deal, someone would have known."

From the bedroom, Lucas lets out a long, hungry wail. Tucking my hair behind my ears, I give Jay one last half smile. "You're right," I say. "I'm being paranoid." All the unease and uncertainty are shoved deep when I open the door to greet Lucas.

CHAPTER THREE

Finn

At least in solitary confinement, I don't need my senses on constant alert. That's the only perk to the box. A two-day reprieve from watching my back is a bit like a sensory vacation.

Of course, the real punishment is having to be alone with my thoughts. During the day, it's not so bad. My mind is a projector, and a highlight reel of my greatest hits plays across the cement block wall. Who doesn't love remembering their excellence?

At night, though, something darker streams. I discover my mother has been murdered; Carys clings to me in the interrogation room begging me not to make a choice that's already made; or she lies on the dirty floor of a pub in Ireland on the brink of death. When I wake up shouting, there's no one to hear me. That's the thing about loosening the seal. Thoughts seep in like smoke under a door, choking me, reminding me of how peacefully I slept beside her, however brief that might have been.

When my breakfast is passed through the next morning, the guard says, "Something's coming down the pipe for you, Donaghey."

"Oh yeah?" I take the tray. "Sharing is caring." I smirk.

"Told me to prep you once you're done with your food."

"Prep me?" On my bed, I shovel the porridge and boiled eggs into my mouth. Has Carys managed to have me moved already? Maybe I underestimated her. Or someone. Could Jay do this?

When the breakfast tray is gone, the guard puts on my shackles, and I muse about where I'm going. Would they let me go to a lower-security prison? I've been in a fight almost every day since I arrived. A lot of money would have to change hands to get anyone to sign off on a transfer to a place with *fewer* security measures. Hope stirs in my stomach. If she's managed to get me this far this quickly, then maybe there's something to her escape plan.

The guard radios back and forth with someone about getting me on the bus. "They packed for you," the guard says by way of explanation as we shuffle toward the prison exit used for transfer.

I stifle a laugh. Packed? Like my government-issued toothbrush and my comb? God knows I got nothing else in that cell. "Know where I'm going?" Maybe all she managed was another high-security place. They wanted to put me in the supermax prison at first, but my lawyer was able to argue out of that one.

"They don't tell me shit," he grumbled.

Ahead there's a line of men being clipped into the back of a truck. Guess it'll be shackles for however many hours until we're at another prison. I'm hoping she doesn't opt for a jailbreak out of the truck. Getting tossed around and flipped upside down isn't on my bucket list. Images from *The Fugitive* resurface. Good movie. Not particularly keen to play out parts of it. Still, free is free, and I'm not going to complain if a heist does the trick.

Once we're locked into place, the engine rumbles to life, and we sway with the bumps in the road as we travel. Across from me, a white guy gives me the eye. Not a cue to fight. No, his expression is different. He's trying to decide if he wants to talk to me. I already know I'm not talking. The less people understand about me—beyond my fists—the better off I am.

"You're Finn Donaghey?" The guy's chin flicks toward me like we're buddies.

I stare and don't respond. Unless he's deaf, he knows who I am. The guard said my name as he locked me in. How many men in this prison are named Finn? Ask a stupid question and suffer my wrath.

"Shut the fuck up, Billy," the guy beside me grumbles. "We got hours in this truck before we get to Michigan, and I don't wanna hear you yammering."

Michigan? The only federal facility in that state is a private, mini-mum-security prison. If that's what's happening here, my prospects of escape are quadrupled.

"I got a message for Donaghey, Eduardo," Billy says with an eager voice.

"Yeah?" Eduardo says. "Is it that you're a dumbass? 'Cause anyone who knows you already got that message loud and clear."

I smirk and glance at Eduardo. An attitude I can appreciate.

"When we get there"—Billy ignores my snarky bench mate—"come find me. It's important."

With narrowed eyes, I glare at him. Would Jay or Carys communicate through such an eager kid? There's been nothing discreet about the con-nection he's establishing. The other three guys in the truck will turn over information on us for a shorter sentence or a perk inside in a heartbeat. So stupid to open his mouth with so many crooked witnesses.

"I got nothing to say to you," I tell him.

Billy chuckles. "Right? 'Cause I got shit to say to you. Don't matter. I'll track you down."

Track me down? This guy isn't getting it, but he will if he tries to drag me into something I'm not interested in.

The truck falls into an uneasy silence as we sway in the back. I put my head against the steel wall and let my mind drift to the life I almost had. Carys. Lucas. Cape Verde. Can I reclaim it?

The facility is a vacation resort compared to the high-security prison we came from. No cuffs from place to place. Trips to the yard. No one tries to fight me or intimidate me in the first few hours. In fact, unlike the other facility, no one here seems to know who I am. I've never been much for anonymity, but the reprieve from constant vigilance is nice.

So when Billy comes toward me in the showers a few days after we arrive, my guard is low. In his hand is a shank, and I catch a glimpse of it just before he reaches me. On instinct, I rotate on my toe and aim a right under his jaw. He crumples to the floor, dropping the homemade knife in favor of rubbing his face.

"What the hell?" Billy mutters. Everyone else in the showers has scattered.

We've probably got two minutes before the guards burst in here. I pick up the shank and stand over him. "What the fuck is this? You coming for me?"

"Hell, no." He shakes his head. "Hagen wanted me to deliver a message."

"With a shank?" I keep my face neutral, but inside confusion swirls. Sure, I owe Hagen a few favors, but if the guy has me killed, he's never cashing them in.

"You're indebted to him. He wants Murray dead. I was to give you the weapon." Billy presses on the bruise blooming along his jaw.

I chuckle. "He thinks I'll turn into his errand boy? I'm keeping this." I wag the knife at him. "I'm not killing anyone for Hagen Volkov."

"He's not going to be happy." Billy props his back against the shower wall. "You owe him one."

"I actually owe him a couple, but he screwed me over once, so I'm knocking a favor off. As for the other, you can tell him I'll decide when I'm willing to pay up and what I'll do. He might be your boss, but he sure as shit ain't mine."

"He—he knows a lot of people in here. He'll make your life difficult."

"That might be true, but I've gone from a maximum-security prison to this rinky-dink place in the middle of Michigan. I'm not risking my cushy station for anything. He wants to ask me for other things, I'll consider each on a case-by-case basis. Murder isn't on the table." Carys needs me here, and I'm not making a single move to cause my chance at freedom to leak down the drain.

I riffle through my stuff on the bench. Do I take the shank or hide it in here somewhere? Safest to hide it. No need to get caught with contraband. None of the guards came, even though everyone must have poured out of the shower area like the place was on fire. Wonder how much he paid for this service?

"We're done here," I tell the kid.

"For now." Billy rises. The bump on his chin looks like a rounded egg. "You don't want to cross me, kid."

"I got bigger problems than you."

"I'm *in* here, so the way I see it, there's no bigger problem than me."

"Yeah, well..." He runs his knuckles over his bruise. "Hagen's out there, and I got people I give a shit about out there. So you can do your worst to me. But I'm not letting him do shit to them." He punches the shower door when he leaves.

How many times have I heard someone begging for another person to be spared or for me to go easy on their family? Never moved me. You get into this business, and you know what you're in for. Danger. Murder. Life on the line. And if you're doing it right, a shit ton of money. Other than my younger brother, Lorcan, who could take care of himself, I never had anyone in my life to be dangled over the edge of a building as leverage.

I'm not stupid enough to believe I'm invincible anymore. Billy and I aren't so different. We've both got people on the outside we won't sacrifice. The question is: What'll we do on the inside to keep them safe?

Chapter Four

Carys

Lucas is in front of the big ocean-view windows on a play mat, and I'm on the floor with him. He's finally starting to sleep in longer stretches, so when he's awake, I'm not feeling like such a sleep-deprived zombie. Jay's daughter, Rosa, is beside me, rattling a baby toy to get his attention.

"Come on, Lucas. Roll over," she coaxes.

At six, she's baby obsessed. Her four-year-old sister, Luciana, is in the kitchen making lunch with Lena. Jay is at the casino, Dominic is at the door, and Sofia is reading a book on the couch behind me. The hustle and bustle of the house is a level of domestic bliss I never expected to achieve. There's just one person missing.

When Lucas rocks and falls onto his back again, Rosa does a cheer. "So close. Try again." Using the toy, she leads him toward his stomach. When he tries to grab it and flips onto his tummy, his giggle squeezes my heart.

"Oh my god. He rolled over from his back to his front." I glance over my shoulder at Sofia.

She grins. Her long dark hair is in a ponytail, and her curvy frame is encased in a tank top and shorts. She peers over the top of her book. "Now the fun begins. Diaper changes go from a relatively quiet affair to a progressively bigger battle. Who wants to be on their back when they can be on their front?"

Rosa gets him to go through it again, and we clap. His first laugh, his first roll from front to back and now from back to front, his first tooth, his first solid food—I've gotten those moments thanks to Finn's sacrifice. So every milestone is a flood of happiness followed by the bittersweet realization Finn made each possible.

"Go on." Lena ushers Luciana from the kitchen.

She rings the bell on the island. "Lunchtime!"

Every Sunday, Luciana helps Lena make brunch. When Rosa lifts my son into her arms, I have to quell a moment of panic. She's strong for her age and careful, but he's a sturdy baby and not exactly light. At the highchair, I take him from her to get him buckled in. His tray is already filled with Lucas-sized bites. There isn't a day where I'm not grateful for the village I built in this house with these people.

I slide the tray onto his highchair and smile at Lena. "Thank you."

"Anything for that toothy little face." She runs a finger down Lucas's chubby cheek.

The front door opens, and Jay sheds his sandals before coming into the kitchen. "Just in time." His voice is light, but there's tension around his eyes.

Sofia and I exchange a glance. I brace myself for more bad news about either the hotel or the casino.

"When lunch is done, girls, why don't we set up the sunshade on the beach and have a play?" Sofia says.

He kisses Sofia's temple. "Thanks, babe. When Carys and I are finished talking, I'll come join you."

"Whenever you get a chance." She pats his cheek. "I know there's a lot going on."

While Jay and I have spent significant time together over the years, Sofia and his daughters were more of a shadow than a fully-fledged part of our interactions. With them living here, I see their family dynamics up close and personal. The care they have for each other amazes me. As a kid, my house was fraught with tension. I chalked my parents' problems up to my father's affairs and my brother's long illness and death. But now I wonder whether my mother's desperation to escape her first husband hadn't been the main problem. Had she ever loved my father? Or was he the lesser of two evils?

Chatter happens around me, but I'm lost in my own thoughts. When it's time to clean up, Lena shoos me away. "Go put him down for his nap." She nods at Lucas.

"Are you sure? I feel like I never help."

Lena laughs. "You raise your miracle baby, and I'll keep the kitchen clean." She winks. "Least I can do for giving me a house filled with so much happiness."

Happiness. Tears spring from my eyes, and Lena rubs my back in soothing circles.

"You'll get your happiness."

"That's just it," I say. "I *am* happy and then I feel guilty."

"He wanted you to be happy. Seeing what you've built here, he'd never begrudge you a full life." She gives me a side hug. "And soon, God willing, he'll be here too."

Finn doesn't want God to have anything to do with his fate. He hasn't lived a holy life. "I hope so." We're going to need more than hope to see our plan through. As Evander keeps reminding us, in an escape this complicated, there are a lot of moving pieces. If even one of them misses their slot, the whole jailbreak could fall apart. Depending on whether we're in the planning or execution stage, Finn could be moved to the supermax prison after all. If that happens, Evander says it'll take years before he'll be able to maneuver Finn into a position to try for another break. *Years.*

After washing his face and hands, I pluck Lucas out of the highchair and head to the master bedroom at the back of the bungalow. At the moment, the master acts as our sleeping quarters and the place where I do the most worrying. When the renovations on the house went so well, I expected the same outcome with the casino and hotel. With my son tucked into the crook of my neck, I rock him to sleep. Nothing better than baby snuggles. My heart stretches in my chest. I may not have everything, but I've got him, and that's a lot.

Jay clicks through his phone, a frown on his face.

"Are you going to tell me?" I ease into a high-backed chair across from the couch.

"Not much to tell. Everything is delayed. Shipment is stuck in customs. Some permits are on hold, and they're the ones we need to move forward."

I sigh. "Can we throw more money at it?"

Jay laughs. "'Course we can. But I'm starting to wonder if that's part of the problem. We encounter an obstacle and out comes the checkbook.

This place is small, and I'm thinking they're putting the squeeze on us to see how much cash they can bleed out before we stop paying."

"So, we stop gushing money?" I sit up straighter in my chair.

"I don't know. When I ask around, I get the"—he rubs his fingers together in the universal symbol for cash—"from everyone. But they also give me a sly smile, which makes me believe we're being hosed." He tosses his phone onto the couch. "It's frustrating, but if we hold off on paying anyone for a while, we send a message. We don't pay anybody until something starts to go our way."

"No one?" My instinct is to disagree. The ruthlessness I sometimes need doesn't run very deep in me. What would Finn do? Probably start shooting people in the knees until we got the answers. Not my style. Money is a powerful motivator in either direction. As much as I don't want to create bad blood here, Jay is right. We can't keep going on as we've been doing.

"No one. Not a cent comes out of any account for anyone until there's movement. We're not a bank, and people on Boa Vista need to stop treating us like we are."

"Going to Praia, the capital, hasn't helped speed anything along?"

"People talk. Everyone knows we've been throwing money around like we're flush. A good strategy until it isn't. Screwing us is shortsighted. The luxury resort and casino will bring a significant influx of tourist dollars to this island. Our negotiation with the government was very reasonable because we wanted in here so badly. It's part of what's so frustrating. Why is there so much foot dragging? Everyone benefits when the resort is done."

"Okay." I nod. "We'll hold back on paying people, see what happens." I check the clock by the front door. "What time is Evander arriving?"

He follows my gaze. "Should be any minute. At least that scheme seems to be ticking along."

"As far as we know," I amend.

Dominic pokes his head in the door. "Mr. Williams has arrived."

"Let him in." Jay stays in his seat.

Evander enters carrying a long cylinder. "Game plans." He holds them up and comes to the coffee table. "A strategy is starting to take shape." He taps out the prison blueprints, and once again, I'm impressed at his efficiency. The maps and architectural drawings are highlighted in various colors. The legend has them marked as Plan A, Plan B, Plan C.

I scan the pages. "Three plans?"

"Sort of. Each plan is a series of contingencies." He points to the first place on the drawing where three lines branch off. "Plan A is the fastest, most efficient way to get Finn out of there. Plan B is if something in Plan A falls apart. Plan C is a last resort. There are several more risks in Plan C than in either A or B. At that point, we'll just be trying to extract him alive."

My stomach swoops low. I lace my hands together and press them against my nose. "That's not comforting."

"I'm not here to comfort you. I'm here to be honest with you about the risks. Seventy percent of the time when I formulate a plan, we never deviate from A because we strategize that sequence of events so meticulously." His dark eyes meet my gaze. "We'll get him out. The exit might be neat and pretty, but it might be messy and dangerous."

"Do you have any idea of when?" Jay asks.

"A few more weeks. We've got the best route, now we need the best people in place. That might take some hiring and firing and shift changes to ensure we're on the same page."

"You can do that?" I'm doubtful.

His jaw tightens. Any time I second guess his abilities, he gets his back up. I suppose Finn would too. "Yes. That's the easy part. Knowing *who* to put in there is the hard part." He gestures to the papers. "Any questions?"

Jay leans over the pages, riffling through them, and I trace the different routes with my finger. He asks a few logistical clarifications, and I try to absorb as much of the information about where Finn is located as I can. I haven't been to a visitation at the new place yet.

"So, he's here?" My voice is rusty when I point to a squared-off cell on the page.

Evander shakes his head and points at a circled cell in another block. "This is where he is. I need to get him moved to this spot before go time. Tactically, this location gives us the three options. If he's over here, it's more complicated."

"Moving him won't be a problem?"

"They're my problems, Carys, and I can handle them. If I didn't think I could do something, I wouldn't plan like I could." His tone is snappy.

Jay slides me a glance. "I'd appreciate if you didn't speak to her like she's being ridiculous."

Warmth spreads across my chest. He's been my right-hand man for years, but since he spent so much time with Finn, he's become more assertive when people are trying to walk over me. He told me, after Eric was dead, that he regretted not being more forceful with Eric when he was taking advantage of me. It's been a rough few months, and I appreciate any support I can get.

Evander's jaw tightens, but he meets my gaze. "My apologies. I didn't want to be short with you. Occupational hazard."

"Probably helps you get the job done," I admit. "But you're the only person I can get reassurance from that this is going to go as smoothly as it can. I'm paying a lot of money for your services, and I'm trying to respect your process. Doesn't mean I won't have questions, even if you deem those questions silly."

He gives a curt nod. "Ask your questions," he says. "I'll take a deep breath before I answer."

A smile tugs at my lips. Would Finn like him? Hard to say. Two rams, probably butting heads. "I appreciate that."

He rubs his face. "All right, fire away. Whatever you want to know, I'll tell you as much as I can, given this stage of planning."

For the next hour, Jay and I pour over the different routes and ask logistical questions. At no point does he indicate he doesn't have an answer, but sometimes he has more than one solution to a potential problem.

When he leaves, I meet Jay's calculating stare. "What'd you think?"

"I think I want to give him the hotel and casino project on top of Finn's escape. There wasn't a single question he faltered on. He had an 'if this, then' for every scenario we posed."

"Any doubts I had are gone," I agree. Rather than the unease that's been building in me, hope is taking its place. Evander's plan is solid.

"Now we wait for the cogs in the machine to line up."

Chapter Five

Finn

When the guard comes to tell me the warden wants to see me, I figure Hagen has him in his pocket too. What'll he want now? Despite my bravado with the kid in the shower, his boss realizes my weakness. If he threatens Carys or her son, I'll roll over.

All the way to the warden's office, I theorize what Hagen might ask me to do. Drugs? Seems the most likely step removed from murder. Would the prison warden be in on that scheme?

The guard knocks on the door, and the warden calls us in. He's a man in his late fifties with bushy eyebrows and a kind face. I suppose since this is a low-security prison, maybe he doesn't have to be such a hard-ass.

"Have a seat, Finn. I'm Jeffrey Lim, the warden here." He motions to the chair across from him. The guard stands beside the door to oversee the two of us. *Must not trust me too much. Shouldn't trust me at all.*

I stare at him in silence. Whatever he wants to say, I'm not giving him an easy opening. Working for Hagen is very far down my list of fun things to do in prison.

"I asked you here today because I have someone who'd like a private, secure meeting with you. We could have done it in one of the lawyer rooms, but I didn't want to take the chance of anyone seeing you together."

Aww, shit. Hagen's *here*? Harder to refuse him in person when he's sneering in my face and I can't retaliate. No matter what, I'm not getting shuffled to maximum security.

"He's not quite here yet. Are you settling in okay? Has everyone been treating you well?" The two caterpillars above his eyes rise.

"Yeah. It's been fine." The guard behind me was on duty the day the kid came after me in the showers. I'm no snitch, and if Hagen's the one running this place, I might as well look like a team player.

There's a knock on the door, but I don't bother turning around. No point in acting surprised when he makes his appearance.

"Ah, here he is. I understand you know each other?" Lim stands and motions to the now-open door.

Reluctantly, I turn in my seat. Well, knock me over with a feather. Not a Volkov after all. I haul myself out of my chair and prop my ass against the warden's desk. These aren't the kind of people to watch a guy's back—more like stab him in it. "That guard." I point to the prison security by the door. "Needs to be gone."

"Pete, these men can handle their own security." The warden shoos him out.

As soon as Hagen's Payroll Pete is gone, I survey the tall South Asian man in an expensive suit and his two comrades behind him. Will Pete be a problem later? Does he understand who these men are? "F-B-fucking-I."

Zahir's lips tip into an almost smile. "That's right. F-B-fucking-I. We were hoping to have a little discussion with you, Finn."

"I have a choice?" I smirk. "No, I will not have a discussion with you." I glance at the warden over my shoulder. "Thanks for inviting me here, Lim. But I'm taking a hard pass."

"You may want to listen. We have quite a proposition for you."

"A proposition? Well, then." I rub my hands together. "Is it a sexual one? I didn't realize the FBI was in the pimping business, but hey, who am I to judge? Nights get dark and lonely."

Zahir raises an eyebrow. "A prostitute? How would Carys feel about that?"

Before I can school my face, a scowl mars it. "You don't talk about her. Her name doesn't cross your lips, you got me?"

"This is a pretty cushy setup you have in here." He comes deeper into the spacious office and leans an elbow against a bookcase. The other two men take up watch on the other side. Whether they're lackeys or security doesn't matter. We understand who's got the power in this room, and it's not me.

"I was a good boy in maximum, so I got rewarded."

He scoffs. "Your girlfriend is a rich woman, and so you bought yourself a better prison." He ventures to the window behind the warden's desk and stares out. "Time outside." He glances behind him at my hands and feet. "No cuffs. Pretty sweet deal you've got here."

Where are these comments going? Did he come to take me to a higher-security prison? Did they set up the equivalent of a Google alert on me? I've only been here a few weeks, and I've kept my nose, mostly, clean. Until I figure out where this conversation is headed, I'm not saying another word.

He rotates so we're facing each other across the desk; the warden is the monkey in the middle. The walkie-talkie on the bookshelf goes off, and the warden crosses the room to turn it down.

"Your girlfriend was in the market for a new man, did you know that?" Zahir asks.

I stiffen, but I'm not taking that bait. Whatever he's alluding to, he wants me to jump to conclusions or say something incriminating. Not happening. "She's free. So, I suppose she can do what she wants."

"Ah, yes. Free. Great word, isn't it?"

I purse my lips and stare. The warden clears his throat, and we both ignore him.

"Your girlfriend has been meeting with Evander Williams. Are you familiar with him?" Zahir asks.

"No." *Fuck, yes. Shit.* A sheen of sweat surfaces on my palms.

"He's very good at getting people out of sticky situations. We've actually used him before in a particularly time-sensitive matter."

"Couldn't be seen getting *your* hands dirty." I try to stifle the panic rising in my chest. They realize Carys is working on breaking me out.

"You should be grateful for how dirty I'm willing to get them now." He nods toward the warden. "Carys is trying to break you out."

"I'm in a federal prison. She doesn't have the resources for that."

Zahir chuckles. "Correct. But Evander Williams has them, and Carys has the money. A perfect combination, wouldn't you say?"

"I signed off on every single charge you laid on me, even shit I didn't do so you'd stay away from her. We have a deal." If this conversation goes where I think it's going, I'll tackle him and beat the crap out of him in front of these witnesses. I didn't like the smug prick when we were hashing out the terms of my surrender, and I like him even less now.

"What if I said we'd let you escape?"

I go still. "If I was trying to escape, I might wonder what you'd want in exchange."

"You've heard of the PLA? Irish organization bent on creating havoc?" He slides into the warden's chair and leans back, the chair creaking as he rocks.

"Wannabes, yeah." Carys and I thought they robbed her warehouse in Russia. Opportunists, nothing more. Poor employees at Van de Berg Ammunition and a distracted boss gave them an opening.

"The CIA and FBI have been communicating about some developing problems on both sides of the ocean with the PLA. We need an informant deep in the organization, and our time to get someone in there seems to be narrowing. We've tried to plant a few people, and while they're in, they've had trouble establishing street cred for various reasons."

"You think they're planning something big."

"From the intel we've managed to intercept, yes."

"What has any of this got to do with me? My little brother is the do-gooder. Ask him. I'm sure you've got a beat on where he is." The last time I saw him, his Irish accent was more pronounced. Have they already shoved him into this shitstorm?

"We'll let you escape in exchange for you infiltrating the PLA organization."

I laugh. "What?"

"You heard me."

"No." I shake my head. If they're ramping up like he says they are, Carys will end up in the line of fire. Too many people connected to me know she's my weak spot. If I fuck up with the FBI or piss off someone from the PLA, I don't want her suffering the consequences.

"This is your one chance out of here. We're not letting you escape unless we've got a deal in place."

"I never expected to get out anyway." I grab the chair across from the desk and plop into it. "It's a no from me."

Zahir gives me an assessing look and taps his lips. "Is this about Carys?"

I don't answer and just stare at him.

"The connections between the PLA and Van de Berg Ammunitions are interesting, don't you think?"

"I don't think much about it at all." Though a few months ago when Carys was being accused of colluding with them, I thought about it far, far too much. Two plus two did not equal four.

"You're worried about her being in danger if you get involved." Zahir shrugged. "We believe she's in danger already."

"Who's 'we?'" I growl.

"Mostly the CIA, but the FBI has a few loose ends from her almost-trial that seem to indicate Van de Berg Ammunition is connected to the PLA or an outright target."

"Nah." I pretend indifference. "You're fishing."

Zahir scans my face. "Very well. If you're not interested now, perhaps you'll take an interest later. If anything changes, ask for a meeting with the warden. He'll call us, and we can work out the terms of our arrangement."

"I won't be calling." I'll rot in jail before I put Carys in danger.

He jerks his head toward the exit for the two silent agents by the bookcase. When they're at the door, I don't turn around, but instead face the warden who looks as frustrated as I feel. There's a heavy pause, and I sigh, turning to him. He wants my attention? Fine, he can have it.

"You realize why you're in here," Zahir says, "don't you?"

"Yeah," I say. "I took a dive."

"For Carys. Desperate times called for desperate measures. You remember that."

Did he just threaten her? I shoot out of my chair and storm toward the door, but the two other agents intercept me. "You stay away from her."

"It's not me you have to worry about," Zahir calls over his shoulder. "Contact the warden when you change your mind."

The prison guard lumbers along the hallway toward us as I seethe.

"You know," the warden says behind me. "You may not be the only one who's desperate. Keep that in mind if you end up back in my office."

"No need to worry about me," I grit out. "If they're knocking at my door, they've already reached the bottom of the barrel. The stench of desperation coats them. But our interests don't align."

"You care about her so much you're throwing away your chance for freedom?" Disbelief cakes the last word.

Does he think the FBI would set me free? Release me as their trained monkey, maybe. Dangle Carys over a cliff to keep me in line the whole time I'm out. I'll die a thousand deaths if it means she's safe. She's not a risk I'm willing to take. "I'd like to go to my cell."

"As you wish." The warden sighs. "Pete, take him back."

Chapter Six

Carys

Sofia takes Lucas from my outstretched arms, and I slip on my sandals. "Holding off on their pay worked, huh?"

Jay chuckles and drops his phone into his pocket. "The project manager is very excited to present the progress they've made. We're cooking with gas, literally. The natural gas hookups were installed yesterday."

"I'm glad to hear things are finally starting to fall into place over there." I kiss Lucas on the head and grab my purse. "You're good with his schedule?" She is, but I can't help asking. She's the person who helped me figure out a routine.

Sofia's lips twitch. "I got it. You're a short drive away, and my husband is never far from his life force." Her tone is teasing. But the other day she threatened to throw his phone across the room if he checked it one more time while they were talking.

"Please. If I had to make a choice between you and my phone, I'd still pick you, babe. No worries." He tugs her into a side hug before giving Lucas a quick kiss on his temple. "You look good with a baby in your arms."

She wags her finger at him. "Someone else's baby. We're not having any more."

Jay chuckles and leads the way out of the house. We both climb into the rear seats, and Dominic slides into the driver's seat. Now that Jay's taken on a more formal role organizing the hotel and casino, my security has fallen to the locals we've hired. Dominic is quiet but efficient, and the rest of his rotating crew is similar. Bringing in new staff made me nervous, but since I'm building a life here, I have to commit to the place and the people.

"We're booked into a hotel not far from the facility in Michigan. Gonna feel a bit different." Jay gives me a side glance. "No glass partition at visitation."

My heart kicks. We'll be able to touch. A thrill of anticipation shoots through me. "Seeing him with fewer restrictions will definitely seem like we're a step closer. We leave in three days?"

"That's right."

Dominic drives across the dirt and sand acting as a parking lot for the build, but there's only one other car. Is the project at another standstill? I smother a sigh of frustration. "What's going on? Where is everyone?" In front of us, the building is a concrete skeleton. Better than a foundation, which is what we had a couple weeks ago, but we must be falling behind.

Jay's brow creases. "What am I missing, Dominic?"

"Today is a holiday." He gets out of the car. "Only the manager will be here to show you around."

"I need to update my phone with local information." Jay takes it out of his pocket. "Why wouldn't he have told me when I asked? We could have come any day."

"Probably better this way," Dominic says. "Otherwise, it'll be very noisy."

That's true. The site doesn't have the same sense of urgency and pace when it's quiet. "Where are we meeting him?"

"In the lobby." Jay nods toward the framed entrance.

As we walk to the roughed-in door, the wind swirls the sand at my feet. In the distance on either side of our hotel and casino are other hotels, but we're the first casino on this island in Cape Verde. A feather in our cap if we can get the damn thing up and running. Initially, the construction sped along, but then we hit roadblock after roadblock. At least the outline of the buildings is here, and I can identify the size and scope of each section.

A man comes out of the front, and Jay grins. "Adiel! Thanks for meeting us. You could have mentioned it was a holiday."

"No problem. No problem." He waves off Jay and extends his hand to me. Dominic is a few steps behind us, and the two men exchange a nod of acknowledgement. "I'm happy to show you the great progress we've made since the permits have come through. So much government red tape." He ushers us into the building.

We follow him around the construction site as he recounts everything that's been done in the last few weeks and what his team is planning to have completed in the weeks to come. We pore over plans and discuss whether we need to move the completion target.

"No." Adiel smiles. "We can make the original date. With the red tape gone, we'll have no problems."

Jay and I exchange a glance behind Adiel's back. Is he blowing smoke up our asses, or is his claim accurate? "No problems," I clarify. "We'll have to start marketing and promotions on an international scale soon to drum up interest. If you can't make the date, now is the time to be cautious, not confident."

Adiel's face clouds. "Yes, of course. When do you need a firm yes?"

Jay whips out his phone and scrolls through various emails we've had with our team. "You've got about four weeks."

"Lots of time." Adiel's expression clears, and he gathers the plans into a neat pile. "I will have a solid date for you in one month."

I smother my smile with my hands. His reaction isn't funny, but when it's not Adiel's skin on the hook, nothing appears to be pressing. He has a month—he'll take the month. Schooling my face, I meet Adiel's gaze. "Great."

We walk to the front of the building to Dominic, who has been keeping watch. He was right about the site being quieter. The eeriness is probably my imagination because I expected the build to be a bustle of activity.

We're almost at the exit when a familiar smell assaults my nose. "Is that..."

"A gas leak," Jay confirms, his hand on the small of my back, ushering me toward the door. "We gotta get out."

My foot hits the sand, and I half turn to ask Adiel about the shutoff valve. A deafening roar rises behind us, and then I'm lifted off my feet, flying through the air. Like any moment when something bad happens, time slows, narrows. Jay disappears from my side. It's like there's a hand square in the middle of my spine, propelling me farther and farther from the building. Every bone in my body loosens and vibrates with the tremendous force. Am I going to die? I'm rotating, out of control. I don't want to die.

Finn. Lucas. I'm so sorry.

The ground rushes at me unchecked. I hold out my hands to break my fall and brace for the impact.

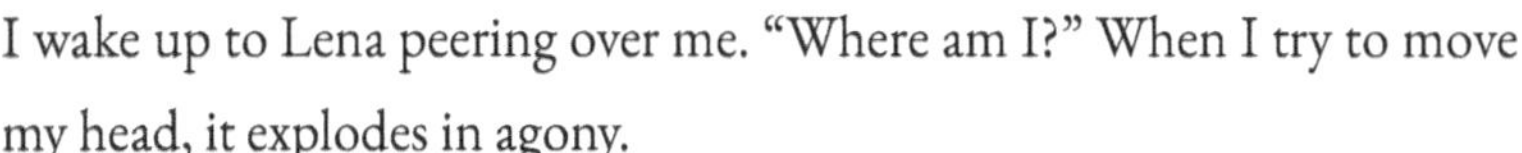

I wake up to Lena peering over me. "Where am I?" When I try to move my head, it explodes in agony.

"Hospital. Someone blew up your hotel." Her expression is resigned. "More trouble following you around. You're lucky to be alive."

A crease forms in my brow when I attempt to remember what led me here. Hotel. Looking over the plans. *Jay.* "Jay was with me. Oh, God. Jay!" I struggle to sit up. Sharp beeps fire in the room, and a nurse rushes in.

"You've got to stay calm," she chides as she checks the wires coming out of my body attached to machines. "You've had a nasty accident."

"Jay's okay." Lena's palm is on my chest. "Adiel got the worst of it, and he's still alive."

I ease my hand across my forehead. "Sofia has Lucas?"

"Yes. Everything is taken care of. You need to look after yourself."

My right wrist is heavy, and I dig it out of the covers. "Shit," I mutter. "I broke my wrist?"

"Doctor says you're lucky it wasn't both. You must have tried to break your fall."

My hand shakes when I press my fingers to the bridge of my nose. Better my wrist than my face. "Where's Jay?"

"Next room. They're releasing him today. Minor scrapes and bruising. He didn't lose consciousness, so he was able to call for an ambulance for you, Adiel, and Dominic."

"Dominic?" My brain is fuzzy, and I forgot about him. "He would have been farther away."

"Got hit with debris. A concussion, but otherwise minor injuries. Adiel has a concussion and two broken legs."

"A bomb?"

Lena shakes her head. "An explosion of some sort. Jay says you both smelled gas just before you were knocked off your feet."

"There are gaps," I admit. "The last thing I recall is Adiel saying he'd have a firm completion date for the build in a month." I swallow. "How long have I been in here?"

"Not long. Maybe two hours?"

"I was out the whole time?"

"They put you under while they set your wrist. You don't remember coming in?"

"No," I whisper. "Is my face okay?" I search for any signs of trauma with my fingers.

"Your face is as lovely as ever. A few minor scratches. No scarring or bruising," Lena assures me.

Jay appears in the doorway. There's a bandage on his forehead and another on his cheek. He may not be so lucky with the scarring. "You're awake."

"You're alive." I smile in spite of my pounding headache. That brief moment of panic about his safety still lingers underneath my good humor. He's been my rock since Finn went into custody, and I can't imagine being without him.

"The only part of me that suffered substantial injuries is my life force." He gives me a wry grin and holds up his phone. Spiderweb cracks obscure the screen. "Hard to read."

"Your wife will be pleased," I tease.

"Because I'm alive or my phone isn't useable?" He lifts an eyebrow and comes over to stand beside my bed. My smile widens.

"Do I need to remind you two of the seriousness of what happened?" Lena puts her hands on her wide hips.

The smiles drop off both our faces, and I scowl. She doesn't. We could have died if we'd still been in the building. Any way I look at the accident, we had a lucky escape. "Are the police on site?"

"They are, yeah. Preliminary assumption, based on both of us smelling gas, is there was a leak. Then something ignited the gas."

"Someone," Lena says. "Mark my words, it won't be something but someone."

I frown. "Adiel, Jay, Dominic, and me. We were the only ones on site. None of us was in a position to ignite the gas."

"Doesn't take much if there's enough. A spark. But yeah, I'm not convinced about the cause of the explosion," Jay admits.

"How bad is the building?" I wince at the thought of the progress we'll have lost.

"Hard to say." He scratches the back of his head. "I was busy looking after all of you until the ambulances arrived. I'll have to assess when the investigation is over."

We'll have to check into it when we get home from visiting Finn. My gaze lands on my cast. My heart kicks. "We leave in three days for Michigan." Panic tinges my voice.

"I can go. Explain what happened. Keep him from murdering people to escape on his own." There's humor in his voice, but there's no way that plan will work.

"If he thinks I'm hurt, he's not going to listen to your assurances I'm okay." I plop my head onto the pillow and immediately regret the sudden movement. Is this how Finn felt when he woke up in Switzerland? There's no question he's tougher than me. A broken wrist—no knife or gunshot wounds—and I'm spent. My body is filled with lead. I can't believe I had the nerve to tease him back then.

Jay sighs and stuffs his damaged phone into his rear pocket. "He'll lose his shit either way. When he left, he told me I had one job, and where you're sitting means I've let him down."

Lena looks between us. "Are you going to tell him there was an explosion?"

"You couldn't have known this would happen," I assure Jay. The photo of the ocean on the wall at the foot of the bed reminds me of our house. It's a holiday here. I should be home with my family. "I don't want to tell him, but as soon as he sees me, he'll know something happened." My wrist rests against the covers, a stark reminder. "No way to hide this with makeup." I take a deep breath. "If I don't show up, he'll think you're downplaying my injuries so he doesn't kill you. No glass partition, remember?"

"A long-sleeved shirt?" Jay's expression is hopeful.

"If it truly was a gas explosion," Lena says. "Accidents happen. He can't blame Jay for that."

Jay and I stare at each other. She's assuming Finn's reasonable. "I'll try a long-sleeved shirt, but he's going to see the cast right away. The real question is what I should tell him."

"Gas leak," Jay says. "That's all we know. The explosion knocked you off your feet."

"Leave out the concussion and hospital stay." I read his train of thought. The lie sends a spike of panic across my chest. Will he realize I'm withholding information? "I want to hire extra security for the house and for us. That'll be his first question. Might as well get on top of that."

"I can call a few local companies," Lena offers. "Set up meetings for the next couple of days."

Jay gives her a grateful smile. "Thanks. I gotta get a more useable phone tomorrow."

When she steps out into the hallway, I sigh. "I just hope Finn doesn't do anything stupid after he sees me."

He grimaces. "We're getting him out. He has to sit tight and have faith."

"Neither of those are his strong points." I shift in the bed and groan. "Hopefully, my body won't be as sore in a few days. Selling the lie I'm fine will be impossible if I still move like this."

"I'll contact Evander and see whether we're any closer to a date. Maybe I can find a way to get him reassurance we're coming for him soon."

I cover my face and take a deep breath. "I'm really tired," I admit.

"I'll leave you be. Dominic and Adiel are down the hall."

"Thanks, Jay. I don't know what I'd do without you." Have I ever told him that explicitly? Bonuses and gifts, sure, but the actual words?

"Feeling is mutual, Carys. You're one of my people, and I feel awful I didn't protect you."

"Maybe we got too relaxed."

Jay's eyes narrow, and he purses his lips as though something I've said has triggered a thought. "I guess we'll see what the police turn up. Accident or planned attack?"

My body heats and then cools in a rush. If I'm a target, that means Lucas is, too, and I'll do anything to protect him. "Accident," I say. "It must have been an accident."

Chapter Seven

Finn

This visitation is vastly different from maximum security. Gone are the glass barriers and phones. The guard who escorted me down here said I'm allowed a brief hug to begin the visitation and another to say goodbye. Holding hands is restricted to one finger. No joke. One finger. He recommended the index. Made me laugh. Guess they're not a fan of her pushing drugs into my palm. Not that she would. Tripping in here would help pass the time. But I'm not keen to start a drug habit now.

The familiar wash of warmth envelops me the minute I catch sight of her at a small table in a corner. She's dressed for winter, with a heavy coat and long pants. Has she acclimatized to the warmer Cape Verde climate that quickly? It's summer here, and the yard was hot as fuck this morning.

When she rises to greet me, I zero in on the stiffness of her movements. Instead of hugging her when I get close, I cock my head and take her in from head to toe. Something's not right. I search her face.

"No hug?" she whispers. The unease in her voice is obvious.

I loop my arms around her waist and slide my fingers under the edge of her coat, then up her sweater so we're skin to skin. She vibrates under my touch and releases a contented sigh.

"I've missed you," she says.

I dip my head into her neck then kiss her under her ear and squeeze her tight. When I increase the pressure, she lets out a tiny noise of discomfort. Something is wrong. She asked for the hug, but she's only wrapped one arm around me.

"That's enough, Donaghey," the guard calls.

I ease away and trail my hands along her back before emerging again. Before she can move out of reach, I grab the hand that was dangling at her side. A thick white cast rests against her palm, and I jerk her jacket sleeve up. "What the hell?" How high does her injury go?

"Donaghey!" The guard moves from his post.

I drop her arm and step back. He's not removing me before I get answers. "What the hell happened?"

Carys's hand shakes when she tucks a loose strand of hair into her braid. Her hair should have been my first clue something isn't right. She hasn't had it up in months. "There was an accident."

"Sit at the table." The guard looms over the spot we've claimed.

I slide into the chair across from her and watch as she maneuvers herself into a seated position. My gut clenches, and violent emotions threaten to spiral out of control. *Calm down. This might be nothing.* Did she fall? Slip on Lucas's toy?

"What kind of accident?" My thoughts want to jump to worst-case scenarios, but I'm working hard to ignore those demons. She's safe now. I'm in here, and she's safe. Jay promised me she'd be safe.

Zahir's threat echoes in my memory. My conversation with the kid in the shower about the people we love on the outside of this building rises to the surface.

Panic twists my insides. God, I hate being in here. I don't sit around worrying; that's not my style. Action. Chaos. Throw me into the middle of a fight, but don't make me idle on the sidelines.

She swallows and takes my hand on the top of the table. I shift her grip, so our index fingers are latched. I'm already on the guard's radar, and I'm not leaving here without answers. The quizzical look on her face makes me realize she thinks I'm rejecting her gesture.

"Guard said one finger handholds only." I give her a hard stare. "Take off your coat and show me what I'm not supposed to see." As if she tried to hide her injury from me. Like I wouldn't notice. Maybe if we were still behind that partition, but now? There's no hiding from me.

Her jaw clenches, and she shakes her head. "You don't need to see it. I broke my wrist in an accident."

"Like you tripped and fell on a toy? Or stumbled down the stairs—oh, wait—there are no stairs in your bungalow. You're trying to hide something from me, so you already know I'm not going to like it. If it was simple, you'd have led with that." Anger bubbles to the surface. Fuck keeping my emotions under control. Jay let her get hurt. Five months in here, and she's sporting a cast. "You need to fire Jay."

"He's not in charge of my security anymore. We hired island staff."

"Fire them all."

"I haven't told you what transpired yet." She gives an exasperated huff.

"Could this"—I grab her injured hand—"have been avoided?" I assess the way she's sitting at the table. She's moving like an old woman, but I know better than to say that. Whatever happened, it jolted more than her wrist.

She yanks her hands away from mine to lean back in the chair and cross her arms. Other than the initial tug out of my grip, her movements are languid rather than sharp. Her body must be sore. "There was a gas explosion at the new build."

"What?" My voice is louder than I expected. "You can smell gas, Carys," I hiss. "You can *smell* it. Did you hire a security company with no ability to smell? 'Cause I gotta tell you, that's a pretty significant weakness."

She purses her lips, and when she rolls her shoulders, she grimaces in pain. "My security guy was at the car."

"And you were...?"

"At the entrance of the building."

"And the distance between those two points?" I use my hands on the table to demonstrate small versus big space.

"Further than you'd be comfortable with."

I run my fingertips along the edge of the table in quick movements, trying to quell the desire to explode. The table heats under my palms.

"Everything okay over here?" the guard asks.

"Peachy," I grit out, never taking my eyes off Carys.

"We've already hired more security, put additional measures in place. You don't have to worry," she says in a rush.

"I don't have to worry?" I shoot across the table. "I turned myself in to keep you safe, and now I hear you and Jay aren't taking that seriously. My one stipulation when I agreed to the exchange was that he needed to protect you like he would his own wife." My voice cracks, and I clear my throat. Frustration is eating me up.

"I know." Her voice is quiet. "It was a gas leak. An accident."

I stare at her. She and Jay must think I'm stupid. "Gas, even a gas leak, doesn't explode without an ignition source."

Her jaw tightens.

"You realize what that means, right? Your old job was in ammunitions, so you get where I'm going with this, don't you?"

"Don't patronize me. You don't get to be an asshole to me because you're scared and angry, okay?" She leans across the table, and we're so close we could kiss if we weren't both so fired up.

Our gazes are locked. Flint and steel spark off each other. Screw it. I'd rather kiss her than yell. We haven't been this close in so long. I cup her face and drag her onto the surface. She meets my lips in a fusion of anger and frustration mixed with passion that makes my bones ache with longing. As though we've been apart minutes instead of months. She sinks into me.

I'm not so unaware I can't hear the guard stomping over. I lessen the kiss before it can get any more heated or risk my next visitation. A slipup is fine in low security, right?

Her breathing is heavy when we break away and sink back into our chairs across the table. The guard is trying to stare me down, but I'm going to ignore him. I like the view in front of me much better.

"Was that kiss an apology?"

Mostly that kiss prevented me from saying something I'd regret. "Sure." I smirk. "Even though I'm not really sorry."

Her gaze softens. "We are taking security more seriously now. Okay? I promise. We've set more people in place, good-quality people."

When she arrived, I planned on trying to tell her about the FBI, that they're aware of what she's up to. Put a stop to her escape plans. But the truth is I can never protect her from in here. She's in danger from something or someone whether I'm in here or I'm out there. I might have thought I had a choice, but I don't. I'm always going to choose her and her safety above anything else.

I take her in, cataloging everything about her I love, and the ache across my chest flares. I'm no good to her in here. Doesn't matter how much security she's got out there—no one is ever going to protect her like I will.

"Okay," I agree. She smiles, and my heart squeezes at the way she perks up at the agreement. She doesn't understand I'm not giving into her but to something else.

While she tells me about Jay's girls and Lucas, I appear engaged, but inside for the first time ever, I'm counting the minutes until visitation is done. When the bell rings to signal the end of our visit, I hug her longer than I should, my fingers grazing her spine under her layers of clothing.

"I love you, Carys." My voice is gruff in her ear. "You understand I'll do anything to keep you safe?"

"I know," she whispers back. "I love you too. It'll be okay."

It's not right now, but it will be.

On the way to my cell, I tell the guard I want a meeting with the warden.

In less than twenty-four hours, I'm sitting across the warden's desk again, Zahir rocking in Jeffrey's chair while the warden stands uneasily behind him by the large windows. We're in a standoff, but I'm not dropping my figurative weapon first.

"It's a good deal, Finn." Zahir tents his fingers and leans back farther.

"The only arrangement I'm accepting is one that lets me live in Cape Verde without spending even a single day in lockup when this job is done."

"You're serving twelve consecutive life terms. Reducing your sentence to three years in total is more than fair. I've also agreed to minimum security."

"Not where I'm sitting. You want me to ingratiate myself to the organization that at least had a hand in framing Carys, put my life on the line, and snitch on whatever dealings they have going on. My skin is in the game, so I'm telling you what it'll take to make it happen."

"Look." He sighs. "There's only so much I can do. Do we want you? Yeah, we do. We've got intel indicating you're our best bet for an in, and if our crew intercepts the jailbreak, it's a huge bump to their street cred for the PLA. Saying that, I cannot pretend you didn't commit a shit ton of heinous crimes."

"Those days are over." I wave a dismissive hand. "I'm a family man now."

"Not too much of a family man, I hope," Zahir scoffs. "Otherwise, you're no good to us."

"I'll get the job done, but my price is my price." I rise and nod to the warden to call the guard. He holds his radio to his lips.

"I didn't want to do this, but you're not leaving me a choice." Zahir sits forward and braces his elbows on the wooden desk. "I've been ignoring the elephant in the room because I believed you called me here to fall in line."

I smirk. Shows what he knows. I don't fall in line, and when I have to, I don't go down quietly. "You thought I was going to make it easy on you?"

"No, but I didn't think you'd dig in this hard. We've been in here for nearly two hours trying to hash out a compensation plan that works for both of us. I've gone down as far as I'm authorized to go."

"So, call your boss and get approved for the right deal."

"I only got a deal this good because we'd been advised you'd be an 'absolute dickhead' to negotiate with."

"I do enjoy it when my reputation precedes me. Makes things easier."

"Usually, probably." He eyes me. "I didn't want to go here because it sets a poor tone for our working relationship, but you've left me no option."

The guard radios to ask for permission to enter. I wave to the warden to get on with it.

"There was an explosion in Cape Verde last week." Zahir meets my gaze.

For the first time since we started speaking, my heart thumps with dread. I hold up a hand to the warden to stall the guard. "If you had anything to do with that"—I lean across the desk, getting in his face—"I'll fucking kill you right now."

To his credit, he doesn't flinch at my threat. "We didn't." He settles into his chair and examines me. "We both know it wasn't a gas leak."

"What's your point?"

"You're in here. She's out there. That little boy is out there." He gives me a meaningful look but doesn't continue his line of logic.

"If I'm out there working for you, I'm not protecting her anyway." My one hesitation in calling Zahir was the realization I might be putting her in more danger out there than I am in here. If I can get out of my sentence, when this trade-off is complete, I'll be able to protect her from whatever is inching closer.

"Here's the information we have—and I'm giving you this as a show of good faith. Carys started receiving packages at her various houses close to a year ago. Inside each package was an alarm clock, and each had a reference to time running out. Then, the day the FBI raided her Chicago office, a confetti bomb was delivered to her. It had already exploded when we entered."

I stiffen at the new information. She didn't tell me about any fake device in her office. Granted we were busy trying to get her out of jail, but if there was a looming threat, I should have been told. Maybe we wouldn't be in this position now.

"The bomb at her hotel was set off on a holiday when there would be a minimal number of staff. It wasn't strong enough to kill anyone or even to do significant damage to the building. An inconvenience." He pauses and meets my gaze. "A warning."

Carys's broken wrist was more than an inconvenience. My nostrils flare.

"Whoever is after her, they're escalating. Not quickly, but it's happening."

He doesn't mention the shootout at Ricardo's flophouse in Russia or the warehouse theft or how someone either in the PLA or associated with them framed Carys for crimes she didn't commit. The threat isn't just intensifying, it's persistent and pervasive.

"So, somebody has put you over a barrel, but it's not us. Doesn't mean I won't take advantage of it." He presses on the desk with his index finger. "While you're out there, you'll be free to pursue whoever is coming for her. Obviously, not so much that you put your mission with us at risk, but you can help her. We won't stop you."

I sink into my chair across from him and cross my arms. Three years in here afterward is better than never being with Carys again, not being there to raise Lucas. The deal isn't what I want, but I recognize I've got no more room to bargain.

"If you're in here, you're on the sidelines, watching her life potentially collapse around her. Out there, you can prop her up."

He must not think he's won me over, but he has. "Neither you nor the CIA has had anything to do with what's happened to her so far?"

"No." Zahir's voice is firm. "We're aware of everything because that's our job, but we haven't been party to any of it."

I run a hand across the top of my shorn head and stare out the window. There's no question I'm taking the deal, but I need a moment to reconcile the choice. "Will she know the escape will be hijacked?"

"No." His voice is sharp. "She can't be told. We must have every aspect of this appear as authentic as possible, or it'll put our PLA agents in jeopardy."

"She'll track me down." I'm not asking if I can tell her anything because I don't care what they want. Once I'm out, I'm playing by my own rules.

"We're anticipating that."

"What's that mean?"

"We're okay with her showing up, that's all."

I narrow my eyes, my mind ticking through his phrasing. There's something they're not telling me. What aren't they telling me? "That doesn't add up to me."

"I'm sorry your math sucks, but that's not my problem." Zahir rises and extends his hand. "Have we got a deal?"

"I want it in writing, and I want my lawyer to read it." There're not offering me three years in minimum and snatching it away once the job is done. I'm making sure no matter what I do out there, I'm not going to be on the hook for any more crimes.

He nods to the guy by the bookcase, who takes an envelope out of his pocket, reads the front, and tosses it onto the desk. *Three years, minimum* is scrawled across the middle.

"I hate being a foregone conclusion," I mutter.

"If it makes you feel any better," Zahir says, "I didn't even bother drawing up paperwork for the other deals we've discussed the last two hours."

After they leave, I finger the envelope, thinking about what I've agreed to.

"They're desperate," the warden comments. "That's a huge reduction in your sentence."

I purse my lips and glance at him. "It's not me they got over a barrel, it's her. And I'd never let her fall."

"An honorable trait, to love someone that much."

I shrug. "Trust me, if I had a choice, I'd cut the honor out of me." Not entirely true. For a brief moment, my life with Carys had been damn near perfect, as close to true happiness as I've ever felt. The other side of that bliss is what I've been living with the last few months—barely concealed despair. "You'll get my lawyer for me?"

"I will." He heads to the phone on his desk. "I'll call you back to my office when they're here."

"Did they tell you when this is going down?"

He chuckles. "I'm as in the dark as you. Could be tomorrow for all I know, so I'll get that lawyer here today. The FBI and CIA are playing chess—the rest of us are playing checkers."

As soon as I'm out and can see where the pieces are on the board, I won't be playing checkers anymore. No matter what it takes, I'll be capturing the PLA's king and taking down the person threatening Carys and Lucas.

Chapter Eight

Carys

Lucas is on my hip as I make myself a cup of coffee and wait for Jay to get back from his meeting with the police. They claimed to have developments in the bombing of the hotel and casino. My grip on the cup isn't as secure as I'd like it because of the cast, so I don't fill the cup too full. I've had a few mishaps with trying to do too much when I'm not at full strength.

"Jay back yet?" Sofia asks as she breezes into the kitchen. She pours herself coffee in a to-go mug and leans against the counter.

"Not yet, no. They've had two weeks to investigate. They must have an idea of what happened."

She grimaces and sips her hot drink. "Maybe that's the problem. What to do with what they know..."

"You don't think it was a gas leak." I hitch Lucas up higher on my hip, and he tugs on a strand of my hair.

"Jay doesn't like me in his business." Her lips twist. "With a building that open, and no obvious ignition source close, it probably wasn't the gas that sent you flying." She winks. "Might have been a little bit of pillow talk the last few nights while he tried to piece everything together."

Pillow talk. A spike of longing shoots through me, and I cross the floor into the living room to place Lucas on the play mat. I stare into my coffee while he kicks and rattles bar above him. Memories of Finn whisper and threaten to pull me under.

"I'm not supposed to understand what you're doing," Sofia says from the kitchen. "But I've got faith you'll get him back."

I glance over my shoulder. "If it doesn't work, though…"

"Then you'll find another way. One thing I love about my husband is his tenacity. He won't give up, and neither will you."

Before the explosion, before I saw Finn in Michigan, I was high on hope. Evander didn't miss a step in our meeting. Even still, the last few days, my stomach has churned with worry. What if the escape isn't successful? What if he's injured or killed? What if he's caught and sent to the supermax prison? What if, for a reason we can't see, the plan never gets off the ground? As Evander warned us, there are so many moving pieces, it only takes one to slip and we could be free-falling.

The door opens, and Jay comes in carrying an envelope. He kisses Sofia on the cheek and makes himself a cup of coffee. He's processing—stalling—before he acknowledges me. The last lingering hope that the explosion is pegged as a gas leak vanishes. If the explanation is easy, there's no need for him to avoid me.

"I have to pick up the kids from school." Sophia grabs her purse. "Lena is grocery shopping. I'll take them to the park so we're out of your hair for a bit."

"Thanks." Jay gives her a peck on the lips before she slips out the door.

"It's not good, is it?" My morning brew is cooling, but I can't bring myself to drink it. It's too bitter.

With a sigh, he comes over and tosses the information on the coffee table. "No idea what it means, and that's the part that worries me."

I take the manila envelope off the table, and I slide my finger along the seal when there's a knock at the front entrance. Dominic, whose injuries have mostly healed, pops his head in. "Mr. Williams has arrived. He'll be in shortly."

When the door closes, I give Jay a questioning glance. "I thought—"

"He had to rearrange his schedule because of another crisis. Sorry—we changed the time while I was with the police. There's only so much texting you can do when you're supposed to be listening."

A security guard, who was stationed near the rear entrance, comes to the front door, hand on his gun. "Williams is known to you?" he asks.

"Yeah," Jay says. "A schedule change. Sorry I didn't get a chance to loop you in."

The extra safety measures have taken getting used to. For a long time, Jay was my main source of protection. Then in deference to Finn, and because we didn't understand the reason for the confetti bomb, we brought on Dominic and his crew. But now we have three other firms in rotation, and it's easy to forget to tell someone something.

When the guard heads back to his post at the rear of the house, Jay sighs. "If *I* was looking after my ass, I'd be annoying myself. I'm always forgetting to tell people shit lately."

"Do you want me to hire somebody else? Remove tasks from your plate?" I've never had money coming out of my account faster than it's going in, and a brief flare of uncertainty shoots through me. If he needs more help, I can't deny him. Everything hinges on his ability to juggle multiple jobs, and maybe that's not fair.

"Nah." Jay shakes his head. "You're bleeding cash. I need a better organizational system till Finn's out, and then he can take over some of this, right?"

The door behind us opens. "Two days." Evander enters the house. "We're making our move in two days."

I toss the manila envelope onto the coffee table and rise to greet Evander. Whatever bad news is in there will have to wait. "Two days?" Excitement laces my voice, and I am excited, but that familiar unease lurks under the surface. Like anything good—the wait is forever and then everything happens at once.

"I got word the last guard I needed in place is changing shifts tomorrow. So, we should be good to go for the day after that." His cylinder of files is clutched in his hand, and he taps them onto the table.

Jay rubs his hands together. "You're going to take us through your steps now that the plan is set?"

"I am." Evander settles into the couch beside me. He spreads out the sheets and flattens them down. Plans A through D are clearly labeled and color coded. We've picked up an extra plan. If C was risky and dangerous, I'm not sure he needs to explain D.

While he clarifies the various scenarios, I listen, but it's hard to focus when I have no ability to influence the outcome. Do I want to understand what's happening and whether things go smoothly? Yes. Unlike the last time, each explanation doesn't calm me but instead causes my uncertainty to swell.

Jay meets my gaze across the coffee table and gives me an encouraging look. "Nothing obvious you haven't thought of."

Evander chuckles. "I've had a whole tactical team on this. If there was an obvious flaw at this stage, somebody would be getting fired." He looks between me and Jay. "There's one loose end I haven't been able to tie up. Might be nothing, but I have to ask in case either of you knows the story."

"Okay." I take a sip of my drink and wince at the taste. Finn would love this brand of battery acid coffee, but it's not my favorite.

"My sources tell me he's gone to see the warden a few times. Could be nothing, but I was hoping to get a definitive answer. I couldn't get anyone there to talk, which is always a concern."

Jay and I hold each other's gaze for a moment, and I frown. "He tends to get in trouble a lot. Could it be related to a fight or altercation?"

"Could be. I have a source who says Finn was attacked in the showers within the first few days of being there." Evander rubs his face. "Does the name Hagen Volkov ring any bells?"

"Like a choir," Jay admits.

"Would he owe him or be owed anything? I didn't get a lot of information from my contact, but I understand the Volkovs have branches inside this particular prison."

I purse my lips. Finn called Hagen for help when he was trying to track me to Ireland and didn't have enough money or resources to get himself there. "Yes," I acknowledge. "He owes him."

"Experience tells me he's having pressure applied to him in there to do *something*, but we don't have a clue what or when. If he is sent to isolation, and our plan is already in motion, we're sunk." Evander gathers his color-coded sheets. "I wanted to flag the issue before go-time. If you've got any way to get a note to him, I'd do that. If not, we'll take our chances. He's kept his nose clean so far. Much cleaner than at maximum. I don't like surprises, and this situation could become volatile."

Jay takes a deep breath. "I don't know if I can communicate with him in time. I don't want to tip off anyone to what's about to go down."

Evander closes the lid on his cylinder and eyes the two of us. "I can get a message to him, but I don't want him acting out of character either. There's a delicate balance here."

I shake my head. "Let's leave it. He's been steady so far apart from the one incident, right? So, status quo for two more days is risky, but probably no riskier than trying to communicate through someone who could give us away. Right?" I look to both of them for confirmation. Is this the safest decision? Even if Finn knows we're coming, there's no guarantee he'll behave himself. He's not going to ignore a threat.

"You understand him best," Evander agrees. "I'll be here in two-and-a-half days with Finn."

Lucas fusses on the mat, and I set my coffee on the table to pick him up. I follow Evander to the door, my son tucked against my shoulder. "You feel good about this, right?"

He takes a deep breath and gives me a wry smile. "If this didn't feel like the best time, we wouldn't be moving ahead. The window is here, Carys. If we're doing this, we take it now."

His brown eyes are full of sincerity and a touch of impatience. The ball of anxiety bouncing in my stomach slows. "Yeah, okay." I nod. "I want him out."

He rubs my free shoulder. "Two-and-a-half days. Don't dwell on the plan. Dwell on what you're doing once he's here."

"You'll be the one with him?"

"Yes. I hook up with the crew as soon as they're off US soil. I'll bring him here."

We've gone over this, but I need this last-minute reassurance. Lucas wiggles in my arms, drawing my attention from Evander.

Jay comes up behind me and shakes his hand. "Looking forward to seeing you and Finn in a few days. Thanks for your work on this."

A hint of a smile tugs at Evander's lips. "I'll see you then."

Once he's gone, Lucas squirms and lets out a dissatisfied cry. I need to feed him and get him down for a nap, but I also have to go through the manila envelope from the police with Jay.

Just then, Lena comes in, struggling with grocery bags. Without missing a beat, Jay takes the bags from her and carries them to the kitchen. "I'll put these away," he says.

She scans me and Jay. "You're stressed."

"He needs fed and a nap, but I also need to talk to Jay."

"I'll take him." Lena heads to the fridge. "He can drink his bottle, and I'll rock him in your room."

"You're a star." Relief washes over me.

Once I've handed him off, I grab the envelope from the table and bring it to the island while Jay puts away the groceries. Sliding the pages out, I scan the police notes and report.

"A bomb?" I frown and run my fingers over the conclusion. I squint at the partial serial number they pulled off the remnants of the device. "A remote trigger? Someone was watching us and set it off?"

"Yeah. The placement of the bomb and the timing of the trigger suggest the explosion was meant to scare rather than kill. The gas leak exacerbated the situation. Police said if there'd been windows or more of a structure, the blast probably would have killed us even though it wasn't meant to do much damage." He glances at the door. "Didn't want to say that part in front of Sofia."

"Or Lena." Although Lena's affair with my father was a difficult pill to swallow, she treats me more like a daughter than my actual mother. Over the years, we've grown very close. When Finn and I made the decision to quit the arms business and move to Cape Verde, we thought we left our perils behind. Apparently, danger intends to follow us.

"Is that serial number familiar?" Jay opens a top cupboard to put away canned goods.

I scan the number again, and recognition dawns. "Oh my God. That's one of ours. From the warehouse in Russia." When the theft happened, I went over the missing products constantly trying to trace any piece and recover something.

"Yep." He stuffs the reusable bags under the sink.

"What does that mean?"

He grimaces and spreads his hands along the island across from me. "Someone was here in Cape Verde with at least one product from the warehouse. They intended for the bomb to scare us but not kill us." He takes a deep breath. "It means you've got a target on your back, Carys. Leaving your father's company hasn't removed it. And the person doing this? They're escalating."

Chapter Nine

Finn

Billy the kid falls into step beside me out in the yard. I've been waiting for his return, but I hoped to be out of here before Hagen came up with option number two. No such luck.

"Hagen's not very happy with you," he says.

I chuckle. "You think I give a flying fuck if that guy is pissed at me?" I glance at the kid. "You might not know me better, but Hagen sure as shit does."

"How's that hotel your girl is building? No explosive situations?"

My hand is in the collar of his sweatshirt, and he's pressed against the fence before he has time to react. "What'd you say to me?" My spit hits his cheek.

"You heard me." His voice quivers.

"Donaghey," the speaker system booms out. "Release Montgomery."

I tighten my grip on the neck of his shirt to make his breathing uncomfortable. "You don't threaten me." With a violent shove, I let him go.

More than I want to kill this punk, I want out of here. If Hagen was the guy who set off the bomb in Carys's building, he'd better pray I don't slip the FBI and CIA before they can get me in prison. Otherwise, he's a dead man. They gave me carte blanche to punish whoever attacked her, and I'm not leaving a single strand of doubt about who played a role before I'm tossed back in here. Annihilating the PLA is my deal, but protecting Carys is my mission.

"You don't say no to Hagen. He said you needed a reminder." Billy is on the ground, staring up at me, but his hand shakes when he wipes his mouth.

I crouch, careful not to touch him. No need to have the guards on the rampage when I leave the yard. "The only person who needs a recap here is Hagen. Tell him if he comes for me or mine, I come for him. I *never* back down."

The kid leans toward me. "You take down Murray, and this goes away."

Curiosity gets the better of me. Hagen's a braggart and reckless, but he's not persistent to the point of stupidity. "What's his problem with Murray?"

"Money," Billy says. "Stole from him."

I scrub my face. Sure, I've killed for less, but this isn't my beef, and I'm not making it mine. With any luck, I can bide my time until Carys unwittingly works with the FBI to bust me out. "Means nothing to me." I rise and stare at him. "Tell Hagen if I ever get out of here, he'll live the rest of his life with no arms or legs for putting anyone I care about in harm's way. You got me?" I pretend to hold a limb and make a sawing motion. "I'll remove each one with a dull blade." With that, I turn and continue my walk around the perimeter.

"At least"—the kid scrambles to his feet behind me—"at least rough him up a bit or something. I can't—I can't—" His voice cracks. "He's got my kid, okay? He's got my son, and he said if I didn't talk you into getting involved, he's going to mail my wife a piece of him for every day of resistance."

I cross my arms and let him catch up with me. "What are you doing running with the Volkovs when you can't take the consequences?" These stories never moved me before Carys and Lucas. Now, a fire burns in my belly.

"I—I didn't. I wasn't. He came to me at visitation and told me he could get to my wife and son. Gave me that first message for you. I'd never seen him before. But he won't leave me alone. He was here yesterday and said he's got my son."

"Have you spoken to your wife? Asked for proof of life?" Getting involved in this shit is a bad idea.

"Proof of life?" A crease forms in his forehead. "I haven't—I haven't talked to my wife."

"Before you do shit for anyone, you always get proof of leverage. Always." The cast on Carys's wrist rises in my memory. If that was Hagen, he's telling me he can get to her, to them. What he doesn't realize is I'll soon be able to return the favor. "The best proof of life is an answer to a question only your wife or son will understand. Something very obscure. Won't be on social media or a response he can fake."

"Okay." Billy expels a breath. "You don't think he has him?"

"Didn't say that." I run a hand along the back of my neck. "If you don't ask for proof, he can tell you whatever he wants."

"What if he does have him?"

This kid is so green. The logical next step would be for him to gather friends and apply pressure to me. Force me to take out Murray. Or try to take out Murray himself. He doesn't have it in him. Besides being a shitty mafia leader, Hagen is a terrible judge of character. Billy might look hard, but he's as soft as butter. How'd he pick this guy out of everyone in the place? Maybe he does have Billy's son. "Your best bet?"

He nods, eager for direction.

In a circumstance like his, when he's not capable of finding his own leverage, his options are limited. He won't convince me to go after Murray. Hagen doesn't appear willing to give in and ask for something else from me or the kid. Billy hasn't realized yet that morphing into someone he's not is his only choice. "Kill Murray yourself."

He grabs his head and crouches on the ground as though I've delivered him the death blow. When people you love are at risk, you make impossible choices. It's why I'm in here in the first place. Without giving him a second look, I continue on my walk.

There's a chance I'll solve Billy's problem for him before he has to take a life-changing action. If Hagen had anything to do with the bomb that went off in Carys's building, when I get out, he's a dead man.

Chapter Ten

Carys

In twenty-four hours, Evander will be successful in breaking Finn out of jail or will have failed spectacularly. The tension in the house is so thick that Sofia has spent most of the time outside with the kids or at various parks. Lena has been baking as though she's starting her own business. The freezer is stocked. She's earned her nap.

As for Jay and me, we've been trying to focus our nervous energy on getting to the root of the explosion. When Finn gets here, he'll be annoyed we didn't start our search earlier or assume the police were incompetent or incapable. Sometimes it amazes me one person's absence can be felt so deeply, but that's how it's been having him gone for months. I understand the routes he'd take and the things he'd want done, but doing any of them is a Herculean task. His moves don't come naturally to me. Once he's here, safe with us, life will be better.

The security radio at Jay's hip comes alive with chatter. Jay frowns and turns up the volume, listening in. I pause my search through old paperwork related to the warehouse theft to eavesdrop. When I hear two names I recognize, I release a long breath. *Charles and Opal Van de Berg.*

"Why are they here?" I gather everything on the island and stuff the papers into an oversized envelope. "And why are they here *together*?" They were on the cusp of divorce last time I talked to them.

"I'm guessing they finally caught wind of the explosion at the hotel." Jay goes to the door. "Want me to get rid of them?"

My mother hasn't done anything to incur my wrath, but my father's meddling in both the family arms business after he retired and my personal life is part of the reason I'm in my current situation. Still, they are my parents. Even if I don't need them for practical reasons anymore, I have a hard time turning them away.

"No. Let them in." I go to the back of the house to dump the envelope on my bed. I double-check Lucas is still napping and return to the living room to find Jay getting them drinks.

I emerge from the hallway into the gray-and-white open kitchen and living room. "This is a surprise."

My mother scans me from head to toe and lands at the cast. "Are you okay?"

I hold up my arm. "This was two weeks ago. I'm coping fine."

"We just heard about the bomb." My father grumbles from his seat on the couch while he nurses his whiskey. "You should have called us."

"There's probably a reason I didn't." Neither of them makes a situation less volatile. My mother is prone to anxiousness and my father to rash decisions.

"Carys," my mother admonishes me. "No matter what mistakes we've made, we love you."

"How's my grandson?" My father searches the room and rises from his seat. "I'd like to see him."

My heart kicks. So many emotions are tied to my father's connection with Lucas. I wouldn't have my son if my father hadn't deceived me. I will never regret Lucas, but the way the situation played out with my ex-fiancé, Eric, and the Russian surrogacy behind my back, will never sit right with me. "He's sleeping."

"Maybe we'll stay for a while," my mother suggests. She has a glass of wine clutched in her hand. "I'd love to meet him."

"He has long naps," I say. "So, you came here to… check up on me?" If that's true, I'm touched by the gesture, though it's out of character for both of them. At forty-six, I'm not a kid anymore. My parents, who are both in their seventies, are still spry and look younger than they should thanks to cosmetic interventions. Not that I can fault them—I inherited a double dose of vanity.

"You were injured. You could have been killed. Of course we came." My mother perches on the couch as far away from my father as possible. "We lost your brother. We don't want to lose you too."

All the times they haven't shown up for me run in a loop. I've been in Cape Verde for months and neither has visited. Granted, I made it clear to my father he wasn't welcome. He also didn't visit me during my not-so-brief stint in prison. My mother could have come, but the last time I spoke to her, she was rattled by the confrontation with her daughter from her first marriage. She left her abusive husband to marry my father, leaving her very young daughter. She's not the mother of the year.

"Well, as you can see, I'm fine." I hover in the kitchen behind the island.

"Just you, Lucas, Jay, and his family?" My father peers over the back of the couch at me.

He's unbelievable. Lena is here, which he knows because she told him she was finished as his mistress and done working at the house in Switzerland. I clench my jaw. "Just us." Hopefully, Lena's nap is a long one. My mother doesn't enjoy being confronted with my father's indiscretions. She must not realize Lena is here.

"How has everything been going on the island?" My mother's voice is cheery and bright.

I frown. She's not the cheery sort. "We've had setbacks, like a bomb going off, but we're handling the issues."

"Still flying to America every month to visit convicted felons?" The ice in my father's glass clinks as he takes a drink.

A sigh of exasperation almost escapes, but I tamp it down. "So nice that you both came all this way. I hope you booked a hotel. Since we weren't aware you were coming, we've got meetings and other things scheduled. Not much time to visit."

My mother shoots my father a look loaded with meaning, but he takes another drink and only raises his eyebrows. Whatever they agreed to discuss with me, he's not going along with it.

"Have you pinpointed who planted the bomb?" She picks at her skirt, her shoulders tense.

"Not yet," Jay says from his position near the door. "Why?"

"Oh, well." She glances in my direction. "I was at a fundraiser with Hagen Volkov's latest mistress, and she mentioned your name." She takes a deep breath. "And Finn. Your father"—she throws out a hand at him—"also heard something interesting the other day."

He downs the last of his drink and rises from the couch, approaching the island where I'm standing. "I was at an arms meeting, and someone told me the PLA had developed an interest in acquiring Finn Donaghey."

I laugh and hope it hides my thumping heart. "He's in prison, so obtaining him would be difficult, to say the least."

"For somebody who is supposed to be keeping out of trouble, those are big sharks circling you." My father slides his tumbler on the island's surface and makes eye contact with me. "I might not like Finn Donaghey, but if he was out of prison, he'd never stand for these threats against you. They *are* threats." He half turns and stares at my mother on the couch. "Volkov's girlfriend sought out Opal to name-drop. The company I was dealing with brought up you and the PLA without any plausible reason to discuss you or Finn."

"We already had our concerns about the bomb," Jay admits.

"Your mother and I think it's time I step in and help you handle things here."

My gaze flies to his. "No." When he goes to speak again, I hold up my hand. "In the past, you haven't made situations like this better for me. You've worsened them. So, no, you're not welcome. I appreciate your concern, but I'm not having you insert yourself." With Finn arriving tomorrow, having my father here is a recipe for disaster. The last person I'll be telling about the jailbreak is the man in front of me.

"You said things haven't been going that well," my mother tries to reason from the couch. "It seems like the source of your problems could be any of these."

"I love you, Mom. But the last time you came to me with a 'threat,' it turned out to be nothing. Finn and Jay wasted resources trying to track a lead that never needed to be pursued."

She flushes and stares into her wineglass. "I'm not going to apologize for worrying about you."

Her selective worry is the problem, not that it exists. "Jay and I are on top of this. I can assure you we're taking the threat seriously."

My mother tips up the rest of her wine and comes to the island to slide the glass on top. "I'm not pretending I can help with any of this or that I even understand it. But promise me you'll call your dad if you get into trouble."

If I'm calling my father, I've hit the bottom of the barrel. I'm not making that promise. "We're handling the complications. You don't need to worry."

Jay shows them out the door and back to their waiting car. When he returns to the house, we stare at each other for a long moment. "I don't know about you," he says. "But I can't wait for Finn to get his ass here."

"I hope Hagen doesn't get antsy and screw up our plan for tomorrow. If he's sending messages through my mother, he's trying to back Finn into a corner about something."

"Agreed."

"Do you think he had a hand in the bomb?" Most of the warehouse stock had never been found. Pieces of it, or all of it, could have ended up anywhere.

Jay takes a deep breath. "It's possible. There's so much unknown right now."

The baby monitor lights up in front of me, and I pick it up, watching Lucas roll around in his crib. My heart swells when I realize our lives are going to change again. "Finn will be here tomorrow. I can hardly believe it. Part of me is jumping for joy and the other part of me is being eaten alive by fear."

"There's no one better than Evander. We have to trust the process. Keep ourselves busy until Finn arrives."

"You're not worried?"

"Worry won't change the outcome. So, keep the focus on things we can manage or influence."

He gave me the same speech earlier today, which is why we spent most of the day poring over old warehouse files. Today has been long; I can't even imagine how tomorrow will feel.

When Lucas cries, I put down the monitor and head for the bedroom. He gives me a big, toothy grin when he catches me entering the room. I lift him into my arms, and he snuggles into the curve of my neck. As I rub his back, my mind drifts to Finn, to how happy we were as a family for a brief window in Switzerland.

"Your daddy is coming home, Lucas. I can't wait to be a family again."

Chapter Eleven

Finn

Something is different. The guards have been shifting and changing the last few days, but the ones interacting with me today are on edge, anxious. Yesterday, they made me move cells. Is today the day? Evander Williams, the FBI, or whoever is running this escape must have people in their pocket. Not knowing who or where has me on high alert.

"Donaghey," the guard calls from outside my room. "I'm to take you to the infirmary for a checkup."

I'm not sick, but I'm not questioning anything when there are so many moving pieces. On my way out, I toss the book I got from the library onto the bed. It's been a while since anticipation has zipped through me like a drug.

Along the corridor, I walk in front of the guard. His walkie goes off with various things happening around the prison. The urge to ask why I'm going to the infirmary or who ordered my checkup runs strong. If I make it to the medical clinic, I'll be surprised. Tension hangs in the air.

When we get to the right entrance, I hesitate. Maybe we *are* going there?

"Hold up," the guard says at the door. He tugs the walkie out of its holder at his hip. "Donaghey says he's running a fever. I've taken him to the infirmary."

The public declaration of my illness must be code to set something else in motion. But what? I hate being on the outside looking in. If they'd let me in on the chaos to come, I could've helped make it better. Or worse. I might have made it worse. I stifle my chuckle as I step into the infirmary.

"I'll be staying with you to make sure we get that fever looked after." His tone is bland.

From my own various exploits, I realize keeping calm and indifferent is the best way to avoid suspicion. Isn't that how Kimi defeated me in my organization? No matter what I threw at her, she never lost her cool. Titanium nerves. It's weird to be on this side of the action. To know beyond a doubt something is coming and to have no idea what will happen. I like it better when I'm the spider, not the fly.

The nurse nods to me on the way past, and her gaze is wary. Is she in on it? Or do I make her nervous? We walk along empty beds until we get to one near the fire escape. In theory, that exit should lead to another fenced area.

"How are you feeling, Donaghey?" the guard asks, leaning against the wall.

"Like there's darkness all around me, and I want someone to throw me a flashlight."

"Not sure the nurse has anything to cure that."

"She isn't the woman I want playing nursemaid." Not that she's come over. Considering I'm the only prisoner here, she must be in on it too.

The guard checks his watch and moves to block the emergency exit. The nurse ambles over with a clipboard pressed to her chest. She crouches in front of me, a thermometer in her hand. "Under your tongue."

I open my mouth for her to slip the cool metal between my lips.

"There are cameras in here," she says, looking at her chart. "But no sound. Privacy rules." She gives me a wry smile. "In a minute or two an alarm is going to ring. You'll have thirty seconds to make it from the door the guard is blocking to the roof."

"If I don't get to the roof in the thirty seconds?" I ask around for the thermometer.

It beeps, and she removes it to scribble bullshit on her chart. "You'll remain locked in the prison. Your friends might still be able to get you out, but you'll be wasting valuable time."

Bowl over the guard, take the stairs to the roof. Was it really that simple? "What's on the roof?"

"With any luck?" She rises and crosses the room. "Your friends with a helicopter."

My body tightens in response to the quick timeline. My ability to sprint isn't what it used to be thanks to being in here. For some reason, security frowns on sudden bouts of running. She comes back holding a small cup of pills, but before she can pass them to me, the alarm blares so sharp and sudden she jumps, dropping the plastic cup.

Without hesitating, I lunge off the bed and tackle the guard, sending him flying through the fire exit and into the concrete hallway. His head cracks against the ground. The injury will help him keep his job, assuming he's still alive. Ahead is the way out into the fenced yard. Red lights flash in a pattern in the corridor and the stairwell. I take the stairs to the right two at a time.

When I get to the top, I wrench on the door handle. It doesn't budge, and having expected it to be unlocked, I applied too much force. My wrist aches, and I shake out my hand, searching the walls for a key or a way to bypass the lock. They've left me nothing?

This was their plan?

My heart thuds through quicksand. *Fuck. Fuck. Fuck.* Ramming my shoulder into the door repeatedly doesn't move it. Even though I'm sure I've got nothing on me to jimmy the lock, I still pat myself. At the bottom of the stairs, the door to the clinic swings open, and a flurry of voices rises over the sirens.

"Donaghey," a guard calls from below. "You've got nowhere to go."

They're not kidding. With the flashing strobe lights and the number of stairs, I wonder whether they can see me. There are so many voices echoing. Are they here or on the radio? I shuffle to the corner of the wall closest to the door handle. When the light flashes, none of it catches me. They'll have to come up here for me, and I'm not making it easy. It's a narrow stairwell. They'll have to be single file. Take one down, and they'll fall like dominoes.

"Donaghey," the guard calls. "We know you're up there."

Do they? They know I went up here, but unless they've been able to check the cameras, they can't be sure whether I got out. Shouldn't the guard I knocked over be helping me escape?

"I need a medic and backup," somebody calls on his radio.

Ah. The other guard is still unconscious. Where'd the nurse go if they're after a medic?

His foot hits the bottom stair, and I tense for battle. Seems he's on his own. Even easier.

The door behind me pops open, and when it swings back, I almost sag with relief until the lights flash red, and the guard draws his gun.

"Look out!" I holler.

Whoever opened the door lets it partially close, and the guard's firearm discharges. The bullet pings off the metal surface, and I slip out the half-open door before he can get off another shot.

"Holy fuck." I force the door closed behind me. The guard who sprints up the stairs after me bangs on the exit. "What took you so long?"

"Holdup at the airport." The burly Black man hustles me to the waiting chopper.

"Are you Evander?" I hop into the helicopter, and he follows. Before we're seated, we're rising into the midnight sky. The guy who got me out shoves the handle down, locking the door, then buckles himself in.

"Shots fired," he calls to the pilot.

"Are you buckled? We need to bank," a female voice responds from the front, her thick Irish accent a surprise. The broad man beside her is focused out the passenger window. A three-person team doesn't seem like much if shit goes wrong.

"Locked," my rescuer says.

"Loaded." I suppress my grin.

With that, we take a hard bank, and my ass slides toward the secured door. Jesus, that was sharp. A chuckle escapes. Elation is a wildfire running through me. I made it out. Carys's name echoes in my mind, and images of her overlap one after the other.

Us in our twenties, in my bed, with her head on my shoulder and leg slung across my hip as she traced my scars. Then seventeen years later, a Russian hotel, the absolute certainty I'll never love another woman the way I love her, her tears in the interrogation room when she realized I gave myself up for her.

I peer out the window for a moment, watching Michigan fade into the background. Her plan worked, or Evander's did. Someone's plan is so simple yet so effective. Then I realize I don't have a clue who broke me out. Is the guy next to me Evander? FBI? PLA? He never answered.

"You're Evander? Why the hell was an alarm going off? You wanted everyone aware I was escaping."

He narrows his eyes and seems thoughtful. "Probably a distraction. I'm a little fuzzy on the details."

"Why the fuck would you be fuzzy on the details? You *planned* the details." Unless he's not Evander. He fits the physical description, but bulky Black dude isn't a detailed list of attributes.

His lips twist, and he faces me. "I'm Noel, not Evander. I'm a junior lieutenant in the PLA. The two people up front are Lachlan and Kim."

That gets my attention. When I glance at the pilot's seat, she holds my gaze in the mirror, a hint of amusement in her black depths. Well, fuck me. "Lachlan, you said?" I lean forward, sure I'm right.

The man in the passenger seat shifts himself sideways, and his hazel eyes meet mine. The same eyes I looked into for years while we planned takedowns and business expansions. He's not Lachlan. He's Lorcan, my baby brother.

"Aye." His Irish accent is thick and deep. "You can call me Lachlan." He extends his hand, and I shake it, squeezing ever so slightly.

His goatee is gone, and they've dyed his hair a dark brown. Hardly a disguise for anyone determined to dig. But we were never much for taking pictures, and neither of us owned a single social media account. Hopefully, the FBI hasn't sent him into this assignment to die.

He drops my hand, which reminds me we don't know each other in this world. Guess I better keep playing along. Their interception of my return home should be a shock. "I was under the impression Evander

Williams and his crew were breaking me out? What's with the change of plans?"

Noel glances at Kim and Lorcan and seems to be weighing his words. "The PLA has an interest in acquiring your services."

I chuckle, but it holds no humor. "Too bad I'm not interested in serving them. Any two-bit mobster could accomplish the things I've done." Not true. I've done lots of cool and illegal shit during my mafia career. Loran's lips quirk up at my modesty. He's never heard me downplay anything before.

"Once we're finished with you, we'll make sure you get to Cape Verde." Noel's tone is mild, and he raises his eyebrows toward Kim's reflection in the mirror like I'm an idiot. As though he believes he's in total control. *Not today, you fucker.*

In one swift movement, I unclip my buckle and lunge at him, my hands gripping his throat. "They sent a lieutenant?" I spit into his face. "Should have sent the general. I don't answer to you. Or anyone at the PLA. And if I have to wrest the controls from her fingers, we'll be going to Cape Verde unless you can give me a good reason to cooperate."

Lorcan reaches over the seats and tears me off Noel. He's been working out. I don't remember him being that strong. Of course, prison has made me weak. Between solitary confinement and fights, I didn't get much time for the gym.

"Get the hell off him," Lorcan growls. "Everything will be explained to ya when we get to Ireland."

"That's not good enough." I match his fierce tone.

His annoyed expression speaks volumes. Am I overselling this? If I didn't know this was how things would go, I'd be livid. I haven't taken control of the helicopter or shot Noel. Though I do have his gun now—snatched that while Lorcan heaved on me. No one has noticed yet.

Noel rubs his neck and glowers at me. "Christ, settle down. The PLA wants your assistance, and when you're done helping, you can do whatever you want. If you won't help us, we don't have a problem going after the things that matter to you."

Lorcan tenses in front of me. Did he just threaten Carys? I unbuckle my seat belt and lunge at him again. Kim banks the copter, and I topple forward into Lorcan's arm instead of wrapping my hands around Noel's throat again. Boy doesn't learn. Lorcan bunches the material of my shirt into his fist and glares at me. We stare at each other, neither of us budging. He tosses me into my seat without a word. *Message received, brother. Message received.*

"You want me to listen to you," I snarl. "You don't threaten me or anyone associated with me." I tug Noel's gun out of my waistband and point it at him. "Better not bank again there, Kim. My trigger finger is itching for a workout."

Noel meets my gaze, and his jaw is set with determination. "You got my gun. So what?"

I chuckle. "So, I'm keeping it. Finders keepers and all that shit." A smirk plants itself on my face. "Next time you take a jab at me, remember I've got this, and I'll be using it to put a bullet in your brain if you so much as *think* about coming after me or mine. You got me?"

"Didn't have to be this way, man."

"You're right. It didn't. So, when we get to Ireland, lieutenant or not, I'm not talking to you. Him"—I gesture to Lorcan—"or her." I nod at Kim. "Not you." I slip the gun against the small of my back. "Next time you whip out your dick, make sure it's bigger than mine."

Up front, Lorcan lets out a bark of laughter before he smothers it. When I stare out the window, I swallow my answering grin. Been a while since my brother and I were on the same side. Having to put up with the prick beside me just might be worth it to reestablish the camaraderie we lost so long ago.

Chapter Twelve

Carys

Lucas is restless. When I put him down at his regular bedtime, I hoped he'd sleep through the night. Rocking him isn't going to work. He's wide-awake, and my nervous energy probably makes him think it's the middle of the day. Evander should have been here an hour ago. Hitching Lucas onto my hip, I head to the living room.

Jay is sprawled on the couch, and he glances over the back when I come out of the hallway. "Little guy can't sleep?"

I laugh. "Can any of us?"

"Apparently my wife and kids aren't having any trouble." He yawns and checks his phone.

"Anything?" Hope rises in my chest for the millionth time since the jailbreak started. Evander said we wouldn't get any updates until they walked through the door. If the plan went sideways at all, he'd be putting out fires. The news broke the story of Finn's escape an hour ago—when Finn should have arrived. He's out. We don't know why he isn't here. "Are you getting worried yet?"

Jay's my barometer for how much I should be panicking. So far, he's been relaxed on the couch. No pacing; no frantic internet searches.

"Nope." He sits up and rests his forearms on his knees. "Evander had a contingency plan for everything. Has something gone wrong? Yeah, I think so. But no news is good news. Whatever has happened, he's fixing it or tracking it or rerouting."

"Right." I take out a bottle, heat the water, then mix the formula. Lucas makes happy noises while he waits for me to stop shaking. "Bubba?" I meet his gaze, and he makes a fist over and over, the sign for milk.

Sometimes when I look at him, I see Eric. For most people, genetics are a marvel, and something to be celebrated. His dark hair and eyes mimic his biological father, and the reminder is a tender spot in my heart. Such an awful man gave me such a precious gift. As my son gets older, I hope his personality outshines any remembrance of Eric. He'll be Lucas, and the shadow of Eric won't loom so large.

I take a seat on the other end of the couch, with my baby cradled in my arms while he drinks his bottle. Talking is pointless, but I want to spew out useless words as though they'll ease my twisted gut. What is there to say when nothing is known? Speculation will drive me insane. He's out of the prison, and he's on his way here. He has to be.

Jay's phone beeps, and he checks the screen. "Dominic says there's a car coming down the lane."

My heart leaps into action as though it's been whipped. The sudden gallop makes me press the heel of my hand to my chest. "He's almost here."

He smirks and rises. "See? Nothing to worry about. A delay. Nothing catastrophic." He tips his head toward the door. "Want me to take Lucas? You can meet them at the entrance."

I nod and pass him off. The heat of anticipation rises to my cheeks. This is it—the happy ending I wasn't sure we'd get, and we're grasping it with both hands. Jay juggles my son while he texts Dominic to let Finn and Evander in straight away.

When the door opens, I bounce on my heels, ready to fly into Finn's arms. God, it's been so long. Evander enters first, his expression grim, but I ignore him and peek over his shoulder. Where's Finn? "Is he still in the car? Was he hurt?" My racing heart stutters. "Oh, God. Has he been hurt?" There's agony in my voice. "Do we need to go to a hospital?"

I clutch onto Evander's arm, trying to see past him into the dark-tinted windows. He'd take Finn to the hospital before coming here if it was serious, wouldn't he? Or have a doctor on standby? Had that been one of the contingency plans?

"You're gonna want to sit down." His tone is gentle despite the frustration in his gaze.

"No." I shake my head. "I don't want to sit. I want to be told where Finn is."

The door to Lena's room opens, and she comes down the hall in a rush. "Is he here?"

"No," I cry, the sound of my voice almost a wail. At the noise, Lucas's face puckers, and he reaches for me. Jay holds him tight, and Lena intercepts.

"I'll take him to your bedroom, Carys. I'll see if I can get him asleep." Her expression is pinched when she removes Lucas from Jay's outstretched arms.

Jay's hand slides along the small of my back. "Come on, Carys. I'm sure Evander's got things he needs to tell us. We gotta keep calm to find the best path forward. There's always a path forward."

That's been our mantra for years. Impossible isn't a word we use. When we want something enough, there's always a route to take or a path to explore. The question is whether the consequences of taking those paths are ones a person can live with. Right now, I'll go down any road that leads to Finn. He's not here. He should be here. I swallow my sob and nod, heading to the couch. There, I perch on the edge as though I'm going to fly out and rescue him myself. Where *is* he?

Once we're seated, Evander lets out a long breath. "Finn's not with me."

"No shit, Sherlock," Jay mutters in his first sign of any emotion since the night began.

"Where is he?" I am desperate to keep my voice rational and even. I've been in enough meetings with men to realize any woman's emotions are viewed as weak or unstable. A man can rage or scream at people in frustration, but a woman can't. I can't. Steady. Calm. Find the way out of the maze without losing my cool.

Evander rubs his face. "I'm still gathering intel."

"You must know something." Jay's tone borders on threatening. "Or you wouldn't be here."

"I came because you'd be worried, and any time a plan goes this wrong, I make it a priority to speak to my clients in person."

"You don't have a clue where he is," I whisper. The realization causes a ball to rise into my throat. The urge to let out a huge, wracking sob is almost more than I can bear.

"I'm hoping to get more information while we're talking. I have a crew piecing together where he might have been taken."

"Taken?" I latch onto the one word. Of course, it makes sense. He was coming to me, and he would never go anywhere else. "We had a bombing here." I glance at Jay. "A few weeks ago. Do you think Finn's kidnapping and that are connected?"

"I wouldn't rule out anything at this point," Evander admits.

"The Volkovs?" I peer at Jay, trying to get a beat on where his head has gone. Mine is spiraling, searching for any answer to make sense of Finn disappearing.

"Could be." Jay frowns. "I got the impression whatever Hagen was after was *in* the prison not out of it."

Evander let his phone rest on the coffee table and steeples his fingers. "Here's what we know. My crew got him to the emergency fire escape that links to the roof. They use the platform to helicopter patients out of the infirmary. During the escape, he knocked a guard unconscious. That wasn't unexpected. We wanted the jailbreak to look like Finn had manufactured it rather than inside help. Protect people's jobs in case I need them again later." He takes a deep breath. "Shots were fired in the stairwell, but Finn did get out." His phone beeps, and he picks it up to check the message before setting it down. "My helicopter crew was intercepted by a group of three at the airport. What I don't understand is who these people are connected to or where they've taken him."

"As far as you know, he's alive?" My voice is little more than a whisper. The thought of him dead is enough to make my knees weak, and my stomach rolls.

"According to my inside contacts, the cameras on the roof show Finn rushing into the helicopter willingly with a big Black man. He probably assumed it was me. We've never met, but I have a certain reputation."

"Finn's led a colorful life," I hedge.

"Colorful?" Evander chuckles. "Bloodthirsty is more accurate. He's got a lot of enemies. Conversely, the talent for blood and mayhem can be appealing to people or organizations." He rubs his neck. "We have a tracker on the helicopter, and when it's apparent exactly where they're headed, we can narrow the field of suspects." His phone buzzes, and he hits the answer button and heads into the kitchen.

"Oh, my God," I mutter, dropping my head into my hands. "We've lost him."

"Whoever took him didn't kill him, at least not right away. So, either Evander is on track and they want to use him for something, or the grudge is personal," Jay reasons.

"That's supposed to make me feel better?" I snap. "We don't have him. He's a wanted criminal. He's got enemies everywhere. Someone sent us a warning weeks ago, and we're still no closer to figuring that out. Do you really think none of this is connected? There's no such thing as coincidence." God knows I heard those words often enough from Finn.

Evander returns to the living room and stands in front of me and Jay, tapping the phone against his palm. "They've landed on a remote airstrip in Ireland."

"Ireland," I breathe. Relieved and anxious because Ireland could mean so many things.

"Who owns it?" Jay asks. "Mafia?"

"PLA," he admits with a grimace. "Not worst-case scenario, but they don't play around. They've been rapidly gaining power. The guard at the prison confirmed he was able to get a microtracker on Finn while they were in the infirmary. So, in the morning, we should have a lock on his exact location. We can go in and extract him."

"I don't understand," I admit. Why would the PLA kidnap Finn from a jailbreak? Why would they need him at all?

"My guess?" Evander glances between me and Jay. "He has the blood-lust they like. As the head of his mafia organization, he annihilated several competing groups. He's a strong tactician."

"I bet you any tactical plans came from his brother, Lorcan, not him. Finn isn't subtle," I say.

"Subtle isn't necessary most of the time. They like effective." Evander shrugs. "Besides, his brother is dead, right?"

"Right." I try not to make the word sound hesitant. Lorcan isn't any more dead than Kim is. I run my hands through my hair and try to gather my thoughts. When the CIA detained me in Ireland, Kim appeared quickly. Would they have tried to insert her in the PLA? Would Lorcan have gone with her? "An extraction?"

"I'll fly to Ireland to get a lay of the land. I've got people I can work with to get him out."

Jay glances at me, and we hold eye contact in silent communication. Whether this fuckup was Evander's fault or not, it happened. He's not running the show solo.

"You're not doing this rescue without us." Jay slides his phone into his pocket.

"This isn't a mission for amateurs. The PLA isn't an organization you want to fool around with."

"Doesn't matter." I steel myself. "We're coming."

"I'll be making decisions quickly and decisively. If you're tagging along, you're not to interfere, you're to observe." Evander pins us both with his gaze. "I'm the leader. There isn't room for more than one."

"Fine," I grit out. His attitude is nothing new, though I'm not sure Finn will be so keen on obeying anyone once we get him.

"Make your arrangements. I'll text you as soon as I've got a definite lock on his location."

"Okay." I follow him to the door, my mind churning with everything I'll need to arrange. Lucas can't come because the situation is too dangerous and unpredictable.

Once Evander is gone, Jay says, "You think Lorcan and Kim are undercover?"

"That's my first thought." I grab my laptop off the side table and open it.

In the search engine, I type Lorcan Donaghey and then navigate to images. Surely there must be a photo of Lorcan somewhere. As I click through page after page, I have to admit the government did a good job of covering his identity, at least superficially. Did they manage to scrub his image from everything? Otherwise, having him undercover would be a liability. When I examined my pictures from various events after Kim's betrayal, her absence from photos was obvious. She had a sixth sense where cameras were concerned, and while she climbed the ranks of my business, she was never keen for accolades that might lead to public praise.

"What are you looking for?" Jay peers over my shoulder.

"Lorcan. But other than his name, his image isn't anywhere. As far as the world is concerned, he is dead."

"At least if he's part of this..."

"Yeah, I agree. He and Finn have their problems, but they're still brothers." I snap the laptop closed. "I hope, whatever is going on, we aren't walking into a trap."

Chapter Thirteen

Finn

When we land, Noel is the first one out the door. The sun is peeking out of the horizon, creating a glow across the sky. We've landed somewhere resembling a field rather than an airstrip—the advantage of a helicopter.

"Where the hell are we?" I grumble, even though this must be Ireland. Northern Ireland, I'd wager.

"The home country." Noel smirks.

When Kim and Lorcan climb out of the helicopter, I get a better look at them in the half-light. Other than Lorcan's hair color being darker and his lack of a goatee, he's the same. Kim hasn't changed a thing. Long black hair, eyes like coal, and tall—a smidge taller than me even. Her appearance might not have changed, but she's a chameleon, able to alter her personality to lure in whomever she needs. Lorcan was always like that too—his accent shifting on a dime from Bostonian to Irish. Eager to please, to fit in, and to do the right thing. He was born into the wrong family. He physically resembles our father, but I'm our father's son, as much as that realization might sting. The old man was a first-class bastard. I have no regrets over the part I played in his death.

"Can you two handle him? I need a nap and then I've got shit to do for PJ," Noel says.

"Aye." One of Lorcan's eyebrows lift. "'Tis nothin'."

"He needs to be at headquarters by eight tonight. Feed him, or whatever, but keep him holed up in your apartment."

"Sounds grand." Kim's accent takes me by surprise. It shouldn't. She'd want to blend, but it's flawless, as though she was raised here.

Noel gets into a waiting car, and the driver zooms off. Lorcan and I face each other. "He's in charge of things? He sounds American."

"Aye, he is. He's a useless scut if ever I seen one. Means to an end." He gestures to the small compact in the parking lot. "This is the closest we've gotten to breakin' into the inner circle. The PLA attracts all sorts."

"Why do you need me?" I hitch up my government-issued track pants, and my mind drifts to Carys in Cape Verde, realizing her hard work was for naught. There's no doubt she'll come for me, and then I'll tell her everything.

"How about we grab breakfast," Kim suggests.

Lorcan runs a hand along her back as though she needs reassurance. Is she still not over me shooting her? I thought we cleared that up in Cape Verde before they helped me make my deal.

"We've got clothes for you in the car."

Her accent is something I'll have to get used to. Each time she speaks, I'm tempted to gawk around for another person. "I haven't had anything that wasn't government issued in months."

"Breakfast it is." Lorcan unlocks the car.

Kim sweeps the booth for bugs while Lorcan and I order meals from the bar. We stand in companionable silence, and I take deep breaths, wondering when my freedom will set in. Probably not until I lay eyes on Carys. The rest of this'll fade to the background.

"You gonna fill me in?" I ask once the bartender has punched in our orders.

"No." Lorcan takes money out of his wallet. "Best wait for Kim. CIA isn't so sure about this arrangement 'tween you and me."

"What aren't they sure about? The fact we've shot each other or the fact we ran a mafia empire together?"

Lorcan's lips twitch. "I suspect both."

"They figured assigning us to the agent who fell in love with you was the winning strategy?"

The smile drops from his face, and he grimaces before meeting my gaze. "They reckon I'd never do anything to hurt her. They're not wrong."

Message received. I'm still lower in the hierarchy of his affections than she is. Not that I'm keen to test that anytime soon. One family shootout is enough for this lifetime.

"You'd better ask any questions you've got tonight. Once you're in place, it'll be too risky to appear overly familiar with each other."

"I'm not much for pretending." Normally, that's a strength. I am who I am.

Lorcan snorts as he accepts the coffees and the change. "Who's pretending? Kim doesn't like you, and I'm not sure how I feel about you. Should be easy enough." He gives me a hard stare. "Sometimes to get what you want, you've got to be willing to be who you're not."

He sounds like a Dr. Seuss book, one of the ones Carys bought for Lucas. The point doesn't go over my head. Whatever it takes to get back to Carys is what I'll do—including another three years in prison or putting my life on the line. "That what you're doing now? Being who you're not?" I grab my coffee and follow him to the booth in the far corner.

"No." Lorcan's tone is annoyed. "I reckon that's what I was doing before Kim. I've barely got two pence to rub together, but 'tis a much more fulfilling life."

The urge to mock him settles over me, a familiar blanket, but I can't bring myself to joke. I understand what he means. While I missed my money and power when our empire fell, love for a couple people has sprung up in its place. "So, faking your work for the PLA is that fulfilling?" I'm still me—can't help a little dig.

Lorcan slides Kim's coffee to her and slips into the booth beside her. I take the opposite side. We might end up on the same team, but I'm not sure we're there yet. "We're not in with the PLA yet," he admits. "Getting you is our power play for access."

"Why me?"

Her lips twist. "We don't know." The Irish accent isn't as thick, more of an undercurrent than a driving force in her words. "Trust me. We didn't go looking for *this* opportunity."

"You're still pissy about me shooting you?" I eye her over the top of the mug as I sip my coffee.

Her jaw clenches. "Less about that and more about you murdering my brother in cold blood and him literally dying in my arms."

A frown mars my brow. What is she on about? "What brother?"

"Chadwick Lee," Kim seethes. "Ring any bells?"

My back hits the soft cushion of the booth as though she's shot me. That's a blast from the past. His death was one of the life sentences I received. Wondered how the FBI was able to pin that on me. "Wicked Wickie was your brother?" I cock my head, trying to catch any family resemblance.

Maybe a bit. Wickie was Asian, wasn't he? I'm not sure what Kim's ethnic background is. Asian wouldn't have been my first choice. Lee's father was Korean, wasn't he? Then something else clicks in my memory, and I home in on Lorcan who is avoiding my gaze. Dare I bring it up? She must be aware. Would he hide a secret that big from her?

Let's test the waters. "Lorcan, what was the deal with Wickie's father again?"

He winces, and Kim's eyes narrow. Proof enough. We're on the same page. Old me would've rubbed in that piece of information, ground the salt into the wound until we were all squirming. Maybe I've learned a thing or two in the last year. "Appears I missed a step with all the shooting at the warehouse. Care to fill me in?"

Kim and Lorcan exchange a long look. "Want me to tell it?" He rubs a thumb along her cheekbone as though wiping away a tear that hasn't fallen.

She gives a quick nod and stares into her coffee cup, avoiding my eyes. Then Lorcan launches into an involved story of how our family has intersected with and decimated Kim's. When he gets to the end, she raises her head, her gaze defiant when it meets mine.

I huff out a breath and take a sip of my coffee, gathering my thoughts. We have to work together with that baggage, and I need to be sure she'll have my or Carys's back in a tight spot. The urge to remove Kim from this equation is strong. If the situation were reversed and she did what I did, I'd put a bullet in her spine at the first chance.

"You still want to kill me?" I stare at her. She might have been a double-crosser, but she was never one to sugarcoat her feelings.

"Some days, yes." She doesn't break eye contact. "Do you ever have any regrets?"

I toy with my cup on the table. How do I answer that? "That's who I was then, and if I think back to him, then no, I don't." I shrug. "Sounds unfeeling, I'm sure. But I didn't let myself give a shit about people. Empathy had no place in my life." I meet her gaze again. "The guy I am now, though?" My mind grapples for the right way to explain the changes I've undergone. "I'd never willingly cause you or my brother pain again." It's the best I can offer. I'm still not a good man, but I'm better than I was.

Emotions flash across her face in quick succession, but her disappointment is clear. Maybe I should've lied.

"I guess that's something," she says as the bartender arrives with our food. Lorcan's hand slides along her back, and she gives him a grateful glance. Their connection, a buzz under the surface when we were in the same house, shines out of them now. Unmistakable. The dimmer on a light bulb turned to full wattage. Christ, I miss Carys.

We eat in silence for a few minutes before I decide to broach the other elephant in the room. "You really don't understand why the PLA wants me?"

"No." Lorcan sops up his egg with his toast. "Reckon it could be any number of reasons."

Kim eyes me, an internal struggle evident on her face. "This is nothing we've been told, but I wonder whether your involvement has something to do with the Van de Berg family?"

Carys's family? "They set her up to take the fall for several PLA arms deals."

"I'm aware." Kim's tone is sardonic. "I did warn her."

"Why the fixation?" I slice into my fried tomato and take a bite. Charles did business with the PLA when he was in charge of Van de Berg Ammunitions, but Carys stopped those transactions when she took over. Were they pissed at her? Frustrated by her morals? Did they have something against women in powerful positions? "Who runs the PLA?"

"PJ." Lorcan cradles his coffee cup in his hand. "Pierre-Jacques, a French national with a hot temper. At least that's what we've surmised. Haven't met him yet."

"That's who we'll see at eight?"

Kim's cutlery rattles against her plate when she finishes her last bite. "I'd think so. PJ wanted you. We're delivering. Noel went with us as assurance everything was on the up and up."

"So, despite the fact he's a lieutenant, he must be expendable."

"Aye," Lorcan agrees. "He's important enough to babysit us, but not a loss if we killed him."

"Curious strategy," I admit. We never let our babysitters get overwhelmed by the ones being babysat. Too risky. When someone needed killed, we did it ourselves. "A loyalty check?" If we outnumbered Noel and could have taken him down and chose not to, it's an interesting gauge of character.

"Perhaps," Kim concedes. "If so, we'll have passed when we turn up with you as directed."

Tiredness seeps into my bones. With the five-hour time change, I'm fading fast. It might be morning here, but it's still the middle of the night in Michigan. What time would it be in Cape Verde? Two hours behind here. She'll be pacing a hole in the floor or on a flight if Evander figured out the switch. "When Carys turns up, I need to be told."

"What makes you think either of us will hear?" Kim raises her eyebrows.

"Zahir said he was fine with her being here. So, I'm guessing they've got eyes on her, and someone will let one of you know." I push my empty plate into the middle of the table between us. "'Cause I'm not sticking around to help anyone if I can't see her."

Lorcan lets out a deep sigh. "Aye, we'll be informed when she arrives. We've been told to let you meet as long as it's safe."

I scrunch up my face as I contemplate his answer. "Seem odd to you? Them being so willing to throw her into the middle of this?"

"As we said"—he drains his coffee—"the PLA has a hard-on for the Van de Berg family. Perhaps Zahir believes Carys will be leverage."

Realization sinks in. The FBI or the CIA *want* her here. Otherwise, they wouldn't be this agreeable. She's my flight risk, the reason I'd ditch and run. So, what are they expecting when she appears? "I want to see her, but then I'm sending her home."

My brother meets my gaze, and there's sympathy in his depths. "A wise decision, I'm sure. Nothing good can come of having her in the middle of this."

PLA headquarters is a run-down, partially converted castle. Looks as though someone tried to turn the ruins into a mansion and got bored halfway through. We're somewhere in Northern Ireland. Kim and Lorcan are vague and won't let me check their phone or search the map. If they're not willing to help me, I'll add a phone to my list of demands from Pierre-Jacques. Pretentious fucking name. Doing other people's dirty work has never appealed to me, and I've got a feeling they want me to climb into the mud for something. What will it be?

After we're searched, we're taken to a ballroom that looks as though it was remodeled in the seventies. A bit garish for my taste. The only piece of furniture is a throne. Well, two. They sit to the left of the oversized double doors. Each one is a deep red with PJ embroidered into them in a crisp white. Is this a joke, or are these people insane? I glance at Lorcan, who is grimacing. Bet he's thinking the same thing as me.

"You made it." Noel breezes through the doors.

Kim shoves her hands deeper into the pockets of her leather jacket. "Thought we were meeting with PJ?"

"If we're not meeting with somebody who can tell me why you've kidnapped me, then I'll be catching the next plane out," I say.

"Oh?" Noel grins. "With what money?"

I chuckle to hide my annoyance. "You think I can't come up with enough cash for a plane ticket?" I cross my arms. "When I want something, I get it."

"Which is exactly the kind of winning attitude I need." A man wanders into the room through the same doors as Noel. His outfit is rumpled, and his too-long brown hair curls at the ends. He's younger than Kim. Must be in his late twenties, maybe early thirties with his baby face. Slight frame, average height.

A sheep. Is there a wolf under that façade? "Oh yeah?" I raise my eyebrows. "It's my winning attitude you need." I smirk. "I coulda loaned you that from a distance."

"Oh, no." He wags his index finger. "I like up close and personal much better." He throws himself into one of the thrones and gazes at the three of us in silence.

"PJ?" Kim hedges.

"Pierre-Jacques." He removes a knife from a holder on his hip and presses the tip into his index finger, peering at us over the top. "Kim and Lachlan?" There's a touch of a French accent, but no lilting Irish.

"Aye," Lorcan agrees.

At some point, I'm going to screw up his name. They're close, but not quite the same. Will I be able to plead ignorance? Definitely can't call him my *deartháir beag,* or I'll have a hell of a time explaining that one. Who calls a stranger their younger brother?

"Finn," Pierre-Jacques says. "We have a job for you."

"Didn't realize I was looking." I want to snatch the knife from his hand, but we're not positioned close enough to make that easy. As annoyed as I am by this government assignment, I'm aware of my role. Whatever this guy is after, I have to go along with it... eventually.

He grins and spreads his hands. "When we are done with you, we'll send you home. Not to worry."

"What is it you're after?" There's no getting around my commitment, and I'm not in the mood to play hard to get.

"Two things." He holds up the corresponding fingers. "We've found ourselves in a bit of a dispute with the McCaffery family. You know them, yes?"

Lorcan, Kim, and I tense at the same time. Jesus. I haven't thought much about them since one of their crew almost murdered Carys eighteen years ago. Going after them won't be a hardship.

"Ah." Pierre-Jacques points to the three of us. "A name you all recognize. Excellent." He tucks the knife into the carrier on his hip. "We want to do business with the Byrne family, and they won't meet with us. We want you to go to them on our behalf. You know them as well, correct?"

I squint in wariness. "What kind of business?"

"Mutually beneficial." Pierre-Jacques's expression is calculating.. "I hear you can be quite persuasive."

The truth is, I like Thomas Byrne and his family. When Carys disappeared last year, snatched up by the CIA for questioning, he milked his contacts to get me information. I owe him. I'm not sure coming to him with a PLA deal is going to go over well. "What do I get out of this?"

"Your freedom." Pierre-Jacques shrugs as though that's obvious.

I chuckle. "You think I couldn't get that right now?"

"Oh, I am sure there is someone in the world you care about, who you would not want to let down with any foolish behavior. No?"

I grit my teeth and force my shoulders to relax. If I had any doubts about sending Carys straight back to Cape Verde, he just eliminated them. That threat was thinly veiled. "If you wanted my help, I'd need more information."

"Of course. Of course." Pierre-Jacques rises from his seat. "Tomorrow, I will give you more details." He focuses on Lorcan and Kim. "For your help in this matter, I can offer you money or a job."

"I like earning my way," Lorcan says.

"Me as well," Kim agrees.

"A job it is. It's actually perfect. Noel doesn't like Finn, so it would be better if he stayed with you tonight. Can you handle him for one more night?"

Kim and Lorcan exchange a glance. "We can," she says.

"Lunch. Tomorrow." Pierre-Jacques wanders toward the double doors. "Bring whoever you want. The more the merrier."

As soon as he's through the door, I want to start talking, but I know better than to tip my hand. Instead, the three of us show ourselves out, collecting our weapons at the front and heading for the car.

When the last door slams, Lorcan shifts to examine me. "You caught his meaning?"

"I did." I stare out the window, my heart thumping an irregular beat. Anticipation and dread. "Carys is in Ireland." The one person I'd do anything to protect is within sniper range of the enemy. "We need to track her down and send her home."

CHAPTER FOURTEEN

CARYS

Our plane lands in Belfast, and as we wade through government red tape, I wonder how the PLA avoided the same process. Maybe they bypassed the whole thing. It's what I would have done—found a loophole. Finn has nothing but the prison clothes on his back. No passport, identification, or money. Evander tracked him and the helicopter to a northern village. He's brought a small team with him to negotiate his release.

We pile into the rented van, and one of Evander's men navigates us north. Finn's presence in the same country is a homing signal, flashing to the beat of my heart. "How long?" I peer out the window as Belfast falls away along the roaring highway.

At one time, Van de Berg Ammunitions had a plan to build our European office here. When I took over from my father, I decided not to pursue the investment, instead favoring more travel for our employees. The terrain around Belfast is familiar given the number of times we came to investigate the possibility of reorganizing. Between Finn's spirit and a forgotten potential investment, the anxiety bubbling in my stomach decreases to a simmer.

"Ballycastle is about an hour from here," the driver says.

"Is that where he is?"

"Not quite." Evander passes me the map app on his phone. With his finger, he indicates a location outside Ballycastle along the coast. "The helicopter landed here." He pinches the screen and points to a road. "His clothes ended up here, or at least the tracker did."

Despair creeps up my spine. It's a guessing game. "So, we don't know where he is."

"We've got a place to start. I'm sending my team out tonight to ask around, observe, see what we can come up with. He's here somewhere. You and Jay will get a good night's sleep at the hotel. In the morning, we'll put together ideas based on where he's located."

"You're not leaving us out of the plan," I warn. The last thing I want is to wake up and find more things have gone wrong.

"No intention of leaving you out." He closes his phone. "But we have got to be smart about this. The PLA has taken him for a reason." He grimaces and examines me. "Is there any chance he's working *with* them by choice?"

I rear back as though he's slapped me. "No. No. He wants to be with his family." There are few things I know for certain, but that's one of them. Finn's unwavering loyalty is an absolute. He went to jail for me. Between death and jail, he always said he'd pick death. For me, he sacrificed his freedom. He would never betray me.

"The PLA framed Carys for the crimes her father perpetrated or for crimes none of the Van de Berg family committed. What exactly went on there isn't crystal clear," Jay admits. "Finn wouldn't agree to work with them."

But he would take them down. They tried to destroy me, and Finn has never taken threats against me lightly. The McCaffery men who came after him in the Irish bar eighteen years ago almost killed me by accident.

Finn tracked them down and murdered them—over an accident. What would he do to the PLA who willfully and intentionally went after me?

I shudder and meet Jay's gaze. The troubled expression on his face tells me everything I need to know. We're on the same page, but for some reason, both of us aren't giving Evander the full picture. Have we lost faith in him? Do we both suspect something larger is at work here? Even if Finn is going after the PLA, it doesn't explain the interception of the jailbreak.

"All right." There's skepticism in Evander's voice. "We'll continue under the assumption Finn has been kidnapped against his will. We'll formulate an extraction plan once we confirm his location."

"Yes." My tone lacks conviction. "He wouldn't choose to work with them."

"We'll go to the hotel first so you and Jay can get settled, and I can determine next steps with my team." He goes back to his phone. A frown mars his forehead as he clicks through various messages.

I stare out the window as my mind ticks through the possibilities. Did he screw up the extraction? Could the Volkovs have anything to do with the PLA? Someone at the prison was applying pressure to him for something. Is Finn trapped by the PLA against his will? If he agreed to the interception, why wouldn't he have given me a way to see it coming?

Evander checks us into our rooms and then disappears into the conference center with his team. Instead of insisting on joining them, Jay and I are in the hotel's bar and restaurant. Huddled together in a dimly lit booth, we pick at our food. Normally, I'd be relishing in the old-world atmosphere. But unrelenting thoughts keep tumbling through my mind.

"Are you thinking the same thing as me?" I ask.

He nods and takes another bite of his beef pie. "Likely. Finn's not someone who goes quietly anywhere he doesn't want to go. For him not to have gotten any sort of message to you since the jailbreak means one of two things. Either he's in no shape to contact you, or he's going along with this bait and switch for a reason."

"But why?" Him injured or incapacitated is too much to contemplate. He's larger than life—unstoppable—he's survived shootings and stabbings. He's been the conductor of his own fate for so long it's impossible for me to believe he's not still in control somehow.

"My gut says to take them down. The better question is: For who?"

"Hagen?" I murmur.

"Evander told us he was having pressure applied to him in prison. Could be Hagen's got a hand in this. Might be unrelated." Jay polishes off the last of his meal, and I envy his ability to eat in a crisis. My appetite vanishes at the hint of stress. "I think we should ask him how smoothly the jailbreak went. We haven't asked a lot of questions about the process. Was it Plan A?"

I consider the implication of his words. "You think one of Evander's men might have aided the PLA?"

"If the plan went off like clockwork except for the interception of the helicopter, then yeah, I think he's been played." He rubs his jaw. "Or he's been playing us. Something is off if there were no issues other than the chopper being stolen."

I cover my face with my hands and rest my elbows on the wooden table. "What if we find him and he won't come back with us?" The truth in that question terrifies me. We waded into a mass of risks to bust him out, and there's still a chance I'll return to Cape Verde without him. He won't leave a threat to our happiness unanswered.

"I'd like to tell you that won't happen." Jay's expression is layered with sympathy and concern. "We both know that'd be a lie. Finn's a wildcard. The lack of communication from him is troubling. He'll realize you're frantic with worry, maybe even capable of doing something rash or dangerous as a result." He shakes his head.

"At this point, do we stick with him or try to go our own way? If Finn *is* there of his own free will, we could be putting him at risk, not to mention Evander and his team." My thoughts are jumbled with the possible scenarios. Not all of them end well, with Finn in my arms, with us on our way home. I didn't take this very dangerous path to have any of us dead.

"We wait until morning to see what Evander's team comes up with for a plan and for intel into where Finn's located. Maybe he'll have contacted you by then. Maybe this worrying will be for nothing."

Jay often tells me worry is a wasted emotion, but his words can't stop the rising tide of it, sloshing away in my stomach. "I admire your optimism." I push my plate into the center of the table and tuck a stray strand of hair into the bun at the nape of my neck.

"No matter what else is going on," he says, "you're Finn's priority. You and Lucas. Without a doubt, if he can contact you, he will."

Hope swells in me, pushing out the worry. Jay's right. It's a truth I've known this whole time, but it's hard to have faith in something so big and impossible. Whether or not he's been kidnapped, Finn will reach out. I'm going to cling to that even as we try to get to him.

Chapter Fifteen

Finn

What game is Evander playing? He used real names at the hotel check-in, no aliases, a flare in the sky to anyone looking. Who is he trying to flush out? Me? The PLA? Someone else? The bombing in Cape Verde and the confetti bomb indicate Carys has powerful enemies. Does Pierre-Jacques have eyes in the hotel? Contacts at the airport? He knew she arrived in Ireland before we did. Them tracking her makes my blood boil.

Lorcan, Kim, and I circle the hotel several times before they leave me at a rear entrance to enter the lobby without me. Since no one is supposed to realize I'm working for the FBI and CIA in a joint operation to take down the PLA, I'm a wanted fugitive. Being out in public, somewhere as high traffic as this is risky. No matter the consequences, I need to see Carys and make her return to Cape Verde. I don't know what the PLA is up to, but if they're okay with her being in the country, and Zahir cleared her interference with the government, she needs to be far away from whatever happens. I don't make bets I can't win, and I sure as hell am not playing with Carys's life as currency.

The back door pops open beside me, and Kim is framed in the doorway. She blocks my entrance.

"Where's Lorcan?" My tone is wary.

"*Lachlan* is on the third floor as backup for your tryst. Jay is in 320, and Carys is in 322. They're both eating in the hotel restaurant right now."

Annoyance zips through me at being babysat by my little brother, but I tamp it down. My priority is getting her out of Ireland, and if I have to put up with Kim and Lorcan thinking they're in charge, I can do that. "Key?" I hold out my hand, and she drops a metal key into it. "I didn't realize places still used these."

"All over Europe." She rolls her eyes and steps back to let me enter. "Stairs are to your right. You've got your phone?"

After our meeting with Pierre-Jacques, I convinced them to stop and get me a burner. It doesn't connect to the internet, so it's useless apart from numbers already programmed into it or ones in my brain. God forbid they give me too much freedom. At least I'll have a way to check in on Carys once she leaves, and the ability to maintain contact with Lorcan and Kim if we're split up by the PLA. Just because Pierre-Jacques thinks they're valuable now doesn't mean he will later. I'm well aware of how allegiances and loyalties can change with unproven staff. As far as he knows, they're disposable, even if for some reason I'm not.

I wave the device at her, but before I can leave, she grips my forearm. Glancing at her hand, I slowly lift my gaze to hers. She snatches her hand away as though I've burned her. We're not friends, and I won't pretend we've buried the hatchet. It's still possible she'll bury hers in my spine. Lorcan has been the buffer between us for the last twenty-four hours, and without him around, I don't have a clue what will come out of her mouth.

"You need to stop calling him Lorcan, even in private. You're used to bucking authority and doing whatever you want. I get that. But you're playing with his life. Consistency is key. Lorcan is dead. As far as the world knows, you killed him. Lachlan isn't your brother. You don't know each other."

The key is heavy in my palm, and I study her. Her distaste for me radiates off her. The speech is authentic, though. Was she like this in my house? We danced around each other, and I was never sure if we were going to rip each other's clothes off or murder one another. At the time, either outcome would've been fine. I bet it irks her that she ever desired someone as evil as me, somebody who played a hand in the destruction of her family. Doesn't mean the pilot light wasn't on, waiting for us to flip the switch and ignite the flame. To do this job and love every part of my brother, there has to be darkness in her too. Maybe, believing it's the light in my brother she loves helps her sleep at night. Her hands aren't clean. Reminds me of what I love about Carys—she never pretends to be something she's not.

"Consider the message received." I amble toward the stairs.

"You're going to make Carys leave?" Kim calls after me along the deserted hallway.

I chuckle. "You think she listens to me?"

"It's not safe here for her." She follows me. "She's better off in Cape Verde." When I don't turn around, Kim lets out a frustrated noise. "I can't imagine you putting up with somebody who doesn't obey you."

I smirk at her over my shoulder before heading into the stairwell entrance. "Ah, see." I put my foot on the first stair and face her. "This is when you don't know me as well as you think. Even I understand relationships don't work that way." Then I take the stairs two at a time, content to leave her stewing in her assumptions.

She's not too far off about my character, or at least who I used to be. I've never shared authority before, not even with Lorcan when we were business partners and brothers. I might have taken his opinions into consideration, but the final decisions fell on my plate. With Carys, I don't have that luxury. Any time we make choices without each other, we're slaves to our weaknesses. So, while I'm prepared to tell her she can't stay, I'm not naïve enough to believe she'll listen without question. That's not how we work best.

When I reach her door, I spy Lorcan at the end of the hallway near the opposite stairwell. He ignores me and gazes out the tiny window. Both our phones go off at the same time. When I check mine, there's a message from Kim. Carys has left the restaurant. My phone buzzes again.

Just a reminder not to scare Carys. Her scream would break your cover. Keep a light on in the room so she sees you.

Irritation makes my jaw clench. Kim's going to be a thorn in my side, reminding me of my shortcomings at every turn. Under different circumstances, I might have sat in the dark, but I'm not an idiot. I close the message without responding. Maybe if I don't engage with her, she'll stop treating me like a loose cannon. After I enter the room, I decide maybe I will respond after all.

If you hear her screaming, it won't be from fear.

Satisfied, I slip my phone into my pocket and turn on both bedside lamps, but I leave the main lights off. No point in flooding this tiny place with light. If Carys booked the hotel, she'd have sprung for a suite. She's not going to be pleased with this shoebox, whether or not it's a standard European size.

The lock flips, the door cracks, and my heart thuds. Outside the doorway, Carys speaks in low tones to Jay. If she peered in now, she'd see me. The anticipation of being with her makes my cock twitch. I've missed having her close enough to touch. Conversations that can last as long as we want, or cover any topic we want, because no one is looking over our shoulders. Other than our brief meeting in jail a few weeks ago, I haven't been able to come near her. My last memory of holding her tight is when I turned myself in. Not the most pleasant recollection.

Her head is down when she enters the room, and she pushes the door closed. Her forehead falls against the old wood. Her hands are braced on either side of her, as though she's shoring up her strength to keep going. Probably a long day of travel for her on top of countless hours of uncertainty. Still, I drink her in.

From the edge of the bed, I observe her for a beat. So sad, but so fucking lovely. "I didn't mean to worry you." My voice is gruff.

She jumps and gasps, then whips around to face me. Surprise and shock register on her features before she takes the three steps from the door to the bed and tackles me. As soon as my shoulders hit the mattress, she straddles me and buries her face in my neck. Her lips tremble against my skin, and I ease my hand along her narrow back. *So good*. She presses her forehead to my temple, and a strained noise escapes. Then her body is wracked with deep, unexpected sobs.

"Hey." My tone is gentle. "Hey. What is this about?"

She clings to me and cries, and I hold her, unsure if I should say more or say nothing. After not being allowed to touch her for so long, she seems fragile—tiny—in my arms. I run my hands along her body, categorizing everything from her arms to her ankles. I savor the feel of her, lingering on her cast, forcing down my fear and anxiety that anyone got to her. I wasn't there, and someone hurt her. Is she crying because she was afraid? My gut clenches. I should have ignored Zahir's directive and contacted her anyway.

"I wasn't—" Her voice hitches. "I wasn't sure I'd ever get to do this again."

My heart softens, and the tension in my body leaks out of me. Her tears aren't from fear; they're relief. I squeeze her tighter and let my joy seep in. Maybe I don't deserve to have somebody love me like this, but I'm not giving her up. She's my home. Wherever she is, that's where I intend to be when my prison term is done. Having her secured in my arms is the best thing to ever happen to me. No matter what, we'll be together.

Then I remember I have to ask her to leave, and we're probably going to fight. If I was a better man, I'd meet the conflict head-on. Tell her straight up she can't stay.

But I haven't been this close to her in months, this free to touch her or revel in her curves and the lines of her face. I haven't been able to brush away her tears with my lips. I wasn't there when she broke her wrist or when she was too tired to get up with Lucas at night, when she needed the release only I can provide. Most of those, I still can't do and won't be able to do for years. Three years is better than never. So, I'll cling to that glimmer of hope while I give her what I can now.

She sits up and wipes her tears with her palms, then searches the room for tissues.

"Behind you," I say, gently. "On the nightstand."

She climbs off me. My urge is to dig my fingers into her hips and will her to stay where she is. The better man in me might emerge if she isn't flattened against me. For months I've been keeping my longing for her at bay for fear of going insane. When she's not so close, rational ideas return. I have to tell her to go.

In the tiny en suite, she calls out to me, "I'm such a mess. God, this is not how I pictured seeing you again."

I chuckle and follow her into the bathroom. She's the sun I rotate around, unable to stay away, even when I should. She's puffy from crying, and her mascara has smudged under her eyes, but she'll never be anything but beautiful to me. I frame her face and kiss her. Tenderness for her is an ache in my chest. When I pull away, she searches my eyes, the questions she's not asking float across her expression. But none of them stick. Maybe she can sense she doesn't want the answers.

"We can do this," she whispers. "There's no one telling us we can't be together anymore."

In the instant I have to set her straight, I can't do it. It's not in me to hurt her again so quickly. Then she rises on her toes and her lips are on mine. Slanting to deepen the kiss, her fingers dig into my neck. Our tongues tangle in a dance we've done a thousand times. The reasons I should step back and suggest we talk first fade away. Reason and ration can wait. There's nothing I want more than to drown in her. I'm going to let myself sink in; sink so far in I'll have to use superhuman effort to haul myself out. We've got tonight, or however long Lorcan and Kim give me before they pound on the door, and I'm not going to waste a moment of it second-guessing myself. Carys is mine, and I intend to remind her that, at least in some ways, I'm worth the wait. I'll be worth the wait forever.

Chapter Sixteen

Carys

He walks us back to the bed, and we're shedding clothes at a frantic pace, desperate to be as close as possible. When I'm naked, the only thing still covering any part of me is my cast. Most of the time, I don't even notice it anymore. It's amazing how I got used to the awkwardness of hauling the dull ache around. I suppose the physical ache matched the constant longing in my heart.

He runs his fingers along the plaster, and his head is bent over my arm. He kisses above it and every finger on my hand. "I hate that this happened to you. That I wasn't there to protect you."

I don't want to fight so I don't tell him I'm not sure if even he could have prevented anything. A broken wrist was probably the best outcome given the circumstances. A bomb and a gas leak are volatile and unpredictable. Could he have smelled the gas? Sure. Known about the bomb? Extremely doubtful.

"I'm okay," I whisper. "I'll heal." I run my hand along the top of his head, and my palm rests on the back of his neck.

He glances up so our gazes connect, and there's so much love and sadness in his icy-blue depths that my breath catches. "I'll find the person who caused this." He brings my cast to his heart. "And I'm gonna rip their fucking heart out."

His words shouldn't make my knees weak; he means them. I don't want any more trouble. While I understand his need to balance the scales, we've got a baby in Cape Verde. I'm not willing to raise Lucas in the world we both grew up in. Saying any of that is another route to a fight.

"I don't want to talk." I skim my knuckles over his cheek. "I want to be so close to you that I don't realize where you end and I begin."

He doesn't need to be prodded twice. His lips capture mine, and he slides me onto the bed, his body covering me. The graze of our skin is an ecstasy I've dreamed about for months. At first, when I closed my eyes, he appeared, sometimes like this, all over me, waking up my body. Other instances the dream would be the two of us in bed, chatting as though we had all the time in the world. To know I'll get both tonight heightens my desire. Whatever happened to lead him to my hotel room doesn't matter. He's here, slipping his fingers inside me while his thumb circles my clit.

"Oh, God, that feels so good," I cry out as his teeth graze my nipple before he takes the whole thing into his mouth. When he parts my legs and his tongue flicks across my center, I buck against him, as my hands dig into his scalp. He's always known how to pleasure me, how to bring me to the brink, and then over it again and again. "Please, Finn," I plead.

At that, he rises over top of me, and our gazes connect. A key sliding into a lock; a puzzle solved. When he enters me, even that isn't close enough. All those months spent apart make me want to cry from the pleasure now, and the pain of before. He presses his forehead against mine as he moves inside me.

"I missed you so much." He kisses my temple before angling his lips over mine again.

His pace is exquisitely slow, as though each touch of our bodies is a gift and something to be savored. His hand snakes under my ass, tightening our seal. He presses my core against him with each movement. I raise my hips, the friction ratcheting me closer and closer to orgasm.

"Oh, Finn," I murmur, unable to get out anything else.

He lifts his head from my neck, gazing at me, his eyes filled with unmistakable desire. "I want to watch you come."

"I'm almost there." My voice is strained. "But I don't want this to end."

He pushes into me a little harder, and I dig my nails into his biceps, so near to toppling over the edge, my vision is blurry.

"Are you—are you close?" My words are garbled and sluggish.

"Yeah, Carys." He kisses me. "Come for me, baby."

Our gazes are locked, and he rocks us one last time. I cry out, my body spasming around him, and I clutch his arms as though I might fall through the bed.

He thrusts into me two more times, and then he's pulsing inside me with his face pressed against my neck. I wrap my legs tighter, locking him in place. A sigh of contentment escapes me. I can't remember when I was so happy.

The questions I realize I should be asking him float through my mind, but instead of speaking, I run my hands along every inch of his body as we cuddle in bed. He's here, and we're together. Nothing else matters.

"I'll have to call Evander so he can stop the search. I should tell Jay to prep the plane to go back to Cape Verde." My voice is sleepy to my ears. When did I last have a restful, uninterrupted sleep? A year? More, maybe.

Finn kisses my temple, but he's gone tense beside me.

"You don't want me to do that?" I peer up, trying to read his expression.

His fingertips dance along my spine, and he sighs. "I'm not coming back with you."

I sit up, clutching the sheets to my chest. "What?"

He follows my lead, the sheet pooling around his waist when he leans against the headboard. His defined, muscled body is a distraction even now. Will I always respond like this to him? We're in the middle of a crisis, on the brink of a fight, and the urge to straddle him, worship him with my hands, and pretend he didn't say those words is overwhelming.

"I don't even know where to start." He meets my gaze, and unlike before, there's a steely resolve. "I'll tell you whatever you want as long as you promise you'll go back to Cape Verde. You can't stay with me."

I let out a frustrated noise and move farther away from him. "No. I'm not making that promise. But you *will* tell me everything."

He rubs his crown and then crosses his arms. Any hint of the yielding lover is gone. He's in full business mode. He climbs out of bed and starts sweeping the room for bugs. "Evander must suspect I came here willingly."

I clench my jaw. "He does. Did you?"

He shrugs and keeps checking the places a listening device could be used. "It's complicated."

Once he's satisfied, he tugs on his boxer briefs and sits on the edge of the bed. When we're touching, my brain doesn't function. His distance is a relief and an annoyance. "You understand that's not an answer I'm going to accept for anything."

He draws a hand down his face, and then he levels me with the full weight of his gaze. "Evander's not as clever as he thinks." Then he continues with a story about the FBI, a deal with Zahir for a reduced sentence, a jailbreak that almost didn't happen, the inclusion of Kimi and Lorcan, and then meeting Pierre-Jacques, the head of the PLA.

My mind bends and weaves around the information he's dumping on me. There are so many problems with this plan, I'm not sure where to start. Instead of speaking once he's done, I climb off the bed and dress. "They're going to reduce your sentence to three years?" It's better than the twelve consecutive life sentences he was supposed to serve, but it's not the happily ever after I envisioned when I hired Evander.

"If I help take down the PLA." Finn doesn't meet my gaze, and I wonder whether he's thinking the same thing as me. The deal is very good—maybe too good. It's easy to give exceptional deals when the FBI doesn't believe the person they're dealing with will survive to cash it in. "You can't stay."

"Why not? As far as I can see, the danger is to you." If he's in danger, I don't want to leave. Even if I trust Lorcan, I'm not sure I trust Kim, and I don't trust the FBI or CIA. "You need someone who has your back."

"Kim and Lachlan are doing that." Lorcan's new name gets stuck on his tongue for a moment.

"I'm not leaving. I'm not leaving until you can come home with me."

"Apparently, you didn't listen to my whole story very carefully. The PLA knew you were in Ireland before I did. They tried to frame you for crimes you didn't commit. They were probably meeting with Valeriya when she was murdered. Pierre-Jacques practically invited you to lunch tomorrow." He thrusts out his arms, annoyance sparking off him. "The FBI and the CIA are both okay with you being here."

"If I'm here, I can help you get to the bottom of whatever is happening. They want me here for a reason."

"Which means it's not safe."

"You think I'm safe in Cape Verde?" Throwing this in his face might not help me and acknowledging the danger causes my stomach to roll with anxiety. Jay and I left Lucas, Sofia, Luciana, Rosa, and Lena on the island because they were safer than here. None of us knows if that's true. "My hotel was blown up a few weeks ago by a remote-controlled bomb. The day the FBI raided the Van de Berg offices in Chicago, someone sent me a confetti bomb. It appeared real."

"A bomb threat you never fucking told me about," Finn growls.

"It didn't seem important then," I mutter and rub my temples. Not exactly the truth. The threat was important, but I needed to be out of jail to address it and to talk Finn out of a murderous revenge spree if he found out who'd done it.

"Not important," he scoffs. "A threat to you outweighs anything else. You got me? I went to jail believing you were safe. Protected. Both you and Jay woulda known that wasn't true."

"Yeah, well, you didn't exactly run your plan to turn yourself in by me, did you?" The memory of seeing him outside the glass window in handcuffs causes my stomach to flip. He blindsided me.

"The safest place for you is on the island."

I clench my jaw and stare him down. "The safest place for me is with you."

"That's not true." He shakes his head, but his resolve is weakening.

I hold up my casted wrist. "The last time we were together, I was grazed by a bullet. You saved me from something worse."

"I can't always save you. There's a scar next to your heart as proof."

Shit. Shit. Stupid. I walked into that one. I'll lose this battle, and he'll send me home if we end on this note. I crawl across the bed and straddle his lap, so we're eye to eye. The physical contact causes a shudder to go through me. We stare at each other in silence, and both of us are convinced we're right.

"Sometimes." I test out my answer. "We have to save each other."

He searches my face then he cups my cheek. "If anything happened to you because I let you stay, I'd never forgive myself."

"Would you forgive yourself if you shipped me home and something equally bad happened?" It's a low blow, but we've never been on the same page about my safety versus our happiness. At every turn he'll choose my safety, and even now that I have Lucas, I'll grab my happiness wherever I can.

When Finn's not with me, I can almost convince myself I can be happy without him. As soon as we're breathing the same air, I realize I haven't taken a long, deep breath since we were together. Being without him is a slow suffocation.

His jaw tightens, and he breaks eye contact. His hands form fists at his sides.

"Would you forgive yourself if you sent me back and Lucas was hurt because they want me here, and I went home instead?" Cracking his resolve in half might be cruel, but I'm not any safer in Cape Verde. When I think about our situation too much, panic creeps up my throat. I left my baby on the island, and while I'd never admit this to Finn, he *is* safer there than here. I'm not convinced the same applies to me. "There are no guarantees." I caress his jaw and rotate his chin to force him into eye contact. "As long as we're together, we know the score, right? Safe or unsafe, we're in it together."

"You have to fire Evander." His voice is rusty, as though the words were dragged out.

I frown. "Fire him? Can't I tell him I found you?"

"The fewer people we have to explain ourselves to, the better." He lifts me up and sets me back from him. "I can't think straight when you're this close." A strained chuckle escapes. "Maybe I'm thinking about the wrong things." He smirks.

I can't disagree. He's a drug to my system. The more I get, the more I want. "That's it? You don't want to explain yourself?"

"Is he gonna believe I agreed to work for the PLA without a fight? That I'd rather do that than go with you?"

I flush. He might have if I hadn't been so confident otherwise. "This is why we need to keep each other in the loop. I *could* have convinced him of that if I'd known I needed to."

There's a light knock. "Housekeeping," a female Irish voice seeps through the wooden door.

"Kim," Finn mutters as he grabs his clothes off the floor and gets dressed.

"Kim has an Irish accent?" Not a surprise, really. I had an inkling this is what was going on with Lorcan and Kim. "You can't go yet." I follow Finn toward the door.

He takes out his phone, and a few seconds later, mine vibrates on the bedside. "My number." He pops open the door, and the openness of his expression turns wary. "Be there in a sec." He shuts the door before I can catch a glimpse of Kim. "Fire Evander. Tell him he's shit at his job. Whatever you need to do to get rid of him. I'll be in touch."

My stomach drops, and I put my hand on the door before he can open it again. "If you're lying to me—if you don't come back for me—I'll never forgive you."

"I gave you my number." He searches my face. "We've got lunch tomorrow with the PLA. You can stay—for now. At the first sign of more trouble than I can handle, I'm shipping you outta here. You got me?"

I nod. Does he realize I won't leave regardless of what he wants? May not matter, because I can't imagine him admitting a situation has gotten out of his control. I throw my arms around him, desperate for one last embrace. He squeezes me tight.

"I love you," I whisper.

"I love you too." His voice sounds hoarse.

He hasn't uttered those words to me in months, and my chest expands in relief before he pulls away and disappears out the door.

I press my back against the wood and sigh. I don't have a plan if he doesn't call me tomorrow with a time to meet him. Honesty. That's what I'm banking on.

The door vibrates against me with a knock. I check the peephole before opening it to Jay on the other side. He slips past me when I give him room to enter. For a moment, he gazes around the room.

"So, he found you, huh? But he didn't stay?" Jay pins me with his gaze. "What's going on?"

I shut the door and frown. "How did you know he was here?"

Jay's eyebrows lift. "For one, these walls are thinner than they look. You two are *never* quiet, much less after you haven't seen each other in months. For two, I opened my door as he was going past. He muttered, 'do fucking better,' as he walked past me." He shrugs. "Probably lucky he didn't stop to deliver a right hook with it as well."

"I have so much to tell you." I nod toward the one cramped chair in the corner of the tiny room. "You should sit down."

Chapter Seventeen

After he finishes sweeping the place for bugs, Lorcan passes me a beer in the kitchen of their tiny one-bedroom apartment. They've got some kind of blocker installed in their car, but everywhere else could be unsafe to speak.

Earlier today, sleeping on the couch didn't bother me. Tonight, knowing I could be in Carys's hotel room mean these cramped quarters will be a hell of a lot more uncomfortable.

"She's not leaving?" He eyes me from the other half of the kitchen with his back pressed into the counter.

"Nope," I admit. "I'm getting soft in my old age."

He chuckles, and one side of his lips quirks up before he takes a sip from his beer. "Maybe you're getting wise."

"This seems wise to you? Letting her stay? 'Cause if I let my brain lead, it feels reckless to me."

"Par for the course, then." Lorcan downs more of his beer. "Kim's none too pleased."

"Not a surprise." I roll the bottle between my hands. "What's the PLA's beef with the McCaffrey family?"

"Nothin', as far as I can tell. I reckon they came up with that bullshit to get you on board. Your murdering spree to avenge Carys's wound is legendary in certain circles." Lorcan shrugs. "Pierre-Jacques is unhinged enough to go after the McCaffrey clan for sport. Motives are secondary."

A twinge of recognition stirs in my gut. Not that long ago, that was me. Murder for sport. "You must have considered me unhinged all our lives."

Lorcan chuckles and grabs another beer from the tiny fridge. "Indeed. Though now I reckon it was because you didn't have anyone to hinge yourself to."

"You're saying Carys is a good influence?" I squint and ponder the implication.

He purses his lips and narrows his gaze. "You're not so cocksure anymore. When you've got something to lose, life is infinitely better and worse. You're always on the cusp of having everything you want or losing it forever."

"Thanks for the recap." I grab my beer cap off the counter and flick it toward the garbage.

His words hit me right in the chest. We've never been the type of brothers to have a heart-to-heart about our feelings. We both lost our mothers—in different, horrific ways. Both of us understand the unrelenting ache of loss, even if he let himself feel it more than I ever could.

"How do you reconcile having her in danger all the time?" I'd never choose a life of danger for Carys, but it's been finding us and hunting us.

He stares up at the ceiling before meeting my gaze. "I fell in love with a woman who inserted herself into our lives. She seeks the thrill." He splays a hand on the counter. "Bit like you, really. She walked into the warehouse trap set by you, hell-bent on saving me rather than keeping herself safe. I love her bravery." He takes a drink of his beer. "Even as it almost kills me every day."

I ponder his words and the notion of bravery in the face of danger. I would've stepped into the warehouse. Not sure I'd label it bravery. Nothing to lose versus everything to lose. "Carys told me she was no safer in Cape Verde than she is here."

"And you believe that?" Skepticism coats every word.

I grimace. "There was that bombing at her hotel."

"Heard about that."

"You know anything?"

"No. Not us, far as I understand. Though they were definitely keen to get you locked in."

I doubt the FBI played dirty to secure my cooperation, but it does mean there's someone else out there with an axe to grind. With me? With her? The unknown is the hardest to overcome. I fiddle with my bottle. "If she's here, at least I might see the danger coming. If she's there—I've got no chance."

The apartment door pops open, and Kim enters the kitchen with two bags of groceries and more beer. Lorcan takes the bottles, loading them into the fridge, while she ignores me to unpack the food.

"Maybe you caving to let her stay isn't as selfish as I thought it was," she says, without looking at me.

I almost spit out my drink. "You were eavesdropping?"

She shoots me a sly grin. "Occupational hazard." She nods in Lorcan's direction as she shoves a box of crackers into a cupboard. "He would have told me anyway." She slots the last thing into the fridge and leans against Lorcan. His hand rests on her hip.

"Bad fucking habit." I slide my beer onto the counter. The kitchen is too closed in for us. Actually, this apartment is going to drive me insane. It's only slightly bigger than my prison cell.

"Except if you're a spy trying to stay alive." Her lips twist in annoyance. "You're one to talk. Given the chance, you'd do the same thing."

Is that what bothers me about her? We're too much alike? Or maybe it's that she doesn't hide her dislike for me? There's no veneer of civility between us. We rub each other in the wrong ways.

"Can you ask Carys to record her conversation with Evander when she fires him?" Kim takes a pack of gum out of her pocket and pops a piece into her mouth.

I eye her warily. It's a good idea, and one I hadn't considered. "I can." Evander is connected to so many people and organizations, he might let something slip in their discussion.

"I'd text her." She keeps focused on putting things away. "But we're not friends again yet."

"You think she can forget your betrayal?" I smirk.

She meets my gaze, defiance in her black depths. "She took you back, so I figure anything is possible."

Lorcan tugs her against him and murmurs something in her ear. The tension dissipates, and she turns to bury her face in his neck.

"Tomorrow." He looks at me. "Pierre-Jacques has a history of keeping his key people on site. It's likely he'll ask you, and perhaps Carys, to remain on the property."

My forehead puckers at the notion. "Then she'd be in constant danger. She can't stay, even if I do."

He gives Kim's ass a gentle swat as she heads out of the kitchen. "If you don't let her stay with you, you might as well send her packing to Cape Verde. If she's not tied to you, I reckon the PLA'll consider her fair game."

At every junction, her safety is compromised. I rub my face. "I don't know the right move here."

"Trust your gut." Lorcan polishes off his second beer and sets it in the sink. "Your head'll overthink, and your heart'll be too cautious."

My gut tells me to keep Carys close. While my presence might be a danger, I'm also sometimes the thing standing between her and something much more terrible.

We're in the tin can car Lorcan and Kim use, and Carys, Jay, and I are crammed into the back. If this was one of those older girly sitcoms Carys used to make me watch, there'd be a laugh track attached. My shoulders feel like they're wedged into a vise.

"Can you play it again?" Kim asks from the passenger seat, half turned to see us.

Carys hits the button on her phone again, and the conversation between her, Jay, and Evander streams through the tiny speakers. While we listen, I try to hear whatever Kim's picked up. Most of it is Evander warning Carys against going after the PLA to rescue me herself. He managed to get information in the twelve hours between arriving and being fired. They're planning a big, complicated job, and no matter what reasons they might have given for wanting me on their team, none of them are likely to be real.

"If the McCaffrey vendetta and the negotiation with the Byrne family aren't legit, that's going to be clear very quickly." Jay reads my mind and slides a glance in my direction.

"Right, yeah." Kim dismisses him, her gaze getting far away as the recording plays. "What he says right... here."

Carys gives an exasperated sigh. Neither of us has much patience for Kim. "He calls him a sociopath."

"Not that." She makes a rewinding motion with her hand. "Go back again."

Carys slides her thumb across the screen, and Evander's deep voice pours out again.

PJ is a wild card. But so are a lot of the people around PJ. There's a shuffling noise as though Evander is standing up or moving around. *Watch yourself. I'm not sure the structure of the organization is what it seems.*

His last warning could mean anything from PJ isn't the real person in charge to PJ doesn't have control over his men. Either scenario isn't good for us. I glare at Jay. "You didn't push back on that comment?"

"We fired the man and told him we thought we could handle your extraction from the PLA better than him. You wanted me to milk him for details?" Jay meets my glare with one of his own.

"Until his tits ran dry." I let out a frustrated huff. "He was offering that information on a silver platter."

"What information?" Jay tilts his head. "The 'I'm not sure' part probably indicated, oh, I don't know, that he's 'not sure' about what he's saying. We weren't being served anything but speculation."

I tighten my jaw in annoyance. When the hell did Jay take his balls back?

"Still," Kim says from the front seat. "We need to be on the alert for shifting allegiances, anything that's out of the ordinary, unexpected people, pieces that don't fall in line with what we think we know."

I hold my burst of annoyance. *Way to state the obvious again, Kimi.* I liked it better when I was bossing her around. "What *do* we know?" I ask. "They terrorize people but not enough to actually get caught by any law enforcement agencies?"

"Bit like us at one time," Lorcan says. He makes eye contact in the mirror. "Human trafficking, drugs, weapons. An anarchy claim supported by almost nothing. Pierre-Jacques says they're going to start seeking revenge on their enemies. What enemies? No one seems to have a list yet." He taps the steering wheel. "Very scattered. From what I've seen, I don't understand why the CIA is so worried about them. No tactical core."

The Irish scenery zips by before we turn down the narrow laneway to the PLA's run-down castle. Tactics were always Lorcan's strength. I brought the muscle and the will to win at any cost, and he created the plan to make it happen.

When the car stops and we've squeezed out, Carys's face scrunches up at the decay. "They live here?"

I try to see the building through her eyes. A pale brick and stone castle with missing windows on one half and a clear remodeling attempt in the 1970s on the other. While we've been referring to the place as a castle, the actual building looks like it has a split personality. Run-down castle here and remodeled mansion there. It *is* huge, even if it's not particularly attractive.

"Not exactly your penthouse suite in Chicago." Kim leads the way toward the front entrance.

Carys's step falters at Kim's comment, but she ignores her. "I hope they have a decent cook."

I slide my hand along Carys's waist, and she leans into me, wrapping her arms around my middle until we're almost at the front. Once we're at the door, she stands up straight and draws her index finger and thumb from her forehead down to her chest. I smirk at her 'game face' routine. God, I missed her.

Just before we enter, I tease up the hem of her shirt to rub my fingers against the small of her back. I've spent months without her. Goose bumps rise on her arms. I want to haul her against me, ignore everyone else, and find an abandoned corner of this place. Shouldn't be too hard.

The guard at the front door clears his throat to separate us for the search. After we've been patted and our weapons confiscated, Noel appears.

"I see you took PJ's claim to bring whoever you wanted seriously. Carys." He nods at her. "Jay." He tips his head. "Welcome."

His knowledge of them sets off an avalanche of tension. My posture tightens, and so does Lorcan's, but Kimi is as loose as ever. She follows Noel toward the dining room, and her hands are shoved into the pockets of her leather jacket. Over her shoulder, her gaze connects with my brother's, and it's the first sign I've seen of unease.

Each seat has a placard by the plate, and when I notice Carys has been put beside Pierre-Jacques near the head of the table, my tension escalates. Jay's name is also written in neat cursive on another piece of cardboard on the opposite end of the table. They've nailed the element of surprise over us. Between each are names I don't recognize.

"PJ thought it would be good for everyone to get acquainted." Noel gestures to the scattered spots across the close to twenty-person table.

I chuckle and snatch Carys's placard from her spot then toss the name tag of the person next to me into the middle of the table. Using both hands, I place her name in front of the plate next to mine. When I meet Noel's gaze, his eyes are bulging. Looks like I shot him. I could shoot him. I still have his gun even though it's at the front door. Might set the right tone for today. Noel is not in charge. Noel is dead.

Was this what Evander meant about the power structure not being firm? 'Cause I can cement this pretty quick.

Carys's hand rests on my forearm, reading my thoughts. "We haven't seen each other in a while," she says.

"Some of these people you've *never* seen." He tries to use her logic against her. "We've got big plans, and you need to understand who's in charge." He glares in my direction.

I smirk. "Nah," I say. "I don't think so."

"Gentlemen." Pierre-Jacques strolls in from one of the side doors. He stops when he sees me and Noel at an obvious standoff. "And ladies." He scans the seats. "The arrangement wasn't agreeable?"

"Noel wants to play musical chairs. It's not really my thing." I grab the discarded placeholder from the center and toss it in Noel's direction.

Pierre-Jacques smiles, but there's a predatory gleam to it. "Ah, yes, he does like his games." He waves a hand in an extravagant fashion, taking in the whole table. "Mix and match as you like." He drops into the seat at the head. "I like my guests to be comfortable."

Noel's movements are tight with anger, but he retrieves the placard from the floor and places it at the empty spot. Other people file into the room. The last woman wears a deep-green gown that hugs her curves and a V-neck that plunges to her navel. It's a dress designed to draw attention. As she takes her seat at the other end of the table, her gaze locks with mine. Carys's fingers tighten on my forearm.

"Quite an entrance," she mutters under her breath.

I raise her hand to my lips and kiss her knuckles. "She's got nothing on you." I mean that, but something about this woman is eerily familiar. Have I met her before? Her shoulder-length hair is chestnut brown, and from here, her eyes appear to be a dark brown as well. Maybe my age or a bit older. No matter what Carys might believe, it's not possible to disguise the aging process, but I'd never tell her that.

Pierre-Jacques rattles off the names of the people around us, and when he gets to the woman in green, he grins like a Cheshire cat. "The vision at the end of the table is my cougar, Jade."

Carys, who has been sipping her drink through the introductions, swallows beside me. Good ol' PJ isn't going to be winning himself any favors with a comment like that.

"I enjoy my women seasoned. Like you, Carys." Pierre-Jacques turns his attention from Jade to Carys, tilting his glass in her direction.

Shots have been fucking fired. I reach under the table and squeeze her thigh, prepared to kick his ass if needed. Her age is the one subject we dance around like it doesn't exist. Forty-six isn't old, but Carys devotes considerable time to maintaining the gloss of youth.

She gives him a demure smile. "Well, bless your heart for noticing."

The steel in her words and the common Southern phrase doesn't go unnoticed by Kimi, who runs a hand across her lips to hide her amusement.

The first course arrives before I have to stage an intervention, and chatter starts up around the table. Nineteen voices talking in various pitches of excitement or boredom. I don't participate in much of it—only when someone directs a question at me. I'm not here to make friends, and these aren't the types of people I'd choose to be friendly with anymore.

"You okay?" Carys whispers to me as dessert is served.

"Peachy. Just waiting for the other shoe to drop."

She frowns and dips her spoon into the mousse. "At least the food is decent."

"Finn," Pierre-Jacques says. "Since you don't have a place to stay, and I've heard Kim and Lachlan's apartment is too tiny, I think you should remain here while your services are needed."

My brother prepped me for this suggestion, and it makes sense. Pierre-Jacques doesn't know Lorcan or Kim very well, and for some reason, I'm a valuable commodity. They've had a couple chances to prove themselves loyal, and as far as he knows, they've been able to keep me in line. "Depends on which side of the building you're offering me. I'm not much for mold and decay. Neither is Carys."

He waves me off. "No one lives on the castle side. It's deserted. A relic. A glimpse of what once was. No, no. We live on the mansion side. You, Carys, and Jay can be accommodated. No problems."

Carys and I didn't discuss where we'd be staying while I worked to disassemble the PLA. Lorcan's advice from last night still rings in my ears. My instinct tells me she's safest with me.

When I don't answer, Pierre-Jacques meets my gaze down the table. "In case I wasn't clear—I insist."

"Oh, I understood." I raise my beer. "I tend to be more wild than tame. Pick your battles wisely."

"So," Pierre-Jacques says, surveying the attentive faces. "Sounds like we understand each other perfectly. Kim and Lachlan—collect Carys's and Jay's things from their hotel. Finn, your room is stocked with clothes. Carys, Jade took the liberty of ordering and having a few items delivered for you since you'll be here longer than expected."

Carys pops the last mouthful of mousse in her mouth and peers at me over the top of the glass tumbler. "Longer than I expected..."

I don't respond but instead tip back the rest of my beer. I figured we'd be here a while, and I should have emphasized the unknown timeline with her when we spoke yesterday. Maybe she wouldn't be here now. I can't decide if having her gone would be better or worse. Better for her. Worse for me.

Whatever plan they're working on must be tough to execute or they wouldn't need me. That's not the part of his speech that bothers me. The PLA understands far more about us than we know about them, and they've been one step ahead of us the whole time. How do I protect her when I can't see where the path is leading?

Chapter Eighteen

Carys

I fling open the closet doors and flick through the dresses, skirts, and tops hanging on the racks. They didn't spare any expense. Eerie how they've managed to pluck items from the brands I love without duplicating anything I already own. When I turn to say something to Finn, he's staring into the top drawer of the dresser.

"They know too much." His tone matches the unease spidering along my limbs.

I check the tags. Every brand is sized correctly, and I'm not a universal fit across these companies. "How long are we going to be here?" I whisper. "Do you think they'll let me go home to see Lucas at some point?"

"If you want out, I'll go tell him now you're leaving. I'll do or say whatever I need to get you outta here." His gaze is locked with mine.

With a deep sigh, I turn to the closet. "We're a bit like flies in a trap, aren't we?" When I look over my shoulder, he's grimacing.

"Not gonna lie. They've got the upper hand. I don't understand why they really need me. No idea on timelines or what they'll ask me to do." He rubs his forehead. "There's something about his girlfriend too..."

"She couldn't stop looking at you during lunch." The few times we made eye contact, there was a glint in her eyes that didn't sit right with me. Was it that her gaze devoured Finn and an old sense of competition rose in me? "Did she look familiar to you?"

I unpack my bag from the hotel. I can't go if he's in danger. The deal the FBI offered him is too good to survive whatever is coming. If I leave and never get to see him again, I'll regret it. Lena and Sofia promised lots of video calling. Lucas is young. I'll have to pray we bounce back from the time we're separated. It's too dangerous for him here. If I dwell on my decision too much, my heart cracks in half. Lucas and Finn. I want them both. Staying here seems like the only way I might grasp my family... someday.

"Did you think so too?" He picks up personal care items laid out on the dresser. "They even bought my deodorant."

I gloss over his astounded comment. They've placed my face creams in the bathroom, including the toothpaste I favor. Unnerving. Frightening if I let it be. "Yes. I've seen her before somewhere. Maybe years ago? It's a vague memory, I think. I can't dredge it up."

Finn's lips tilt up, a hint of a smile. "I've got lots of gaps in my memories."

"Almost dying tends to do that." My mind fumbles for wherever I've seen Jade before. "I want to unscrew my head and extract the memory. Is the remembrance important? It bothers me I can't remember."

"Those gaps are a bitch." He sighs. "They almost let me get taken down."

I can't help my laugh. "She *did* take you down."

He shoots me an annoyed look.

"I saved you." I wander over to him and cup his cheek. "Could have been worse." Though both paths—the warehouse shootout and my rescue—ended up leading him to jail. No point in rubbing salt in the closing wound. We get however long we get together before he's back inside. I'm not going to waste a moment.

He tugs me flush against his body, and his head dips toward mine, and our lips connect. Our tongues tangle, and I fall into the pit of desire. Despite the circling danger, the joy of being this close to him propels logic out. I slide my hands up his taut sides, reveling in the skin-to-skin contact. His shirt is gone, and mine is over my head before a knock sounds.

"Go away," Finn calls out, his lips trailing along my neck.

"You're wanted in the war room." Lorcan's thick Irish accent pierces the heavy wood.

Disappointment rushes into the places desire had already seeped in. I wrap my arms around Finn's middle and put my ear against his chest. His heartbeat is so solid and strong—one of my favorite sounds.

"Give me a sec." His annoyance is obvious.

"Is his timing always this terrible?" I sigh.

"Not when I'm in charge." He kisses my crown and draws away to pick up his shirt. He tugs it over his head and then stares at me for a second. His hands slide along my cheeks before he drags me into a long, passionate kiss that leaves me breathless. "Something for you to think about while you unpack." He brushes his lips against my temple one more time before throwing open the bedroom door. "War room, huh?" Finn says to Lorcan as he shuts the door.

As uneasy as we are about the current situation, the hint of excitement in his voice at the suggestion of violence is unmistakable. He loves a riddle and a worthy adversary. Will they prove to be more than he can handle? Strangely, having his brother at his side gives me more confidence that between the two of them, they'll figure out how to get a step ahead of the PLA. It's a matter of time—both a blessing and a curse, with Lucas growing older each day I'm away from him.

When the last piece of my clothing is unpacked, I check my phone to see a video message from Lena of Lucas in his play area, Rosa passing him toys. My heart softens at the familiar sight. We need to make it out of this alive, and then we'll eventually be together as a family.

There's a knock at the bedroom door, and I exit my messages before cracking it open. Kim stands on the other side, her hands shoved into the pockets of her jacket. We were such good friends for a while that her appearance brings me up short. My instinct is to lean into our old friendship, despite her betrayal. If she goes after Finn again, it's the same as going after me. Can she be trusted? His family is so connected with Kim's. The smallness of the world amazes me.

"Did you need something?" I ask.

"Pierre-Jacques hauled Jay, Finn, and Lachlan into a strategy meeting. No women allowed." She rolls her eyes. "He asked me to keep an eye on you... though he wasn't too thrilled about asking."

"That's because he doesn't trust you."

"Feeling is mutual." She shrugs. "What can you do? We hardly know each other."

A reminder we're playing parts, and in this version of reality, none of us have known each other more than a few weeks. While Kim might be schooled at pretending, the rest of us aren't used to this kind of subterfuge. At what point will we slip up?

"Did you want to come in?" I try to soften my tone to one I'd use with someone unfamiliar. To be effective at our deception, I have to shove my memories of her in a compartment of my brain I don't access and start fresh.

She shakes her head. "It's not like we're going to sit around braiding each other's hair. Why don't we go for a walk?"

I glance at my heels and remember seeing a pair of flats in the closet. My size, of course. "Come in for a sec." I swing open the door. "I need different shoes."

She trails me to the closet after closing the door. When I throw open the double doors, a frown mars Kim's forehead.

"They bought these for you?" She fingers the tags and rears back at the price tags.

"Anything with tags still on it." I take a deep breath. "They know so much about me," I whisper. "What do you think that means?"

Kim leaves me at the closet and sweeps the room, checking lights, under desks, corners, moving items, examining things left behind. Eventually, she goes into the bathroom and turns on the tap and shower. She motions for me to follow her in, and she shuts the door.

"Harder to bug a bathroom with the moisture and sounds." Her lips twitch. "Who wants to listen to people shit?"

I can't hide my answering smile, and I shake my head. "Our room is bugged?"

"You have to be more vigilant and careful than you've ever been in your life. The FBI and CIA are worried about the PLA because there's been an explosion of activity. Once a nuisance, they're now a major player. With that in mind, the CIA wants you here, and the PLA wants you here. Why? A coincidence? For once, I'm going to agree with Finn. Doesn't exist. We can't see the big picture yet, but it's there."

I meet her concerned gaze and ask her the question Finn would never answer with logic. "Should I go home?"

Kim sucks in a deep breath. "I don't know. Your hotel was bombed, right? It's not a straightforward, easy call. I might not like Finn, but he'd give his life to save yours." She leans against the shower stall, and the steam cascades over the top. "Do you trust your security on the island?"

I recall the day of the bombing. Dominic was with me, but as Finn pointed out, too far away to do anything. "I trust Jay, but I'd want him to stay with Finn to help him. My island security firms are new, untested. If Finn asked, I'd say I did trust them, but that would probably be a lie."

Kim laughs. "Lie or face his wrath. Been there."

"Did you get a weird vibe off Pierre-Jacques's girlfriend?"

"You mean his *cougar*?" Her lips purse. "Doesn't that usually suggest the woman is the predator? She's definitely older than him by at least ten years, maybe fifteen or twenty. Like you, her age isn't easy to pin."

That concession makes me feel better after Pierre-Jacques's comment at lunch. In the back of my mind, I was already firing my dermatologist. I don't pay a small fortune to look my age. While Finn has told me a thousand times, I can stop paying for 'all that shit', my vanity won't let me quit.

"From what I've heard from other staff members, they've got a weird relationship."

"How so?" I cross my arms, trying to recall any cues I got from watching them interact at lunch.

"A few comments about abuse." Kim tucks a loose strand from her ponytail behind her ear. "Powerful men often exert their power everywhere."

There was a vibe of authority at lunch. The iron control wasn't any more overt than men I dealt with in the arms business. His boyish looks might downplay his sinister underbelly. He didn't seem like somebody I should be afraid of.

She turns off the shower and sink. Our gazes meet in silent agreement that we're done talking about things we shouldn't discuss. I may not trust her, but it's comforting to unburden myself to someone other than Finn.

"Walk?" She opens the bedroom door.

I follow her along the corridors to the main entrance. When we get there, instead of going outside, she opens another door which takes us into the dilapidated castle area.

"Did they run out of money?" I ask.

"Far as I know, the PLA bought the place like this. So, someone at some point probably did. But not them. They got this place for a song." Her Irish accent which she downplayed in the bathroom is in full force.

We wander through the rooms and hallways in silence, taking in the decay.

Does what we're doing count as snooping? We've been wandering through the open areas for quite a while now. Kim's probably examining the place for hiding places and spots to set up a sniper attack. I'm marveling at the architecture and the loss of history in these stones.

"It's sort of pretty on this side, isn't it? A spot on the brink of ruination." An unfamiliar voice stops the two of us in our exploratory tracks.

We both turn, almost in sync, to find Jade in a lovely floral gown. Her dark hair is pinned, and despite her age, there's something delicate in her appearance. Unlike earlier when she played the sex kitten in the green dress, this outfit isn't meant to inspire lust. Innocence, maybe. Which version of her is accurate? Sex kitten or naïve girlfriend? I can't get an accurate read, but she draws me in. I'm more curious than afraid.

"Jade, right?" I extend my hand to hers. When our hands meet, the shake is limp, like she forgot to lock her wrist.

"That's right." Her smile is shy. "I hope you liked your clothes. I scrolled through so many photos to make sure you'd be happy."

"Photos?" I raise my eyebrows, surprised she's admitting her surveillance.

Her expression turns flustered, and she glances at Kim with a hint of nervousness. "From, um, magazines and things? You used to go to fashion shows."

"The items you picked out were lovely." I attended fashion events before Finn burst into my life. Could she have found enough photos of me online to decide on her purchases? Maybe. Still makes me uncomfortable.

Her shoulders sag in relief. "Oh, good. I was so worried I'd offend you by picking the wrong size. I don't have many girlfriends, so I didn't even have anyone to double-check with."

"Pierre-Jacques doesn't employ many women?" Kim's tone is neutral.

"Oh, no." Jade laughs. "He says we're untrustworthy." She shrugs as though her boyfriend's view is acceptable.

Kim bristles at the implication, but it makes me smile. We *are* deceiving her while standing next to her. At least about us, Pierre-Jacques isn't wrong.

I search Jade's open and honest face for any hint of darkness. Then I recall Kim's claim of an abusive relationship. Perhaps there's an opportunity here. "Women are not that different from men in that regard—some are trustworthy, some are not. I'm not sure how long we'll be here, but I'd love to get better acquainted."

Would Jade be privy to Pierre-Jacques's plans? To the real reason he wants Finn here? In most relationships, there's pillow talk or overheard conversations, something leaks out to places it shouldn't.

She touches her chest as if pleased and surprised by the suggestion, but her gaze slides to Kim as though her presence gives her pause. "I—I think I'd like that."

"Perfect." I smile. "Next time the men get together for a meeting, we can go for a walk or, I don't know, something else on the property?" Can I talk her into showing me areas of the place we wouldn't have access to? Who knows what secrets lurk here?

A wince creases the edges of her eyes for a split second, and I wonder which part of my suggestion she doesn't like. Kim's inclusion? The idea of exploring the property? How much control does Pierre-Jacques hold over her?

"Yes." A wisp of a smile. "Sounds lovely. It would be nice to have a female friend amongst this testosterone."

Kim's phone buzzes in her pocket, and she takes it out. "Meeting is over. I'm sure Finn is keen to get you back." She scans Jade, Kim's face impossible to read. "Nice to see you again."

"Likewise," Jade says before wandering off deeper into the ruins.

Kim watches her go for a beat before leading me back the way we came. As soon as we're far enough away, she mutters, "Something isn't right there."

"She's definitely a chameleon." Jade was friendly and quiet. Maybe even a little shy. Earlier in the dress, with the way she stared at Finn, she was more the predator. She knows more about me than I know about her, but that could be the nature of inviting someone like Finn into the PLA.

"Her accent isn't authentic. I don't know why she's pretending to be Irish when she's not."

"Faking her accent?" I grab her arm to halt our progress back. Once we're in the main house, we could be overheard. "What makes you think that?" I replay everything she said, looking for a break in the lilting speech.

"Things you learn to listen for when you have to. She also doesn't want me along for these get-to-know-you activities. I'll have to make sure I'm at every one. I don't trust her."

"Your Spidey sense *could* be on overdrive."

Kim meets my gaze with an unexpected intensity. "My Spidey sense keeps me alive. It'll keep you alive too. Always trust your gut. Always."

"Maybe we befriend her? Pump her for information."

"Or maybe she's intending to get information out of *you*. She said 'a female friend' which doesn't include me. Somehow, you're a linchpin between the PLA and CIA. Why? We don't know. You've got to tread carefully. I cannot overstate that."

Her gaze is full of so much concern it makes my heart thud in response. She's not sugarcoating anything. While Finn might worry about me, she isn't the type to exaggerate danger.

"I'll be careful," I say.

She nods. "I hope so. You don't go anywhere alone." Then she opens the door to the main house.

Chapter Nineteen

Finn

The war room isn't as good as the one Lorcan and I had in Boston. The space has been ripped out of the pages of a 1970's design catalogue. Whoever tried to remodel the castle had zero sense of taste. In the center, the table is large and wooden, but people have carved their names into it like it belongs in a playground instead of as a symbol of power. Still, the map of Ireland spread out across it makes my pulse race. Is this when I find out what's going on?

Noel is on the other side, as is Pierre-Jacques, and another man whose name I haven't bothered to learn is at the head of the table. He's pale white, like me, but he's got red hair, and his brown eyes are at half-mast as though he smoked one joint too many.

"Daniel will take us through our strategy." Pierre-Jacques signals the redhead to start.

For the next ten minutes, Daniel points to places at random and makes grand proclamations about overtaking munitions sites, raiding money laundering ventures, and oddly, infiltrating a prostitution ring.

My brother nudges me with his shoulder, but we don't look at each other. He has to be thinking the same thing as me. Jay's frown is so deep I'm pretty sure I could plant a garden in it, but he's not asking questions either.

"What the fuck is this?" I burst out when I've had enough of Dopey Daniel.

"Daniel's strategy for taking down the McCaffrey family," Pierre-Jacques says, his tone mild, but his gaze twinkles with amusement. "He's our best strategic person."

Lorcan, who had been leaning over the map, stands up straight and crosses his arms. He's still not offering questions or ideas. Is part of his cover to be dumb? 'Cause there have to be thoughts circling in his head. Planning shit like this is his specialty.

"What's your problem with the McCaffrey family?" I mirror Lorcan's posture. Tactics aren't my area of expertise, but I'm smart enough to realize nothing Daniel suggested will work.

Pierre-Jacques draws the dagger out of its place on his hip and taps the tip against his finger. "They're not nice people."

I chuckle and gesture around the room. "None of us are nice people." Maybe Jay, but that's a weakness here, not a strength.

Pierre-Jacques slides into the chair and stabs his knife into the wooden surface. "I have a big project planned. We need a lot of men. Men who are slaves to money and power. If I have both, they become *my* slaves."

Can't disagree with his logic, but I'm not convinced the desire for those things resembles a plan. "You're going to snap your fingers, and all of it will come to you like magic?" I point at Daniel. "That's basically the nonsense he was spewing."

Daniel's face scrunches up as though he's going to argue then he shrugs. "We need what they have."

I rub my forehead and hope Lorcan speaks up. Then, I forge ahead. "You *can* get it, but what you presented was a wish list, not a plan. What's your timeline?" I fold up the map. "I'll need this."

"One week," Pierre-Jacques says.

"You want to put a plan in motion within a week?"

He shakes his head. "I want to own it next week. Not start. Be done. We're on a schedule."

"Screw your timeline," I say. Even at my most unreasonable, I understood when something couldn't be done. "We're not geographically close to these places in the south you want to raid. Have you got another crew down there? Otherwise, it's not gonna happen in a week." Zahir warned me the PLA has its base in Northern Ireland, but divisions lurked unnoticed in many cities.

Pierre-Jacques steeples his fingers and seems to consider my outburst. "I thought I hired someone capable of getting this done." He stares at me. "No?"

My lips twist with suppressed anger. "Hired? You kidnapped me."

A ghost of a smile flickers across his face. "So I did. But Carys came here willingly, no? Would be a shame if she was not free to leave here to see her baby boy."

Ice shoots through my veins. I've been in enough of these confrontations to keep my features schooled to neutral, but they have to have ears in our bedroom. If Zahir didn't have a leash on me, I'd be across the table at his throat. Three against three, and I have more confidence in my men than in his. "Don't make the mistake of thinking you hold the cards. I killed my brother. Okayed the murder of my father. Consequences be damned, I do what I want."

Pierre-Jacques nods. "Ah, yes. Including murdering that baby's father."

Jay tenses on the other side of me. Pierre-Jacques has to be fishing because no one knows I put a bullet in Eric's head. Didn't use my gun.

No witnesses. "I do what I need to." Gives me more street cred to sidestep the question.

"Good. What you need to do now is find me a way to get what I want. We all win when I am happy. Otherwise," he says with a smile and a shrug, "people start losing." He rises and tugs his knife out of the table. "Cape Verde can be explosive this time of year. I wouldn't want anyone to get hurt."

Jay lunges at him across the wooden surface, and Lorcan wrestles him back.

"You go anywhere near my family, and your men will be scraping your brains off the floor." Jay struggles against Lorcan's tight hold.

I'm not holding him back. My gaze is focused on Pierre-Jacques throat, on the pulse point at the base, at how easy it would be to snap his neck like a twig.

He grins. "My brain splattered anywhere sets off a reign of chaos and destruction. You think I brought someone so volatile to live with me without a strategy? Of course, the children could not come. Rosa, Luciana, Lucas... there is nowhere in the world they are safe from me and the tentacles of my organization. You do your job, and you go home. Everyone is happy. Unharmed. You try to fuck with me, and you pay the price."

His claws are out, and at this point, they're longer and sharper than mine. What does he value? Not his own life. Jade? Maybe. If not her, then I need to understand who or what we dangle in exchange for the people we love. Everyone has a weakness. Sometimes it's a person, and sometimes it's an object. Almost no one travels through life with zero connections. The best of us hide them well, and when we can't hide them, we insulate the people we love so no one can touch them. I was in jail when I should have been insulating. Carys and Lucas are ripe for the picking. I have to be certain their lives don't get plucked.

Pierre-Jacques signals for Noel and Daniel to follow him out of the room, leaving a struggling Jay, Lorcan, and me. When the door clicks shut, Lorcan releases Jay with a grunt.

"He threatened my family." He shoves Lorcan in the chest.

Lorcan's gaze connects with mine, and I'm grateful for the silent brother communication that still exists between us. We can't talk here. If they bugged my bedroom, they sure as shit bugged this room in case we drop any information once they're gone.

"We'll walk you to your car." I keep my voice even despite the fire raging in me.

Pierre-Jacques wants a reaction, to be assured he's picked the right thing to hang over the cliff. Jay gave him one, but I'm not going to give him the satisfaction of making a scene in here.

Jay huffs out a breath but follows us out of the mansion and into the circular gravel drive. At the car, Lorcan stares at both of us.

"I can come up with a plan that'll get him what he wants within a week. Kim will help. We've got enough intel about the other branches scattered around Ireland we can guess at men and logistics. I'll send the plan to your phone. Memorize it and delete it."

"Why didn't you speak up?" I mutter.

"I'm Lachlan Donovan. I'm not a strategist. Might be a tad strange for me to offer a much better plan than you on the spot." He runs a frustrated hand through his hair. "Gotta earn trust. Walk before you can run."

"I can get him McCaffrey's men?" We've dismantled rival organizations before, but our timelines were never this tight.

"It's not impossible. Daniel's incoherent rambling didn't help, though." Lorcan gazes at the mansion. "We should think about moving your families. He's got reach, but only if he knows where they are."

Jay breathes out a sigh of relief at the suggestion, his hands braced on the hood of the car.

"You're not going to like this," Lorcan says. "But your best bet is to put them with a connected family we trust. Makes it harder for the PLA to swoop in without serious consequences."

I swallow, my mind already ticking through the very short list. The Byrne Family would be at the top. With them on the PLA radar, they're not a viable possibility. Volkovs can't be trusted. The other option isn't one I can approach, but maybe Carys can. Wherever they go, we have to be positive we're not dropping them into more danger.

"Leave it with me," I say.

"Jay can you go get Kim for me?" Lorcan tips his chin at the house.

He pushes off the car, and with bowed shoulders, goes back into the house.

"I reckon he's not cut out for this." Lorcan's gaze follows Jay.

"He's worked for Carys since he was young. Never had to worry about his family in the line of fire. Got him in his gut. He'll be all right. He's got a steady hand." Jay's got a lot of faults, but Carys considers him family, so I do too.

A hint of a smile tugs at the corner of Lorcan's mouth.

"What?" I ask.

He searches my face for a beat. "Not clear whether I should be grateful for the changes in you or terrified. To get out of this alive, I reckon we're gonna need quite a bit of the old you."

I raise my eyebrows. "I'm like the Grinch. My heart grew three sizes."

"You? Quoting Dr. Seuss? Never thought I'd see the day."

"Blame the kid."

He eyes me, the hint of a smile dropping off. "You still got it in you?"

"You don't need to worry about me," I say. "I understand what's at stake. Despite what I always told myself, these connections aren't weakening me. They're making me more determined than ever to come out on top. He doesn't get to threaten my family and get away with it. I might have to play the long game here, but I still know how to win."

Lorcan nods and slides into the car as Kim comes out of the mansion. When she and I pass each other, we don't make eye contact.

At the top of the wide, curved staircase I turn left toward the suite we were assigned. The first set of rooms, closest to the stairs, are Pierre-Jacques's. Noel made a note of telling me to stay away from them when he gave us his very brief tour.

When I wander past, the door is cracked, and voices explode with anger. I should keep going, but instead, I pause at the door and catch a glimpse of Pierre-Jacques and Jade arguing. He grabs her forearms, dragging her against his chest, her floral dress whirling around her legs. Her breathing is labored, and she turns her face toward the door. Our gazes connect for an instant before she turns back to Pierre-Jacques, her chin thrust out in defiance.

He eases his hold on her, but she rises on her toes, pushing against him. Their eyes are locked, and silent communication happens. What is she trying to tell him? He drops her forearms and slaps her across the face. The smack of his palm on her cheek echoes in the hallway. She cries out and staggers, falling to the ground. Her gaze slides to me in the cracked door.

I cock my head. The exchange should be shocking, but it's like I've witnessed a performance, a dance. Does she think I'll interfere? Step in and defend her? Or is there something else at play?

I'm weighing the pros and cons of interfering when Pierre-Jacques looks in my direction. He crosses the room in three quick strides and slams the door in my face.

Chapter Twenty

Carys

Jay and Finn pass each other in the doorway, and the expression on Finn's face is puzzled. I can count on one hand the total times he's been baffled by a situation. Jay told me about Pierre-Jacques threatening the kids, and Finn's uncertainty doesn't ease my anxiety.

"Please tell me you have a plan."

He sighs, and his gaze darts around. "Did he search the room?"

"No." I'm tempted to mention Kim, but she went to such great lengths earlier to turn on the water and close the bathroom door before talking to me I don't suppose she'd want me saying that out loud.

He lets out a frustrated noise and doesn't talk to me while he tears the room apart. When he finds a listening device the size of his fingertip, he holds it up before replacing it. He takes his time putting everything back in its place.

"I've been considering our options." He winks at me, but his voice remains concerned. "I've got no plan. No clear way out. He's got us by the balls. The bastard is clever."

Since he showed me the bug and winked, none of this is what he believes. The compliments are for whoever is listening in. Are we going to leave the device in place? I frown. "Should we go for a walk? Fresh air might help."

"Yeah," Finn says slowly.

I change into my flats again, and I lead him toward the castle side of the property. When we get to the door, he points to the front entrance instead. We walk the long gravel path, well beyond the house, and then Finn says, "Please tell me he didn't say Lorcan's name during your conversation?"

"No, no. He told me he didn't have any idea what you were going to do about Pierre-Jacques's threat. I don't know if he was being careful or if we got lucky." I replay the discussion to make sure. But Lorcan never came up. Jay was too distraught about them knowing his kids' names.

"He threatened our kids?"

Finn shoves his hands into the pockets of his jeans and stares into the darkening fields. The sun has sunk into the horizon. "We'll have to move them."

"Where?" The tail of my braid rests on my shoulder, and I give it a little tug. I'm trying to keep calm because he always has a plan, and when he doesn't, the two of us make one. He won't let me down.

"Lachlan..." The name sticks to his tongue. He avoids addressing his brother whenever he can. "... suggested we need a connected family to give them the greatest chance at maximum protection. I don't disagree."

I shake my head, a laugh escaping. "None of them like you. Every family you're associated with wouldn't be keen to offer you any favors. Hagen was your best bet, but my parents said he was sniffing around you in prison."

A frown mars his forehead. "Your parents?"

"They came to see me because of the explosion." I hold up my cast-ed hand. "My father told me I've got sharks circling me. PLA, Hagen Volkov, who knows who else." If I asked my father to keep the kids, Lena, and Sofia safe, I'm sure he'd employ the best people, spare no expense. I won't let them stay unprotected, so I'll ask if I have to.

Finn nods, his gaze focused on my hand. "Come here." His voice is gruff. "Nobody is getting to you while I'm still breathing."

I snuggle into his chest and wrap my arms around his waist. "What's your plan?"

"I need you to call Demid Kunznetsof. I can't rely on the Volkovs or the Byrne family." He tightens his grip on me. "I don't know where else we turn."

"My father," I whisper. Even suggesting him sends a surge of anxiety through me.

"He can't be trusted. Charles's first priority is Charles." Finn rests his chin on the top of my head. "Will you call Demid?"

"Yes." We had a good working relationship until his daughter, Valeriya, turned up dead in an Irish harbor less than a year ago. Eric, my former fiancé, was the likely culprit since they were having an affair, and she was pregnant. The memory makes my stomach roll in protest. "He'll take them in. I'm not certain what he'll want in return."

"Call, but make the call from outside. Somewhere out here or in the fields."

"We're not going to remove the bug?"

Finn chuckles. "What's the good in that? They'll put another in there, and we might not find it next time. We know the room is bugged. They can listen to us have sex and talk about skin creams and whether my black shirt matches my jeans."

I smack his chest. "We've never had those conversations."

"We do now." A hint of a smile plays at the corners of his lips. "We'll bore whoever is listening with innocuous day-to-day ramblings, and they'll never see the knife we're going to shove into their back."

His arm stays around me while we amble toward the mansion again. "Kim and I ran into Jade today while we were out exploring."

"Did you?" His voice has a wary tone I don't expect.

"She seems lonely. We could befriend her, maybe get information from her."

He grimaces. "There's something off with her."

"What do you mean?"

He stops walking and turns to face me again, his expression pinched with uncertainty. "You won't believe me."

Finn doesn't lie to me, so the fact he thinks I won't believe him explains the way he's been acting since he returned to the room. Is his hesitation about how I'll interpret the incident? "What happened?" I give him a beat to answer and then add, "Did she make a move on you or something?" Jealousy sours my stomach, an emotion I haven't experienced in years.

He chuckles. "No, nothing like that."

He must not have noted how Jade feasted on him rather than lunch when she first noticed him. But then when we met each other in the ruins, she was so shy and meek.

"I saw Pierre-Jacques slap her across the face."

"What?" I clutch my heart, Kim's warning about abuse rising to the forefront of my mind. "Kim said she heard he was abusive." I try to catch his gaze. "Did you say anything?"

"They were in their bedroom. The door was cracked a bit." Finn gives the width with his hands. "Him hitting her wasn't what bothered me."

"Him abusing his girlfriend isn't a problem for you?" I cock an eyebrow, and annoyance spills out of me.

Despite Finn's penchant for violence, I've never worried he'd take out his frustrations on me. Even when we were young and he was fighting for his life in The Cage, the minute his rage dissipated, it was like it had never been there at all. Now that he's older, he's mellowed. Though Finn calls it 'getting smart' about how and when he attacks.

"Wouldn't be the first man I knew who controlled a woman with his fists." When I open my mouth to protest, he holds up his hand. "I'm not saying it's right."

"So, you stepped in? Said something?"

"No, I—" He scratches the top of his head. "The fight might have been real, but the slap—I don't think it was."

"Did he hit her?" I cross my arms. What is Finn trying to say? The notion of Jade being abused stirs my protective instincts. My relationship with Eric was fraught with abuse—more psychological—but any way you examine it, she's being hurt.

"Yes. He hit her. She fell to the ground."

"He hit her that hard?"

"That's not—" He groans. "You weren't there. She saw me watching. She got in his face, as though she was challenging him. I think she was giving him a cue. She was very aware I was there."

I glare at him. How can a man who is so smart not recognize this as a cry for help? "Did it occur to you that maybe she wanted you to *do something*? Maybe somebody would witness her suffering? Someone strong enough, tough enough to help her?" I managed to claw my way out of a relationship with Eric, but we continued to fall back into unhealthy patterns. Finn invading my life snapped my relationships with everyone in my life into focus.

He shakes his head. "That wasn't the vibe."

"And you're an expert on domestic disputes?"

He returns my glare. "I'm an expert on manipulation. On people trying to con me. On power dynamics."

"You're telling me she *wanted* to be hit? The sole purpose of him hitting her was to *manipulate* you?" The idea is ludicrous. What woman would agree to be slapped so hard she tumbled to the ground? Will she have a bruise tomorrow?

"I'm saying there's something off about their relationship, and it's not the domestic abuse. You weren't there. The energy in the room..." He fumbles for an explanation, flustered. "It wasn't right."

The wind lifts the few strands of hair that have escaped my braid. I tuck them behind my ears as I consider Finn's words. How does he not see this for what it is? "I think you've been so used to being the most powerful man in a room, you can't understand a woman's fear and how it might look to someone else." God knows the number of times I've had to conceal my fright are too numerous to count. The result isn't always neat and tidy.

He purses his lips, and when our gazes connect, his is brimming with the same stubborn determination as mine. "Maybe I'm wrong. It'd be a first." His hands rest on his hips, and he takes a deep breath. "Don't let your guard down with her. I might not understand *exactly* what happened between them, but my gut doesn't buy what my eyes saw."

"What woman would welcome the abuse? That doesn't happen, Finn." I can't hide my frustration. She's trapped in an abusive relationship and rather than helping her, he walked away. I love him, but at times like this, I don't *like* his stone-cold facade. "Whatever our plans to get out of this end up becoming, we need to keep in mind she might be a victim too."

Finn runs the palm of his hand across his shorn strands. "What'd Kim think of Jade today?"

A lie forms, and then I reconsider. We have to survive this as a team. "She said something seemed off with her."

He raises his eyebrows in the closest he'll come to an *I told you so* with me. "You've got a good heart, Carys. Someone with a black heart, they'll take advantage of your kindness in an instant."

"I'll be careful," I murmur. "Doesn't mean you're right."

He loops his arm around my shoulders and brings me to his side, his lips pressing against my temple. "Except I'm always right." I shove his side, but he tightens his hold on me with a chuckle. "Let's go back to our room and give them an earful."

"We've got some lost time to make up for." I rise onto my toes and kiss his jaw.

CHAPTER TWENTY-ONE

FINN

Instead of memorizing the plan, Lorcan and I meet on a deserted side road, well before he's due to arrive at the mansion. He walks me through the takeover strategy he and Kimi brainstormed the night before. Solid. Not brilliant, and certainly not without complications, but better than anything I'd have come up with in less than twenty-four hours. Our meeting is to make sure I don't have questions about the plan before I present it to Pierre-Jacques, Daniel, and Noel. Otherwise, how do I respond if they push back on something?

"The PLA believe I'm capable of this." I wave over Lorcan's detailed scheme. "We both know if you weren't here, my action items would not be so... subtle."

He chuckles and rubs his cheek. "Not much subtle about our ideas either. Calls for the murder of the oldest McCaffrey son to guarantee obedience."

"None of the others are strong enough to step in and take over?" If somebody had murdered me, Lorcan would have been more than capable of taking the reins for the Donaghey family.

"CIA doesn't think so." He shrugs. "It's the intel we've got, which Kim says is sometimes shit." He squints into the distance. "Think they've got eyes on you?"

"Didn't notice a tail. I ran for about five miles before I started walking. Anyone who might have followed would need a drone, which I would have heard, or be running behind me on foot. Either way, I tried my best not to make the chase worth their time." I stare at his scrawl on the page. "They've got ears on us. In the bedroom."

His eyebrows lift. "You and Carys are being careful? Jay knows as well?"

"We're going to kill whoever is listening with mundane chatter. This morning's topics were the effectiveness of antiaging face creams and blow jobs."

Lorcan snorts. "Blow jobs? Those two are connected?"

I chuckle. "Nah, but the stupid conversations have been making Carys laugh." A bonus for me. Since Pierre-Jacques threatened the kids last night, and I didn't buy into her 'scared woman' defense of Jade's behavior, things have been strained between us. If Demid agrees to take everyone under his protection, maybe that'll ease her mind.

Lorcan taps the roof of his car and stares at the deserted, winding country road. "You got any questions?"

"I gotta go there to execute your plan. So, if I have to leave, you need to be here to protect Carys."

"I won't go south." He leans against the vehicle. "McCaffrey family would recognize me right away. Bullseye between the eyes. I'm the spitting image of the old man."

The same goes for any interaction with the Byrne Family. They'd recognize him in a heartbeat. No goatee and a different hair color aren't much of a disguise. The CIA may not care if they've got one less operative, but I've only got one brother. He's the sole surviving member of my family. Despite our history, I'm not letting him walk into a trap.

"Pierre-Jacques can't trust me yet. I reckon he'll send Daniel or Noel with you. Keep you in line." His lips quirk up at the suggestion. He flicks the paper in my hands. "Memorize this and burn it, yeah?"

I take out a lighter from the pocket of my running shorts and wag it before sliding it back in. The PLA did think of everything. The gym in the basement of the mansion, which I've nicknamed the dungeon because it amuses me, fulfills my need to lift heavy things and get out my frustrations. I'm still not sure why *I'm* the best person for the jobs they've set up. Could be as simple as muscle for hire. The equal focus on Carys is what messes with my head.

Lorcan nods and climbs into his compact car. It's comical watching him fold himself into such a tight space. "If you need me to say something at the meeting, ask. Otherwise, I'm keeping a low profile."

"Got it." He starts the engine, and I say, "I'm surprised Kimi let us meet alone."

He purses his lips. "She trusts me. CIA might not. FBI might not. But she does. I'm not fucking that up for anyone."

At every turn he's cautioning me not to put him in another situation where he has to choose. I'm not intending to go rogue. As long as Carys, Lucas, and the rest of our crew is safe, I can play along with whatever the CIA wants me to discover or dismantle. The immunity on crimes committed for the PLA during my stint on the outside doesn't hurt. I'm leashed and unleashed. Could be worse.

"I'll see you later." With a tap on the hood, I wander into the fields. I've got a few miles to walk and memorize before I burn this sheet far from the prying eyes of the mansion.

------◆○◆------

The setup for the conversation with Pierre-Jacques pisses me off. Instead of being in the war room, he's summoned me to speak, literally, in front of his throne. Like I'm some kind of peasant. It's insulting, and a power play in the most obvious way. He's seated in one throne, and Jade, black eye on prominent display, occupies the other. Didn't look like he hit her that hard. Noel and Daniel hover on either side of them, obedient dogs.

Behind me, Jay and Lorcan are listening to me lay out the plan. Without a map, the ideas are jumbled words to me. I've got no idea how Pierre-Jacques is following the rotation of places, the modes of attack, the number of men needed. They seem bored by my chatter, which is *really* annoying. I didn't ask to be his lackey.

Pierre-Jacques sighs loudly. "Will this get me what I want?" His expression is bland.

"Yes," I grit out, ready to tell him that if he didn't give a shit about the actual plan, he should've sent me south with no restraints and let me blow buildings up. I memorized that sequence for nothing.

"Go ahead, then." He waves me off. "Take Lachlan with you and go to the southern faction. You've got one week to bring me Donal McCaffrey's head on a stick, literally. On a pike." He mocks driving it into the ground. "So I can display it on the corner of the castle ruins."

Jade tenses beside him, obviously not impressed with his suggestion. She places a hand on his forearm, and he gazes at her, their eyes locked in silent communication.

"Fine," he mutters before turning back to us. "A box or some such will do. I can have someone here put his head on a stake afterward." He makes an impatient gesture toward Noel, who winces in response.

"Jay, not Lachlan." I glance over my shoulder at the two of them. "I trust him."

Pierre-Jacques barks out a laugh. "Well, I trust Lachlan, Noel, or Daniel. Pick one. Jay is not an option."

I stare at Noel and Daniel. Noel is a dick and won't follow my orders. I'm as likely to have a knife driven into my back with him along as I am to get Donal's head on a stick. Daniel is more pliable, but that doesn't make him any safer as an accomplice. Guy is so medicated he can barely prop his eyes open. A drug addict, a dickhead, or my brother. Choice is easy.

"Lachlan." I don't look at him. How we'll keep him safe and away from anyone who might recognize him in the south is a problem for another time.

"Leave today. I want this done quick, quick." Pierre-Jacques dusts his hands off and rises from his seat, offering Jade his open palm. "You can put Francois in charge once you've got the McCaffrey men in line. He'll be your contact in Cork. Good enough to direct the symphony from there. I require you to conduct other business afterward."

I frown and cross my arms. "McCaffrey family used to deal primarily in Dublin, not Cork."

"Yes," Pierre-Jacques agrees. "They did. Funny how things change with time." With that, he leads Jade out of the large throne room and into another section of the mansion I haven't had a chance to explore.

"Come with me." Noel gestures for me to follow him. "I'll give you Francois's information. I'll also give you a PLA car. That piece of shit Lachlan drives isn't suitable for such a long drive."

Means the vehicle will probably be bugged. Pierre-Jacques might have claimed he trusts Lachlan, but I don't believe him. Mindless chatter for six hours. Fucking amazing.

"My car is good on petrol." Lorcan reasons from behind me. I wonder if he's also dreading the six hours of stilted conversation.

"PLA's got bank. We don't care about costs." Noel opens an office door for us and directs the three of us into it.

But they're concerned for our comfort? *Yeah, right.* I whip out my phone and open the contacts page.

"We'll also provide you with a phone." Noel eyes my no-frills device. "Preloaded with the contacts you need. You'll return it to us when your work with the McCaffrey family is done."

Nothing about this setup is comforting. Their phone, their vehicle. They may not have cared about the actual plan, but they're hell-bent on catching me doing anything I'm not supposed to. I take the phone without a word. Jay's always playing on his. Maybe he'll be able to tell if they've enabled anything on the device that can screw me over. I'm fine with them tracking me, but if I have to be worried about them listening in even when I'm not in the car, that's a problem. Lorcan and I will have to plan and coordinate openly at some point. Too easy to screw up his identity.

Noel hands me a phone, a paper map, a stack of cash, and the key fob for a vehicle. "The vehicle is in the barn out back?" I'm guessing because I haven't seen a fleet of vehicles out front.

"Yeah, that's the one," he agrees, distracted by the ping of his own phone. "I've got somewhere to be. You got questions?"

"None," I say, and he shoos us out of the office as though he's in charge of the world. He rubs me in the wrong places.

We reach the car in silence. There, I pass the PLA phone to Jay. "I need for you to take a look at this."

"Ears?" He's already unlocking the device.

"Yeah. Anything I need to be careful about. I know fuck all." Lorcan and I stare at each other over the top of the tin can he drives. "Their car will be wired."

"Undoubtedly." He grimaces. "Physically more comfortable, intellectually more painful. He doesn't trust me. I don't know what game he's playing."

"You build trust by testing people." Jay's brow is furrowed as he navigates through the phone. "Us standing out here huddled together probably isn't earning any of us points."

I make a frustrated noise and point at Lorcan. "Be back here in two hours. We'll send Kim down."

Before we get to the entrance, Jay puts his hand on my arm. "Something Pierre-Jacques said the other day has been eating at me."

I cross my arms, impatient to get packed and jump this first PLA hurdle. "What's that?"

"Did you kill Eric?" He closes the loaner phone and passes it back to me. "Disabled the microphone. So, if you want to record someone, you or Lachlan will need to enable it again."

"Why has that comment been bothering you?" Answering might open a minefield between me and Carys. I promised I wouldn't kill him, but when he was incapacitated from the shootout at the Russian house,

I didn't hesitate. One less problem for us. Besides, putting him out of his misery shouldn't make me the bad guy. Not sure Carys would see it that way.

"Eric died during the raid. But if Pierre-Jacques knows he was still alive when you returned…"

He doesn't bother to finish his chain of logic. Either the PLA planned and executed the attack on the house, or they know who did. I'm not admitting anything, but Jay's not stupid. I take my opportunities as they come.

"Would also explain why you weren't so keen to figure out who stormed the house." Jay puts his hands on his hips. "You didn't want Carys to find out what you did."

I smirk. "I admit nothing. Supposing the PLA was involved in the raid, and assuming Eric was alive when I arrived, why? Why leave him there?"

"Maybe he was meant to deliver a message." Jay searches my face.

For the first time, a hint of uncertainty sprouts in my chest. "A message?"

"Did he tell you something before you shot him?" There's no judgment in Jay's question, just curiosity and an unexpected urgency.

Eric didn't utter anything of importance, but it wasn't from lack of trying. Instead of encouraging him to speak more, I dismissed his incoherent ramblings. What had he been attempting to say? "Nothing." I twist my lips. "Nothing I could decipher." A chill snakes along my spine at the realization the house invasion in Russia might have had more to do with Carys than I realized. I let myself believe Eric's brutal torture was Demid retaliating for his daughter's death. Pierre-Jacque's comment, and Jay's curiosity, throws a whole new light on that night.

"Something's not right here, man." Jay shakes his head and leads us toward the door again. "I can't put the pieces together yet, but I know they fit."

I rub my face and follow behind him. The wind snaps the Irish flag on the pole above the mansion, and when I glance up, Jade is framed in the window, staring at us. The voice at the back of my mind whispering *trouble is coming* gets a little louder.

Chapter Twenty-Two

Carys

Finn should be done with his meeting soon. Kim and I are headed for a rear entrance that'll take us into the fields for a walk, if anyone asks us. Really, I've managed to schedule a call with Demid to discuss a 'business opportunity' instead of trying to talk him into something via text or email. Maybe if he hears the naked pleading in my voice, he'll be reminded of how much his daughter meant to him and how he was willing to do anything to get her back. Would he wish the kind of pain he suffers on me?

We're at the top of the rear set of stairs Kim found yesterday when I spot Jade coming toward us. Even though we're pressed for time, I tip my head in her direction. "Let's wait a minute and at least speak to her."

Kim's face remains a cool mask of indifference, but she's voiced her suspicions. They may match Finn's, but it doesn't mean I can't cultivate a wary friendship with Jade. My guard is up. I can't stomach leaving a woman in a vulnerable position if we have the means to help her.

When she gets close enough, the bruise around her eye is obvious despite the concealer to mute the black discoloring. "You've hurt yourself." I point to my eye, and I scan the rest of her for signs of violence. "Are you okay?"

Her chin trembles, and she won't meet my gaze. "I—I tripped, and my cheek caught the edge of a table in our bedroom."

Kim remains emotionless beside me. Anger stirs my stomach. She's lying. Does she realize we know or suspect a different reason for the dark bloom?

"I'm sorry to hear that." I keep my voice pitched low. "Sometimes you really have to watch your step."

She brushes away a stray tear, concealer appearing on her finger. She winces at the contact of her fingers on the tender skin. With a deep breath, she straightens her shoulders before meeting my gaze. "Were you serious about us being friends?"

No matter how hard I try, I can't shake the impression I've seen her before somewhere else. There's the vague outline of a memory, as though I could use a pencil to shade over the imprint and fill in the empty space. The flicker of familiarity draws me closer. "Of course." I smile. "Women should stick together."

"PJ needs me right now. But maybe tomorrow, sometime? We could go for a walk or... I don't know." Her expression turns amused. "Share a cuppa and some biscuits."

"Sounds lovely." I take her hand and give it a gentle squeeze, making eye contact. "I'm looking forward to getting better acquainted."

She touches her hair with her free hand in a gesture that reminds me of myself—a nervous habit. I cock my head, trying to decide whether the movement is genuine. Are Finn and Kim right?

"Tomorrow," Jade whispers, stepping past us to stride down the hall.

Kim watches her go and when she's clearly out of earshot, she says, "A cuppa and some biscuits." Her accent is mocking.

I roll my eyes and lead the way to the staircase. "Can you pretend to like her a little? She might be a valuable source of information."

"I cannot believe these words are going to leave my mouth, but Finn and I are in agreement about her. Maybe you can get something out of her. Will it be real? Will the information put you in more danger? She's trying to deceive people with her fake accent. What else is she pretending?"

"That bruise is real enough." I stride out into the fields with Kim a few steps behind me. "Your accent isn't real either." Though, now that she's pointed out the oddity of Jade's accent, it's all I hear when she speaks. Is she attempting to blend in? Or hide another accent underneath? Maybe it's simply PJ's French merging with Jade's Irish. That happens. Couples who spend a lot of time together adopt each other's traits.

Kim doesn't say much while we make our way toward one of the outbuildings. When I find a spot sheltered from the wind and from the prying eyes of the mansion, I take out my phone. I scroll through my contacts for Demid, but before I can hit Send, Kim puts her hand on mine.

"I know why you *want* to believe her. Under normal circumstances, I would too. If she's manipulating the abuse to gain sympathy or if she's pretending to befriend you for a power move, the deception goes against who you are at your core. I get that. Hard to believe she'd do that." We stare at each other for a beat. "But trust me when I tell you, she's not your friend. She'll never *be* your friend. Her loyalty lies with the PLA. I guarantee it."

I clench my jaw with the things I want to say but keep discarding. She and Jade could be twins, given their deceptive natures. "I guess you'd know." Then I hit Dial on Demid's number and put the phone to my ear. I turn my back on her and her hurt expression. Did she betray me when she worked for me? No. Only because I didn't give her the chance. I'm not going to allow Jade the chance either. I'm too smart to be sucked in.

"Carys." Demid's voice washes over me like an old friend.

We haven't spoken since I sent flowers for Valeriya's lavish funeral and made a hefty donation to the charity he named in her honor. I'm hoping he remembers those things during the next few minutes.

"You said you had a business proposition for me?"

"Tied to a favor, I'm afraid."

There's a beat of silence on his end before he says, "Ah yes. Nothing is ever free. For both of us."

"Because I respect our previous working relationship, I'm just going to come out with it." I pause to draw a deep breath of courage. If he says no, I'm not sure what we'll do to protect everyone who isn't here with us. "I'm in a bit of a sticky situation with the PLA. They've threatened my child and my associate's family as well. I was hoping I could call on you to take them in. Offer them protection for the next little while."

He sucks in a breath. "The PLA? Carys, why are you dealing with those thugs?"

"It's a long story. I—I can't get into the details, exactly. I need to know what you'd want from me to help us."

He clucks his tongue and makes various humming and hawing sounds over the phone. Kim raises her eyebrows when I glance at her. My odds are fifty-fifty right now, and the sinking sensation in my stomach is about to drag me under.

"The only thing you can offer me is what you no longer have."

His words are a knife slicing through my heart. "The ammunitions business."

"Your father has not been good to me since he's taken control."

Of course, he hasn't. My father understands money, not loyalty. Demid and I worked well together. Rarely legally, but always well. "Do you want me to talk to him?" I'm not sure what else I can offer.

"In exchange for my risk in taking in your family, I want discounted rates and preferential treatment from Van de Berg Ammunitions." His smile is clear even over the phone. "For life."

Oh, sweet Jesus. My father is never going to agree to that condition. "I must talk to him. I can't make that decision on the spot."

"I understand. *I* am in no hurry. You, however, may be." His thick Russian accent makes the words sound more ominous than normal.

"I'll be in touch," I say and hang up the phone. I tap it against my palm and glance at Kim. "Did you hear?"

"Enough. He's not a quiet talker."

"What do you think?" Words are out of my mouth before I can consider whether I should be seeking her opinion.

"His terms aren't terrible. The issue is that you can't fulfill them without getting Charles involved."

"Yeah. Small glitch." I use my fingers to indicate it's not a big deal even as my heart pounds. "He won't agree."

"Doubtful." She peers into the distance, across the remote fields of the property. "You need Demid."

"What if my father offers to protect them," I whisper the words, not sure they'll be true.

"Your father works with bad men, and maybe he's not a *good* man, but he's not a *bad* man. He won't inspire terror in the PLA. He's no Finn."

I should resent the comparison, as though Finn is the worst of the worst. Instead, a streak of longing runs through me. When my back is against a wall, there's no one else I'd rather have on my side. He'd walk through hell and welcome the flames if it meant protecting me. It's a level of comfort and security I never thought I'd get from a man. "I need to talk to Finn."

"They should be back now. I'll have to meet Lachlan out front. I'll walk you to your room first."

We make our way into the mansion and up the stairs in silence. My mind keeps seeking another way to protect Lucas, Luciana, Rosa, Lena, and Sofia, but I fear Kim is right. My father won't be enough to deter the PLA from coming after my family. We need real consequences.

When I return to the room, the door is ajar. Kim shakes her head and gently shoves me aside to prod it open with her fingers. Finn is packing a bag on the bed with his back to us. At the creak of the hinge, he turns.

"Are we going somewhere?" I step around her.

"I am. You're staying here."

"By yourself?" I ask.

Finn's finger goes to his lips, a reminder about the bug. I suppress a sigh. The worst thing about our time here has been the constant vigilance. Considering how he's packing, it doesn't seem like I'll get to talk to him about Demid or my father. I might have to make that decision on my own.

"Lachlan's coming. Kim, he's waiting for you in the car."

She disappears from the doorway, closing it behind her.

"I was hoping we'd have a chance to talk." I sit beside his bag, wishing I could blurt out the details of my phone call.

"About face creams or blow jobs or something else?"

I give him a wry smile but don't answer. The only positive of the nameless listener is Finn's joking manner. Witty remarks live in him, but most of the time they're hidden under a serious, menacing demeanor.

"Hand jobs?" He shoves the last item of clothing in his bag and zips it up.

"You're putting me to work before you leave me?"

His grin is wicked. "I don't mind doing *some* of the heavy lifting."

Butterflies of anticipation flutter around my stomach. I can't get enough of him. The mere mention of sex, and I'm aching with desire. "Are you calling me heavy?"

"Never." He scoops me up and tosses me farther onto the bed. He rises over top of me, and his lips connect with mine. Our tongues tangle, and I ease him between my legs. He rocks against me, already hard and ready.

"How long will you be gone?" My voice is breathy with need.

"A week at most." His lips slide along my neck. "I'll call you every night to make sure you're missing me enough." He draws away and lifts my skirt, tugging my panties down. His fingers skim my slick folds, and he groans. "We don't have much time."

"I'll take any time we've got if it means I get you." I unzip his pants to release him and run my hand along his shaft.

His eyes close, and his jaw tenses with pleasure.

"What kind of job do you wish me to perform?" My voice is husky. I want to clamber on top of him and ride him until we both get the release we crave.

"Surprise me." A hint of a smile tugs at the edges of his lips, and I close my own around him. "Fuucckk," he mutters as his hands dig into my hair. "God, I love you."

We shed our clothes, and any thoughts of talking turn to finding a few last moments of pleasure in each other. When I climb on top of him, and he grips my hips, our gazes connect. The combination of love and lust in his icy-blue depths squeezes my heart. To be loved by this man is tied for the greatest gift of my life. Not before him, and not after him, has anyone consumed me so fully.

My breasts brush against his chest as I rise and fall over him in the slowest, sweetest rhythm. Being without him again so soon catches my breath, and I kiss him deeply and cling to him. His hand slips between us, brushing against my clit, and I gasp into his mouth as I grind on him, seeking my release.

He tugs me a fraction of an inch closer, and I come apart, gripping his shoulders with the ecstasy, and he follows behind, crying out my name.

Chapter Twenty-Three

Finn

When we arrive at the farmhouse in the rolling hills of west of Cork, we're greeted by two cattle dogs and a six-foot-tall bear of a man with a shotgun.

"You Francois?" I put my hands up.

Lorcan, beside me, also has his hands raised. We've both got a gun at the small of our back. "Pierre-Jacques sent us," he offers.

The man lowers his gun and whistles for the dogs. "Damned PLA," the man grumbles as he motions for us to follow him. We keep our distance as he leads us to one of the barns behind the house. Fan-fuck-ing-tastic. The PLA lives in a barn. My hopes for something better than a seventies mansion are fading fast.

When we get to the door, I eye my brother. We haven't discussed a strategy for the first meeting, but since we don't know who is in the barn other than Francois, sending Lorcan in blind is idiotic. Northern Ireland is generally safe from recognition. We didn't spend much time there in our youth. But the south? We ran around here like a playground while we went to school.

"You stay here. Watch my back."

Lorcan nods and leans against the side of the barn.

"He's not going in?" the bear of a man asks in a thick accent.

"Just me." I motion to the door. "Do you need to tell him I'm coming or anything?"

"Doubt it," the man says. "Just Francois in there, hiding out. My brother is a useless tit who thinks you all can give him more than an honest day's work."

A smile plays at the edges of my lips. He tells it like it is. I've got no problems with that. "He's your brother, and he's named Francois?" I arch my brows.

"Changed his name. The twat. That woman of Pierre-Jacques's gifted him the new poncey moniker."

"It's just him in there?" The realization I'm not walking into a substantial crew hits me between the eyes. Lorcan's plan depended on more than the three of us.

"Aye." He snaps his fingers for the dogs and heads toward the farmhouse.

"It's still too risky for you," I say to Lorcan.

"You don't know everyone I used to know." He scratches the back of his head. "You could call me in there, and I'll recognize him, anyway. Least if I go in, we'll realize straight away what we're dealing with."

I scuff my feet in the gravel outside the entrance and squint into the fading light. Can't disagree with his logic, even when I don't like it. I unlatch the door and step into the barn.

"Francois?" I call out, surprised at how clean and modern the place is. From the outside, it looks like a wooden barn, but inside it's renovated in neutral tones with wood-and-steel accents. Much nicer than the mansion up north.

"Up here," he responds from the loft space. "Be there in a tic. You Finn?"

We're going to need to talk about security. While his bear of a brother might be menacing, he gave up Francois without mounting any defense or question. "Yeah," I respond. "The one and only."

He lilts down the stairs, tucking a wallet into his front pocket. "Right, we have ta be at the pub in the next ten minutes."

"The pub?" I scan him as he rushes from the bottom toward us. Has to be in his twenties. Too young to have been friendly with either me or my brother.

"Right, yeah. That's where the crew is. Dish out the assignments. We've got a week, yeah?" He eyes me. "You're older than I expected, mate."

"You don't have Google?" I give him a mild look and tip my head at Lorcan. "This is Lachlan."

He shakes Lorcan's hand and then leads the way to our PLA car. "I don't know what you've been told, but we've got about twenty lads lined up."

"All trustworthy?" I frown as Lorcan slides into the driver's seat.

"All hungry for money. Best kind of loyalty." He takes out a cigarette and lights it in the back seat. "Finn? Lachlan?" He offers the pack to us.

It's times like this when I start to feel each of my forty-one years. Did I smoke in my twenties? Sure. Now? Not a chance. I got enough things that might kill me, no need adding to the list. "Nah." I wave him off. "We're good."

Francois cracks a window and blows the smoke out as we drive. "You've got the plan, yeah?"

I tap my temple. "In here. Are the lads around your age?"

"Yeah. They're my mates from school." He grins.

How in the hell is the PLA an organization worth the CIA's time when it's run by a bunch of twenty-year-olds who don't have a clue?

"Did you meet Jade?" he asks. "She's fit, ain't she?"

I smirk. If he thinks Jade's attractive, Carys would blow his young mind. "Does Pierre-Jacques realize you've got a thing for his girlfriend?"

Francois chuckles. "I reckon she likes to be wanted. Prancing around in her tiny outfits, flirting with the lads."

Lorcan and I exchange a glance up front. Not the impression she gave us. At every turn, she's got a new face. "She's a flirt, is she?"

"Vindictive tart is more like." He laughs. "I reckon that's why we're after the McCaffrey family. She used to run with them when she was younger."

"Oh." It's the first word he's uttered since his introduction. "Was she shagging one of the McCaffrey boys?"

"Not from what I heard." He shakes his head. "Wanted to, I'm sure. I reckon she's like that." He taps ash out the window.

I let out a grunt. Much better when idiots ramble with the information I want rather than having to drag it out of them. He hasn't realized he shouldn't be chummy with us yet, which suits me fine. Maybe the fact he isn't privy to my reputation will work in my favor. "So, what? She hung out with them?"

"Don't know, exactly." He flicks the butt of his cigarette out the window before rolling it up. "Just heard she used to run with them. Was a long time ago, mate."

Does that explain the familiar feeling I have whenever I look at Jade? Was she in the background when we were younger, toying with the McCaffrey boys? If that's the case, does she know me better than I think? Does she recognize Lorcan? My blood cools and then runs hot.

"We need to talk," I mutter to Lorcan.

"Agreed." He catches Francois's attention in the rearview mirror. "Whereabouts are we headed?"

"Ah, right. Sorry. Left here. Pub's on the right. I've secured you a room above the pub. Nothing fancy, but better than sleeping on my settee."

At the pub, Francois walks ahead of us, and I mutter, "Does Jade know us?"

"Not a clue," Lorcan says. "Her personality is giving me whiplash. There's an agenda hidden under these layers."

"What, though?" I rub the back of my neck. "I'll get in touch with Jay."

"I'll tell Kim they should be on high alert. Jade can't be trusted."

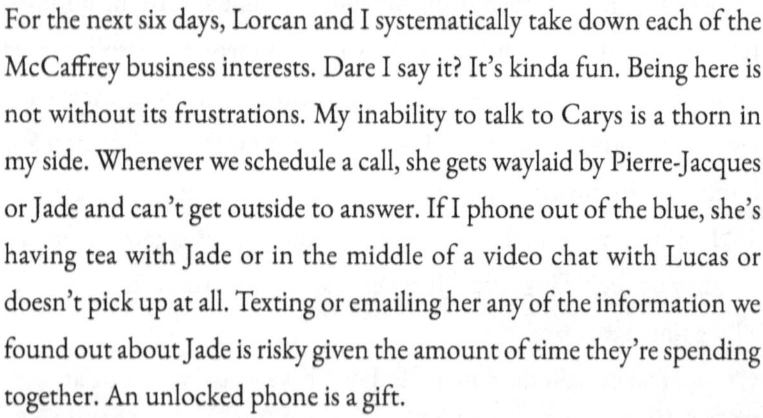

For the next six days, Lorcan and I systematically take down each of the McCaffrey business interests. Dare I say it? It's kinda fun. Being here is not without its frustrations. My inability to talk to Carys is a thorn in my side. Whenever we schedule a call, she gets waylaid by Pierre-Jacques or Jade and can't get outside to answer. If I phone out of the blue, she's having tea with Jade or in the middle of a video chat with Lucas or doesn't pick up at all. Texting or emailing her any of the information we found out about Jade is risky given the amount of time they're spending together. An unlocked phone is a gift.

Other than the constant queasiness in my stomach, I don't have any proof Jade's the devil in disguise. But it doesn't seem right for a woman to wear so many faces or be so adept at adjusting to her audience. Young boys? The flirt. Pierre-Jacques? The obedient girlfriend. Lunch with new contacts? The cougar. Tea with Carys? The lonely, abused woman. Carys says women wear different faces all the time, especially if they feel threatened in a man's world. I suppose that's true of some women. I'm not convinced that's Jade's reality.

"We got him." Lorcan gestures to his phone from the bar where he was ordering us dinner. "Francois called. Sieged the house. They've got Donal waiting for us."

I could have had one of the boys Francois recruited kill Donal or ordered Francois to do it himself. But I have questions I need answered before I'm going for the jugular. "Are you coming?" I rise from the table we've used as command central in the far corner of the pub.

Lorcan grimaces as he wanders closer. "Don't think I should. If they brought him here, maybe. Too many eyes might see something we don't want if I go there."

Like the fact Lorcan Donaghey is still very much alive. Keeping him here coordinating Francois's lads has worked out well. Lorcan could be a central part of the action while meeting very few people. This pub is sleepy and on the edge of a village outside Cork. Not many in or out of the place. To the lads, I was the public face of the operation, going wherever another pair of hands was needed. My brother was the brains and the steady calm in the storm I raged. By the end of the week, most of the men knew if they wanted courage to do a difficult job, they came to me. If they wanted strategy then they went to my brother.

"We've come this far," I agree. "No point in screwing it up now." I squint at Lorcan. "You think he was serious about the head?"

He nods slowly. "Unfortunately, the only way to be sure is to take it." He runs a hand along his neck. "If he meant it, you've done well. If he didn't mean it, the fact you were willing to do it sends a pretty strong message." He stares at me for a beat. "Not sure this needs to be said, but I'll say it anyway. Shoot him dead before you chop off his head."

"Yeah, yeah," I mutter, striding to the front entrance. "Mercy and all that shit."

When I arrive at the country property, Francois meets me at the iron gates. He climbs into the passenger seat for the drive up the laneway.

"Where's Lachlan?" Francois asks.

"Left him at the pub in case anything comes up."

He seems lost in thought for a minute. "The two of you have this…" He purses his lips. "Slick system, as though you've worked together for years."

"Sometimes you get lucky and gel with someone." I shrug. "Doesn't happen that often."

He points to the side of the massive house. "Around the rear. In the barn. Didn't want to make a mess in the house. We've got McCaffrey's men, the ones still alive, digging a grave for the others, cleaning up any trouble."

We do not need the authorities sniffing here, looking for people. "You don't do a mass grave. You need an incinerator. When families ask questions and you've got no answers, they're gonna search this property."

"Won't be our problem," Francois says. "We don't want the land. Just the men and other assets."

I let out an annoyed sigh. The bodies aren't my problem either. Lorcan's been in touch with the CIA since we started this mission, and while they aren't thrilled with our methods, they're more concerned about what comes next. The McCaffreys isn't where the plan stops.

I park the car and follow Francois to the barn door. The structure is newer and smells of hay. Cattle mill around in the pasture, but the swinging doors are closed, keeping them out of the way.

When we enter, Donal is tied to a chair, beaten and bloody. Someone worked out their frustrations while we were gone. Dirt, hay, and blood are mixed together on the surrounding floor.

"Leave us," I say, and his good eye cracks open.

"Finn," he mutters. "'Twas you?"

"PLA." No need to hide the source of his demise since he won't be around to speak to anyone. Everyone but Francois files out of the barn. Guess he thought my order didn't apply to him.

"You're workin' for them now?" Donal asks.

"In a way." I shrug and remove my gun from the small of my back. "You can leave too," I say to Francois.

"Lachlan isn't here. I've been told to make sure you're kept in line." He leans against the barn wall and takes an apple out of his pocket and bites into it. The crunch sets my teeth on edge.

I rotate and fire my gun at him. The bullet grazes his upper arm and lodges in the wood.

"What the bloody hell?" Francois's free hand covers the spot where blood trickles out of the hole in his shirt. "What was that for?"

"'Cause if the PLA thinks *you're* keeping me in line, they got another think coming. I said out, and I meant get the fuck out. That was a warning shot."

He pushes off the wall, cradling his upper arm with his hand, and he leaves without further comment. He finally did an internet search on me midweek. I enjoyed watching the color drain from his face while he read my list of crimes.

"Fucking women," Donal says as soon as Francois is gone.

"I know he looks like a pansy, but he's actually a man." I cock my head. "Well, boy, really." I let my gun hang at my side, and I turn to Donal.

"Not who I meant. PJ's sex toy."

"Jade?" I thought I'd have to bring her up to milk him for information. A stroke of luck or a bad omen?

"Is that what she's calling herself now?" Donal glares at me. "You're the reason she's got her knickers in a twist."

"I'd remember if I twisted her knickers." I smirk. Not that my list of women is short, but I can't imagine *that's* how I recognize Jade.

"You murdered her boyfriend about... What'd it be now? Almost twenty years ago?"

I narrow my eyes. He has to be talking about when Carys was stabbed. When I tracked down each of the men from the bar brawl, a few of them claimed Paddy's girlfriend had been with him at the pub. I found him last. He begged me for his life on his knees in his apartment. After I shot him, there was no trace of a woman. Hunting her hadn't been worth my time when Carys was in the hospital. Looks like mercy might bite me in the ass. *Again.*

"Paddy?"

"Aye. She came wailing to me about wantin' retribution for Paddy's death. We put a bounty on yer head. But you were gone by then. Back to America. Daddy swept in." His tone is mocking. Admirable, given that I'm about to shoot him between the eyes and cut off his head. I'm quite fond of men who don't know when to show their belly.

"You're lucky he did. You would've lost a whole lot more men trying to take me down." I wave my gun. "Why would this takeover have anything to do with her?"

"She reckoned I didn't do enough to avenge his death. Said one day she'd have more power than me. This is her flex, ain't it?"

If her pursuit of the McCaffreys is for revenge, why is she having *me* deliver it? There's a knock on the door, and Francois calls, "Have you lopped off his head yet?"

Donal pales. "My head?"

"In a box. Suppose it's a lover's gift from Pierre-Jacques to his sex toy. I don't find it sexy, but she must. Fetishes. No accounting for them." I raise my gun. "Don't worry, I'm going to kill you first."

"Wait, wait," he cries. "Can't—"

I fire my weapon, and Donal's chin slumps to his chest, blood trickling out of the bullet wound in his forehead, spatter on the barn wall behind him. My mind drums with this new information. Is Jade after me? She could have tried to kill me a number of times already. They could have executed me on the roof of the prison.

What's her game?

Is she really the person in charge of the PLA?

CHAPTER TWENTY-FOUR

CARYS

Jade and I are riffling through my closet talking about fashion. Kim is sprawled across my bed, staring at the ceiling. She probably wishes she was dead right about now. Partly, I'm keeping the discussion with Jade so centered on clothing to irritate Kim. Topics she finds amusing do not include makeup, skin care, or fashion. I've been spinning the chatter in those directions for the last hour. This is the second day in a row.

Jade sighs as her fingers trail along a gown the PLA bought me.

"You like that?" I drag my attention from Kim's disinterested position on the bed to Jade's wistful smile.

"I have it in green." She flicks to another gown. "Pierre likes me in green."

"Do *you* like green?" I keep my voice gentle. She's been funny and sweet the last few days since Finn has been gone. The niggling sensation that I know her has only gotten stronger, but I can't pinpoint where or how.

"Well enough." She steps back from the closet. "Shall we go for a walk? It's a lovely day."

"Oh, thank God," Kim breathes from the bed.

"Oh, um, actually. I was asking Carys. Our conversations seem to bore you so much, I didn't figure you'd want to come along."

"I'd love a walk. See more of the property." Kim sits up. Her midnight hair is free from her ponytail today and cascades in a shiny curtain around her shoulders.

"The two of you and Jay walk the fields a lot. I can't imagine there's much more to explore." Jade gives her a sweet smile.

"Exercise, then. I like exercise." Kim hops off the bed and leads the way to the door. "Shall we?" She raises her eyebrows, and I stifle a laugh. Unless she's is prepared to give a direct order as her boss, Kim won't budge. Despite our mundane babble the last few hangouts, she doesn't trust our host.

"Great." Jade's smile is strained.

We head to the back stairs, and Jay appears out of nowhere, offering to join us. Finn has put the fear of God in him about leaving me unattended outside. In the house, Kim is fine as a companion, but outside, Finn expects someone he can trust when Jade or other members of the PLA are involved. Jay guides us, and Kim trails a few steps behind, not even pretending to be interested in our conversation.

"He must worry about you a lot," Jade says once we're in the fields.

"Who?"

"Finn. Jay protects you. Despite the fact Kim works for me, I suspect she's loyal to Finn. Strange, really, since they hardly know each other."

"He tends to inspire loyalty very quickly."

"Inspire?" She raises her brows. "Or force?"

I chuckle and tuck my hands into the pockets of my jumpsuit. "Depends on the person, I suppose."

"Do you like that?" She shakes her head. "Sorry. That's a very personal question. I shouldn't have asked. I've picked bad men my whole life."

"Oh?" I raise my eyebrows and scan her petite figure. "How bad?" My mind strays to Eric, who might not have been as bad as Finn on paper but proved to be so much worse in reality.

"Thieves, murderers, cheaters... abusers." Her voice grows soft. "You name him, I've dated him."

I weigh my options. Should I give her something personal in return? "Finn isn't exactly a Boy Scout."

"So, you like dangerous, evil men too?"

I laugh. "I guess? I don't know if I would call Finn evil, exactly." He's never been dangerous to me. He does terrible things. Makes decisions I don't agree with. But I can't think of him as evil the way Kim and other people do. He's not that man to me, even if I can recognize his choices make him that for others.

"This is going to sound weird." Jade fiddles with the ends of her hair. "I sort of like the fear bad men inspire. What does that say about me?"

She's hit on my trigger. No matter how wrong it might be, I *am* attracted to Finn's darkness. "The fear they inspire in *you*?" He has never dropped his dark shadow over me. Jade's softening black eye indicates she might not be so lucky.

There's a pause, and she seems lost in thought as we walk. "Not in me, no. Though, there is that." Her laugh is soft. "I suppose, sometimes. Can't help some fear when a man's that intimidating." She gives me a side glance, gauging my reaction. "But I mean seeing *other* people's fear. There's something so powerful in knowin' yer the cause of that."

"Oh." I'm at a loss for words. She gets off on people experiencing fear. The notion sends a shiver down my spine. While I'm not sure I could ever watch Finn kill a man, even if I realize he's doing it, I'm starting to wonder if Jade would enjoy seeing the moment and revel in the pain. Would she be at Pierre-Jacques's shoulder, encouraging him, and delighting in the violence?

She lets out a self-conscious laugh. "Sorry. That's *really* dark. I was raised in a pretty twisted family, and I think it's warped every relationship I've ever had."

I breathe a sigh of relief. We all have dark thoughts sometimes, right? Warped family relationships is a topic I can navigate. "Families are tough. I don't have much of a relationship with my father anymore. My mother self-medicates and lives in denial. My brother died when I was younger."

"How far are we walking?" Jay calls from up ahead.

"Turn down this path," Jade responds. "It loops back to the house."

We walk in silence for a few minutes, and I wonder whether Kim used her superspy capabilities to listen to my conversation with Jade. What would she make of Jade's fear comments?

"I hope I didn't disturb you with anything I said." She glances at me. "I've enjoyed getting to know you the last few days. I've never had a sister or a female best friend. Surrounded myself with men, mostly."

"I grew up in a world of men too." Though I've often had women, like Kim or Lena or Sofia, who I've formed connections with. I meant what I said to her days ago about women sticking together.

"You seem so at ease without Finn around."

My brow furrows at her suggestion. She thinks I'm *happier* when Finn's not near? Has to be projection. "Are you more at ease when Pierre-Jacques isn't around?"

She checks over her shoulder. "He loves me, but we fight a lot. Sometimes he's—sometimes he's rough."

"If you need help to get away—"

"No, no." She shakes her head. "He loves me."

We reach the main entrance of the house, having circled the western edge of the property. Jade's phone pings, and she takes it from her pocket.

"He needs to see me. I should go. Tomorrow?" She gives me a hopeful look.

"Sure." I smile.

She hurries into the house. Jay and Kim flank me on either side.

"Lachlan texted me," Kim says. "They're on their way back." She stares after Jade. "Any news from Charles?"

"Just more back and forth on terms he's willing to let me give Demid."

"Want me to try?" Jay says. "Finn's not gonna be happy if he comes back and we don't have a plan in place."

"Is Donal dead?" I ask Kim.

"The PLA is now in charge of the McCaffrey clan." She tucks her hair behind her ear. "Next up is the Byrne family."

"And we still have no idea what the end goal is," I whisper.

Jay looks down the long gravel drive. "I'm not sure when we'll see what's coming. I just hope we recognize it before it blows up in our faces."

CHAPTER TWENTY-FIVE

FINN

Lorcan glances at the box on the floor of the back seat again. It's wrapped like a Christmas present, a bow sitting on top. Underneath is a garbage bag to keep the blood from seeping into the car mats. Probably been blood spilled in the vehicle before. Not as much as that leaking head, though.

"Bloody hell, you're playing with fire," he says.

"I'm giving them what they want." I've taken the second stretch of driving to get us into PLA territory. We've spent most of the ride in silence since we can't be sure if we're being monitored by someone. If my mind wasn't busy mulling over Jade's connection to Carys's stabbing years ago, I'd be bored out of my skull.

"Indeed. With a 'screw you' flourish." He sighs and rubs the side of his face.

That's been my MO since we were kids. Why would he imagine I'd be any different now? "Think anyone is still awake?"

He squints down the dark laneway, trying to catch a glimpse of any lights ahead. "It's half twelve. I reckon someone will be up as a lookout. Pretty shoddy security otherwise."

As we get closer, the gravel drive crunches and crackles under the tires. There's no silent entrance by car. If anyone is watching for trouble, they'll hear us coming, even if we turned off our lights. I park the vehicle by the front, and framed in the doorway is Noel. I could give him the box now and have him find a spike for Donal's head. Or I could deliver the package as I intended. Easy choice.

From the back seat, I drape the garbage bag over my present and pick it up. The contents aren't heavy, but I don't need to be getting covered in blood when I haven't seen Carys in a week. Not sure how she'll respond to what I'm about to do. She's probably sleeping, anyway.

Lorcan is at my side as we walk toward Noel. "Pierre-Jacques and Jade around?" I ask.

"In the throne room. We heard the car on the laneway." Noel holds open the front door. "Is that...?"

"It is. No peeking." I smirk and shoulder past him.

They follow me to the throne room, and while I hated our last meeting here, I have a feeling this will leave me more satisfied. When we get to the large, open room, Jade and PJ are settled into their thrones drinking glasses of wine as though they are royalty. Ridiculous. I set down the garbage bag and pluck out the bloody, wrapped box. Without waiting for an invitation, I set the box on Jade's lap.

"M'lady. Donal's head. In a box." I give her an exaggerated bow.

She gasps, and her wineglass crashes to the floor. Red liquid spills everywhere. When she glances up at me, shock and rage mingle on her face. "Is that *blood*?"

"Yeah. See, the head is connected to the neck by—" I use my head and neck as props while I explain basic anatomy.

"I know," she grits out. "Why did you put the bloody box in my lap?"

"Oh, sorry." I frown, trying to suppress my grin. "I thought *you* wanted his head."

"You thought wrong," Pierre-Jacques says from the seat beside her. "Noel, remove the box and do as I asked earlier. Head on a spike at a corner of the house."

I quash my eye roll at such a useless display of dominance. Who from McCaffrey's organization will see his head up here? No one.

When Noel lifts the box, Jade's dress is patterned in various shades of bloodred.

"You've ruined my dress," she seethes.

Funny, it's not the blood bothering her but rather the ruined fabric. I focus on Pierre-Jacques and ignore her quiet rage. At least her emotion seems authentic. Apparently, she cares about clothes. She and Carys would have that in common if nothing else. "Francois probably called you already, but the McCaffrey men are yours."

"Did he beg for his life?" Her hands hover over the dampness of her dress, disgust marring her features. When I don't answer right away, she glances up, a cunning gleam in her eyes. "Well?"

"No." I shrug. "He went out like a man."

She glares at Pierre-Jacques, unsatisfied with my answer. "Did you kill the rest of his family?" Pierre-Jacques asks in a leisurely tone.

I chuckle. "Uh, no. Had you listened to my plan, you'd have known who I needed to kill to get this done. Lady Macbeth here has the blood of the only person who couldn't survive in her lap."

Her eyes narrow at my reference. What I'm trying to figure out is whether she's more like Iago. A poison in Pierre-Jacque's ear, partners in the PLA, or is she manipulating him?

"Yes, but you have a certain reputation." Pierre-Jacques flicks his hand. "Kill them all."

"What can I say? I learned a few things in prison about being more economical." Beside me, Lorcan covers his mouth, but he remains a silent presence.

There are more sides to Jade than a house of mirrors, and I can't tell whether she understands why I put the box in her lap or not. If she was at the pub eighteen years ago, she'll have seen Lorcan too. So far, they've given no indication they don't trust him. Trust is earned, but it can turn on a dime.

"Leave us." Pierre-Jacques picks up his wineglass.

"What? I don't get a pat on the head? A cookie?"

His furious gaze bores into mine. "You disrespected Jade, and you're alive. The fact you still have a head is because you brought me someone else's. Leave us."

The instinct to bite down, swagger harder, rises and waits at the back of my throat. I swallow the urge. Until we've got Lucas, Sofia, Lena, and the girls moved to a more secure location, I can only push so hard. Carys wouldn't forgive me for putting them in danger for my ego. The CIA would never pardon me for ripping his head off without knowing the larger PLA plan. Tentacles of the organization lie across the world. Take one off and another grows in its place.

Instead of escalating, I rotate on my heel and stride to the door which leads to the stairs. My brother follows behind as a silent shadow.

"Not you, Lachlan. We have things to discuss."

"Aye." He turns back. "Yes, sir."

I half turn in response, uneasy at the thought of leaving him alone. In this situation, he's not my brother, he's the PLA's hired gun. If they don't suspect anything yet, insisting on staying will raise their ire. Our gazes connect for the briefest moment before I'm through the doors and headed for Carys. There's only so much protecting I can do, and I relied on Lorcan to take care of himself once our father was disposed of. I can't start coddling him now.

In the hallway outside Carys's bedroom door, Jay is playing twenty-one with a deck of cards. "You winning?" I smirk.

He chuckles and sweeps up the deck. "You've returned."

"How were things here?" Even though we chatted a few times, communication was tricky with the distance between us and people on both ends listening in. My respect for Kim's duplicitous nature might have increased a smidge in the last week. Here, in the PLA mansion, I'm just like her. Vulnerable from both sides—two agendas tugging on me for attention. Figuring out which to prioritize, and when, isn't always clear.

"Weird. You?"

"Same, actually." I frown and check the time on my phone. How long will Jade and Pierre-Jacques stay awake? We can't speak inside, but middle-of-the-night trysts came with their own risks. "Three a.m. Field. You got me?"

"I got you." Jay rises to his feet and ambles along the hall to his room.

I slip inside the door, and Carys stirs in bed but doesn't wake. At home, she became a light sleeper with Lucas needing fed. I undress as quietly as I can and slide between the covers behind her. When I tug her flush against my body, she sighs.

"You're here," she murmurs. Her ass moves against my erection. She turns in my embrace and burrows into me. "I missed you. I wish you never had to leave me again."

My arms tighten around her, drawing her as close as I can. The whole week I was gone, there'd been a dull ache under my breastbone. The same one I carried with me in prison. Right now, it's disappeared. Vanished.

I'm never going to get into heaven, but having her in my arms is pretty damn close to perfection. Amazes me, sometimes. I get to feel *this* with her after everything I've done.

She trails kisses up my neck until she reaches my lips. "Show me how much you missed me."

Easy. I'd give her that demonstration all night.

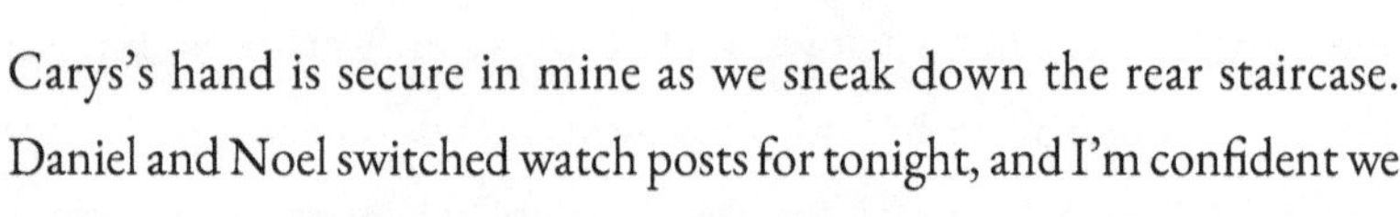

Carys's hand is secure in mine as we sneak down the rear staircase. Daniel and Noel switched watch posts for tonight, and I'm confident we can get to the fields without Daniel seeing us. He's lazy and borderline incompetent. Once we're outside, Jay's build is a shadow in the distance.

We're silent while we trudge through the field to meet him. When we arrive, he says, "What'd you learn?"

Carys wraps her arms around my waist, and I run my hand along her back. Having to meet out here in the middle of the night is inconvenient, but at least we're capable of speaking somewhere. We need to have the same information. "Jade's not her real name. She used to run around with the McCaffrey crew when Carys was stabbed. I—uh—murdered her boyfriend."

"Oh shit," Jay breathes. "Why'd she want Donal's head on a stick?"

"According to Donal? He didn't do enough to get revenge for my murderous spree within his organization."

"But if you killed him..." She gazes up at me. "Why go after Donal? Shouldn't she be going after you?"

Jay and I stare at each other in the dark. "You think she wants to hurt Carys?" he asks.

I shake my head. "If that's what she wanted, she could have gone after her while I was away. I'm confident she has more power than she lets on. I don't know if Francois told me the shit about Jade because he was supposed to let it slip or the guy's an idiot. Spent a week with him. Fifty-fifty either way."

"What's Lachlan think?" Jay asks.

"He's going to check to see if there's any more intel on her. I doubt it. Without a real name, we're flying blind. This alias could have come from anywhere at any point."

"She mentioned she likes to—" Carys seems to search for the right words. "She gets off on seeing people afraid."

I rock on my heels. Well, fuck me. Letting me realize she's a threat and then coiling up like a snake, not striking, but not backing down, is a hell of a message. For the first time, the risk in being here is weighty and solid. She's circling us. Maybe it's because of her dead boyfriend or maybe it's something else. "You talked to Demid?"

"Yeah, but my father won't budge on the terms. Thinks Demid is being unreasonable. Sure—abandon your daughter and grandson to dangle in danger while you determine what's the best deal for you. You know? He makes me so angry. I'd never leave him in harm's way."

"I can't make a move until our families are safe." I rub my face with both hands. "She's got a grudge against me. That much we know. How much does the bitterness matter in the bigger plan? Who really wanted me here? Was it her? Pierre-Jacques? Why do they need the influx of men from the McCaffrey organization? Why do they want to drag the Byrne family into this? Does Jade know Lachlan isn't Lachlan?"

"That's a lot of unknowns," Jay mutters.

"I don't like our odds at the moment," I admit. "We've gotta start slotting pieces into the puzzle. We need time and space to search the place."

"Jade and I are going shopping in Belfast tomorrow. So, we'll be out of the house."

"Not alone."

"Kim's coming, much to both her and Jade's disgust." She laughs a little. "They don't get along."

"But yet Jade tolerates her and is technically her boss." I cock my head. "Why?"

"She likes Carys to think she's weak," Jay says. "She enjoys Carys's sympathy. Almost... preens when Carys gives her undivided attention. If she vetoed Kim, she'd lose the weak angle and possibly Carys's sympathy."

I glance down at Carys. "That what you think?"

She eyes Jay with a hint of a smile. "You've really been paying attention."

"You and Jade have been talking about a lot of boring shit. Makes it easy to read some body language 'cause there's fuck all else to do."

"Maybe she *is* faking it. But we do seem to have a lot in common."

"What's Kim say?" I hate asking, but if someone can spot a fake, I suspect she's it.

"It's easy to become who someone wants when you know them well enough." Carys sighs. "So cynical. I will admit Jade has too many faces to be completely sure which is the real one."

"How'd she respond to you putting the head in her lap?" Jay's eyes gleam in the moonlight.

I wince. Lorcan must have texted him. I can only imagine how that exchange went. I was hoping to avoid the brutal details with Carys around. She's never been squeamish, but I'm loath to push her too far with my ruthlessness.

"Head in her lap?" The furrow between her brows deepens.

"Don't worry." I rub her back. "I used a box."

"Please tell me you killed him first." She squeezes her eyes shut.

"He didn't suffer. No point. Killing him wasn't personal. Not for me." I kiss the top of her head. "As for Jade, I'd say indignant and a bit aggressive. Mostly about the blood on her dress." I consider her reaction for a beat. The dress wasn't the weirdest part. "She also wanted me to tell her if he begged."

She points at Jay. "The way she discussed fear and suffering with me the other day was not normal." She presses her finger into her chest. "For me to say her opinions on those topics aren't normal? Well, you realize she's screwed up."

Carys might love me, but her sense of right and wrong is on a scale others would recognize even if they don't agree with the breadth of her gray areas. *Enjoying* the suffering of others? On a different scale entirely.

I gaze between Jay and Carys. "We need to understand who we're really dealing with as soon as we can."

Chapter Twenty-Six

Carys

We're in the dressing rooms of a high-end women's clothing store in Belfast, and I've already tried on half a dozen outfits. While I might not trust Jade, she has impeccable taste in clothes. I've never been here before, but it's becoming a favorite.

When I emerge from the dressing room, I rotate in front of the bank of mirrors. The deep-purple dress fits me like a glove, and the color makes my skin radiant.

Jay flips through a magazine on a bench meant for beleaguered spouses or supportive friends. Finn didn't trust my safety to Kim alone when we'd be more than an hour away. Jay doesn't glance up from his reading material but still says, "You look great."

"That's a winner." Kim brandishes another dress from the racks. "If I was you, I reckon I'd get it."

"I want to see," Jade calls from her own change cubicle. "Give me a second."

I eye the outfit she's holding and tease a finger along the neckline. The black lace will plunge between my breasts, a deep V, exposing my scar. I raise an eyebrow in question, and she circles where the mark lays. "I can't wait to see her face when she sees this." Her midnight eyes are full of a sly meaning. The comment is loud enough for Jade to hear, but since she can't see us, she won't understand Kim's true intent.

Jade pops out of the dressing room. "That's gorg." She orbits around me, her own dress floating around her legs with a swish. "You have to get that."

"That's pretty." The fabric of her dress slithers between my fingers. "Nice and light."

"Good for summer." She rotates to catch the angles in the mirror like I did.

Another stab of familiarity strikes me. Did I see her at the pub when I was stabbed? Is that why some of her movements and expressions hit me so hard? Last night when Finn and I went back to bed, I tried to remember faces from the crowd. But other than his stricken expression above me, and Lorcan's steady presence, everyone else is a blur, a vague remembrance. It's not a happy memory, one I cultivated, or clung onto. Instead, I worked to suppress the helplessness of that evening. All Finn's strength and cunning were nothing compared to a tiny knife inserted in the right place. Death a hair's breadth away.

I snatch the dress out of Kim's hand. Perhaps she's right. The scar has grown faint over time, and if Jade notices, it'll be because she knows to look. When I've zipped up the back of the dress, I examine myself in the mirror. The scar is framed perfectly by the neckline. One of many reasons why I never wore dresses like this. I tug on the waist and smooth it down. With a deep breath, I open the door.

Jay throws his magazine to the side, ready for his body language study. Kim lounges on the seat beside him, but Jade is back in her room.

"That's a dress stitched to lie on a man's floor," Kim exclaims for Jade's ears. The comment is so obviously a bait, I almost laugh.

"Do you think?" I turn in the mirror.

Jade's door flies open, and she's wearing her own clothes, three dresses draped over her arm. She strides over to me, peering at the silhouette and then homing in on the neckline.

"That plunge doesn't really feel like you." She meets my gaze. "It's very daring. Are you comfortable with it?"

"I like it, actually." I twist toward the mirror, offering her another chance to peek at my scar while I peer at her.

"You've got a mark." She gestures to her own chest. "Just there. What's that from?"

My cheeks warm, unable to help the reaction. Talking about the night I lost my baby with Finn and almost died is one of my least favorite topics. Creating the discussion flusters me. "An old injury."

"What happened?" Jade's eyes are wide while she stares at me. "An accident?"

"A knife," I admit. "Meant for someone else."

"May I?" Her index finger is poised above my chest. She's transfixed by the scar, unable to tear her gaze away.

While I don't want her touching me, I'm interested to see where her behavior leads. Yet another side to examine, dissect. "It's a scar." I force myself to stay in the moment with Jade and not to look at Jay and Kim. "You can touch the mark. The skin's a bit rough."

Her fingertip brushes the raised flesh, and she shudders. With her eyes closed, she says, "He must have been terrified."

"Who?" Kim's voice brims with false curiosity.

Her eyes snap open and widen at the slip. Then a mask falls over her face, and she rubs her forehead. "Oh, I—" She seems to stare through us for a beat. "She said the knife was meant for someone else. I assumed it was a man." A soft chuckle escapes her. "How many women get into knife fights?"

Kim draws a tiny one out of the side pocket of her spandex tights and twirls it across her fingers. "I know a few."

Jade's jaw tightens a fraction before she turns to me. "I shouldn't have assumed. Was it another woman you were with?" Her face is open with innocence again, any hint of calculation gone.

"It was Finn, actually," I say. "He was afraid. Terrified. Scariest moment of his life." He's never said those words, but he's laid his heart bare to me over the last year. Going after the men who attacked him and stabbed me was his way of getting control back. When Finn's backed into a corner, he doesn't cower. He swings with all his might. Exaggerating his fear may elicit more information out of Jade. "He couldn't save me, so he punished everyone else." I hope she hears that because not even God will be able to help her if she comes after me or Lucas. Finn will hunt her to the ends of the earth.

When our gazes meet, Jade's pupils are dilated. Jesus. She's aroused. Was the trigger fear or punishment? "Must be incredible to have that kind of desperate love," she murmurs.

I can't lie. Who wouldn't want someone who'd suffer their own personal hell to save you from yours? I chased the kind of love Finn gives me for almost two decades with other men and had no success. Not everyone can have what we have, and her envy shines bright from her eyes. Does she want Finn to pay for his crimes, or does she just want Finn? "You must have something similar with PJ?"

The reminder snaps her out of a trance, and one side of her lips tilts up. "Pierre-Jacques isn't much for desperate. Too emotional."

Too emotional? Interesting. She drank up my Finn story as though it was the sweetest nectar. She's already told me she values fear. Does she also value love? Or is she like her partner?

Jay clears his throat.

"I can help you with that zipper again, Carys." Kim comes to my shoulder.

"I suppose I should pay for these." Jade stares at the dresses slung over her arm. "Did you want to get the purple one? He won't notice one more in the pile."

I observe her for a beat before saying, "That's all right. Kind of you to offer. I'm going to think about it. My closet is already stuffed at home."

"Ah, yes. Cape Verde. Gorgeous island." She turns and heads for the cash, clearly a little off her game.

In the dressing room, Kim doesn't bother to help me with my dress. Instead, she leans against the wall while I change.

"She was there that night, and she got off on seeing Finn so upset," she whispers.

"That's how I read her too." I slip on my outfit from earlier. "There's something not right with her."

"That was fast," Jay says, his voice raised. "Efficient cashier here."

"They like my money," Jade responds.

Kim takes the black dress and puts it on the hanger and gathers the other dresses lined up, tossing them over her arm. "Are you getting any of these?"

"Not today." The whole experience, fun at first, has been tainted by our final interaction. I'm still not sure whether Jade's after revenge for her dead boyfriend or lusting after mine.

"Dinner?" Jade suggests when Kim and I emerge.

"Sounds lovely." And necessary. Lorcan and Finn need as much time as possible to search the mansion for clues. "I'm in the mood for one of those multicourse places. A real experience."

"Oh." She frowns. "I'm not sure we should be gone that long."

"I've found a place," Jay says. "We can walk there. Only a few blocks."

Jade's bodyguards have kept their distance near the door, and one of them opens it when we get close. "Home?" he says.

"Everyone's hungry. We're going to walk to a restaurant a few blocks from here." She draws her phone out of her purse. "I'll have to let Pierre-Jacques know we're going to be late."

Chapter Twenty-Seven

Finn

The plan is risky, but what is life without a little risk? Carys, Kim, and Jay are supposed to keep Jade and her crew of bodyguards away from the property all day. So far, from Carys's update texts, their piece of espionage is going well.

Lorcan and I have a harder task. "Did you get it?" I mutter when he arrives at the mansion.

"Aye." He glances around the entrance for people listening or observing. "You sure?"

"Might be our best chance." This morning when we went to breakfast, almost every member of the PLA crew was missing, including Daniel and Noel. When I asked, Pierre-Jacques brushed me off and said everyone would be gone for a few days on errands. This plan, risky as it is, came together with the opportunity he presented us—limited security and a mostly empty house.

My agreement with the CIA only holds if I foil the PLA's larger goal. Otherwise, the time I spend here is a vacation from my twelve consecutive life sentences. The push-pull between treading lightly to keep everyone safe and ensuring I get my freedom someday is wearing on me.

Despite the work we did in securing the McCaffrey organization, we're outsiders. I'm not an ass-kiss, and Lorcan is on babysitting duty for me rather than having a real role in the PLA. The inner circle eludes us. Today, I'll either wedge us into the middle of things, or I'll force us to change directions.

He falls into step beside me as we head to Pierre-Jacques's office. We're supposed to be meeting about the plan for the Byrne Brothers. There are only two guards left protecting Pierre-Jacques, and both are off on wild-security-goose chases to the outbuildings. Lorcan's knuckles rap on solid wood. My heart thuds. When he answers, we have to act fast.

The door swings back. The words on Pierre-Jacque's lips die when Lorcan sticks the syringe in his neck. He collapses, and I catch him, dragging him to the couch. I hoist him onto the leather surface and situate him the way I imagine he'd nap.

He shuts the office door and locks it. We sweep for any cameras, but we come up empty-handed. If we're wrong and they're somewhere very covert, we could end up busted. We're living on the edge, and we've got one shot to turn up information if we're caught here.

We search in silence. Lorcan starts with the filing cabinets, and I tug open the desk drawers. The key to a good search is being methodical. No stone can be left unturned, but the area needs to look as though nobody has touched it too. When Pierre-Jacques wakes from his nap, he can't suspect we've been here.

A missed meeting is a mistake because he was too tired or we forgot to show up, but if his office is ransacked, the truth is impossible to conceal.

Lorcan removes papers and bookmarks their slot in the cabinet. I find purchase orders for explosives and put those on the desk, keeping the drawer open so I'll recall where to return them. The process can't be rushed, but we've only got two hours until Pierre-Jacques wakes up. If we've timed it right, he'll be awake and no longer groggy before Jade returns. He won't remember us arriving at his door, and we'll claim we came, knocked, and got no response. According to the CIA, he'll think he slept through any disturbance. The plan is both brilliant and insane—exactly the way I like it.

The middle compartment on his desk is locked. I heave on it, but I can't get it to release. I tip out jars and peer into every nook and cranny. No key. Could it be in Pierre-Jacques's pocket? I'm not willing to risk disturbing him. The drug is supposed to knock him out cold, but if the CIA is wrong, and he wakes while I'm pickpocketing him, the jig is up. If the drawer is secured, it's one I need to access.

"They're right to be worried," Lorcan mutters, flipping through a file folder. "Bombs have been delivered to Chicago, Cork, a small town in the Swiss Alps, Shanghai, Mexico City, Cape Verde, and some shit town in Russia."

"Cape Verde?" I run a hand down my face. "When?"

"Looks like about a week ago."

Not the one that went off in Carys's hotel and casino then. Strange the PLA would have any connections on the island, though the CIA warned Lorcan and Kim the PLA's net is wide and deep. Do they have divisions in those cities? Ready and willing to execute their plan?

I grab a paperclip from the dish on the desk and jimmy it into the shape of a key. My hands freeze on the drawer when the locations on Lorcan's bomb list click into place. "Is the town in Switzerland outside Zurich?"

"I'd have to check a map," Lorcan admits. "Don't know offhand."

The Van de Berg chalet is in a small town outside Zurich. Carys and I stayed there while I recovered from the warehouse raid and then again while we were trying to make a break from Carys's family. "What about the Russian town?" My shoulders tense. "Is it near Volgograd?"

"I don't bloody know. I'm not a walking international map." He snaps pictures of the documents with his phone. "At least we've got an idea where they're targeting now."

Chicago is the head office for Van de Berg Ammunitions. What about the other places on the list? Would I also find Van de Berg properties there? Maybe. Cork didn't fit for sure, but did the others?

"Get that open yet?" Lorcan tips his chin at where my hand still rests on the drawer.

I yank out the paperclip key and let out a frustrated growl. A crowbar would be helpful right about now.

"Here," he says. "Let me. Kim's taught me a thing or two about locks."

"That what you two do for fun? Lie around trading superspy secrets?"

A teasing glint enters Lorcan's gaze while he works to refashion the paperclip. "Among other things. She's quite clever. I reckon you don't want to hear it, but 'tis true."

Whether Kimi is smart isn't the issue between us. I can't trust her knowing what I did to her family. No one forgives and forgets that kinda thing. If anyone murdered my brother in front of me, I'd damn sure be looking for revenge even a hundred years later. Putting her personal feelings aside would make her a much better person than me.

He fiddles with the lock, and it clicks unlocked. On the couch, Pierre-Jacques stirs. My brother checks his watch while he tugs the drawer open. "We should get outta here." He slots the pages he photographed into their file folders, slipping them into the bookmarked areas of the filing cabinet. "Kim says the sedative isn't always an exact science."

Since the drawer is unlocked, might as well search it. I ease it all the way back, and along with the usual office supplies, there's a manila envelope. Peering inside, I chuckle. "Jackpot." I pour the contents onto the desk. Passports. Must be at least ten of them. Different countries adorn each.

Lorcan keeps photographing and slotting, photographing and slotting. A good system for us to examine the details later. I pluck my phone out of my rear pocket and open the first passport. Methodically, I work through documenting them. No two are the same in names, dates, or country.

I'm opening the last one when Lorcan dumps the others into the envelope and says, "We've gotta go. I need to relock this drawer."

Jade's final passport is in my hand. She's younger in the photo, and the passport is close to expiring. It's not her picture or the date that causes the low whistle to escape me, it's the name. "Well fuck me," I whisper. My gut clenches. "I know who she is. We need to get to Belfast."

Chapter Twenty-Eight

Carys

We're seated in our own section of the quiet, upscale restaurant, and we've been here for hours. We've exhausted the polite chitchat topics, and Jade's bodyguards have rotated out, so everyone has had a chance to eat. The bill has been paid, and we're sipping our tea and coffee. Used cotton napkins litter the gray tablecloth.

Jay slouches back in his seat and pats his stomach. "I'm not sure I've got any more room in here."

Jade's phone pings, and her rueful smile slips when she glances at whatever is on the screen. She taps her manicured nail on the case and seems to be running something through her head. She types out a quick message and drops her phone into her purse.

"You okay?" I peer at her, trying to read her mood. She's been quiet and reserved during the meal—more observer than participant.

"Lucas. That's your son, right?" She meets my gaze, but there's been a shift in her brown eyes. The open naivety is gone, replaced with a more sinister slant. The directness of her question is surprising. Despite the amount of time we've spent together, our talks have been superficial. Until this minute, I hadn't even noticed. A frisson of unease snakes down my spine. Kim, who has been lounging beside me, sits up straighter.

"He is, yes." Lucas isn't a secret, though I have been very careful not to video chat with him in my room or anywhere people might overhear.

"But Finn's not the father?" She cocks her head, and her chestnut hair swishes around her shoulders.

"He'll be his father in every way that counts." I sip my wine and flick my gaze to Jay to check if he feels the heaviness in the air too. Alert. Listening carefully. We've noticed the unspoken swing in power. I focus on Jade. She's fishing for something, but I'm not sure what.

"Eric, right? Eric is Lucas's father."

"Biological, yes."

"Hmm..." She drums her fingers on the table, her nails making a soft tap on the cloth. "How did he die?"

Kim's eyes narrow, and she tucks her phone into her pocket. She's read the new tension too. Behind Jade, three of her bodyguards appear.

Did Finn and Lorcan get caught? Kim checked her phone almost an hour ago and gave me the nod to tell me the search was done. Something has tilted, and not in our favor. Anxiety pools in my stomach. None of us has dared to look at our phones while Jade's been at the table with us for fear of tipping our hand. Even Jay has kept his in his pocket.

"Eric was shot in Russia during a raid on a house my father owns." The details are public knowledge, and the way she's behaving, she must already have the particulars.

"By whom?" A hint of a smirk appears on her face. This is not the same woman I've spent so much time with the last week and a half. This is the woman Kim and Finn warned me about.

"I—I don't know." I shrug.

"Mmm. You never bothered to find out? The father of your only child and you dismiss his death like it's nothing?"

I clench my jaw. "You don't have a clue what you're talking about."

"What if I told you Finn shot him?" Her gaze is calculating, angling for a reaction.

"He didn't." I narrow my eyes.

"Oh, Carys. You poor, naïve soul. I almost feel bad for what's coming. *Almost.*" She rises from her chair and drops some bills on the table. "If only Eric had lived, you would have known what to expect. Of course, you would have been afraid this whole time." She grins. "Would've been glorious as far as I'm concerned." She sighs. "Finn's bullet put a wrench in my plans, so I sent you a going away present to your office." She stares at me a beat, waiting for me to catch up. "I must have watched the security footage a million times." Her Irish accent is gone, and in its place is one I don't recognize. Not American. European of some sort.

"The confetti bomb," I whisper.

Kim draws her gun, leveling it at Jade. The three men behind her point their guns at each of us. "I could kill you and save us all some trouble."

Jade tsks. "Murdering me wouldn't solve your problems. Oh, sweetheart. The path is set. Finn didn't mention how empty the mansion was today? The pawns are in place. If you're dead, because you tried to take me out, who's going to rescue Lucas, Rosa, Luciana, Sofia, and Lena?" She shifts her gaze from Kim to me. "The walls have closed in, and you didn't even see them moving."

I want to scream at her, try to call her bluff, but the woman rising from her seat across from me isn't the person who walked in here after a day of shopping. She's cool and calculated. Whatever version of her this is, it's real. All pretenses are gone.

Her bodyguards circle her, creating a protective barrier for her to make her exit. Their guns are still raised, and the few other customers in the restaurant cower under the tables. The restaurant staff is absent. Has someone already called the police? If Jade's threat is real, we have to get everyone moved no matter what we have to do to accomplish it. My body runs hot and cold, and I dig into my purse for my phone.

Twenty missed calls from Finn.

Shit.

Just before she gets to the door, she turns back, giving me a long look. "Give *our* mother my regards."

My stomach drops into my feet, the dip after cresting a hill at high speed. "Our mother?" I whisper in disbelief. *Our mother?* The bells above the door jingle with her exit, and my mind is still scrambling until her words stick.

Oh, my God. *Pearl.* She's my half-sister from my mother's first marriage, the child my mother abandoned to marry my father. My mother warned me about her months ago. A woman who wanted my mother to understand the fear she grew up with because of an abusive father. Finn and Jay searched everywhere and found nothing on Pearl. Not a single blip to indicate she was a real danger, that her threat to my mother wasn't bitter bravado.

Of course, if she's been using aliases for years, they never stood a chance.

Kim grabs my hand and tugs me away from the table. "Back exit is this way." The distant sound of sirens pierces my consciousness. The last thing we need is to get hauled in by the police.

Jay and Kim led me out of the restaurant and into a rear alley. We don't have a car or any means of transportation. Finn and Lorcan are still at the mansion, and Jade has revealed herself. My head is spinning, and my knees are weak.

"We can't worry about Lorcan or Finn until we've secured a place for our family to go. They need to leave the island now." Jay's phone is out, and he's frantically going through his contact list. "Who can we call?"

"You call Demid," I say. "Tell him things have changed. We'll do anything he wants." My voice catches. "Anything. I'll call my father and make him draw up the contract. I'm not having—" My throat closes up, and I have to swallow a sob. "I'm not having my son murdered over money." The thought almost drops me to the ground.

I punch in my father's number with shaking fingers. The phone rings and rings and rings, but he doesn't answer. I glance at Jay, and he's grimacing. "What is it?"

"Demid's dead." His voice is dull. "I just—I just got his man on the phone. Car bomb this afternoon. The PLA must have realized we were trying to move our families."

My breath catches, and Kim's arm snakes around my waist when my knees give out. I clutch onto her, shock hitting me square in the chest. "Dead?"

"Finn and Lorcan are on their way here." Kim keeps a tight hold on me. "I talked to Lorcan, and they're in the car. That must be why Jade decided to tip her hand. Finn found her passport in the office when they combed it. Pearl Jade is her name. Pierre-Jacques must have woken up and realized Finn and Lorcan were missing or the office had been searched—something."

"My son," I whisper. "She's going after my son."

"And my family." Jay runs a hand down his face.

Sirens wailed in the distance. "We need to get out of the alley and away from the restaurant. Maintain a normal pace." Kim points in the opposite direction to what I would have chosen. "This way. We'll find a pub or somewhere to duck into. Keep calm."

My hands shake while we walk onto a side street, away from the downtown core. Our steady pace makes me want to jump or run or scream. Energy courses through me with no outlet. Kim leads us through the narrow streets, the closed shops, as though she knows where she's going, and I'm grateful for her confidence.

With his family at risk, Jay isn't in any position to hold me together. My heart is in my throat. I've wanted a baby since I lost my first with Finn, and to have Lucas now, and to realize he could be snatched from me at any moment is terrifying.

"If Demid's organization is in chaos, who is most likely to step in?" Kim asks.

I take a deep, shaky breath and force my brain to think. "Before she was murdered, I would have said his daughter. Now, I'm not sure." There are black dots on the edges of my vision, and I'm fighting to stay upright. *My baby.*

"Try your father again. He's better than nothing if he can arrange for them to go somewhere or at least get a lot of additional security."

"They can't stay on the island," I whisper. "She's already a step ahead of us. She'll realize how to get to them." Was she responsible for the bomb in my hotel? The one who almost killed me and Jay?

"I understand it's hard," Kim says. "She's counting on fear to drive us. We have to stay rational and logical. We don't have a timeline, but since she's shown us her hand, we have to move now. Do you still have your plane in Cape Verde?"

"Yes," I say. "Why?" Her decisive tone is steadying me, and she drops her hand from my arm.

"Let's get your family on it. Get them headed here, but somewhere in the south of Ireland. If a better option comes up while they're in flight, we'll reroute them. But at least if they're in Ireland, we can conserve resources and minimize worry."

"I'll call Sofia," Jay says with tears in his eyes.

"Have your security detail sweep the car and the plane for explosives before anyone sets foot in either."

"Do you think…" I say. "Do you think she knows who you and Lorcan are?"

Kim shoves her hands deep into the pockets of her jacket. "She wasn't surprised I had no loyalty to her. I held a gun on her, and she didn't flinch, didn't pull rank. Technically, as far as she knows, she employs me." We walk for another moment before Kim says, "If she does realize we're agents, and she doesn't care, she doesn't think we can stop her."

Chapter Twenty-Nine

Finn

I'm driving Lorcan's compact car like it's a Formula One masterpiece. The engine is at full whine while we buzz along the highway to Belfast. We hustled out of the mansion after grabbing most of our stuff without being seen. Carys would have been pissed if I left her clothes behind, and since we weren't being shot at, I stuffed shit in a suitcase. Couldn't get everything.

Lorcan's talked to Kim, and Jade dropped the truth on Carys at the end of dinner, along with a hell of a threat, so our quiet escape didn't mean much. The urge to speak to her is thrumming through my veins, but if her voice cracks, I'll turn the car around and go back to the mansion to hold everyone there hostage until Jade returns.

If her danger is real, confronting her right now won't keep Lucas and the rest of them on Cape Verde safe. My usual slash-and-burn strategy won't work. What I wouldn't give to unleash the full force of Finn off his leash on Jade and Pierre-Jacques. No one has ever stood toe to toe with me and won. They won't be the first.

I can only hear Lorcan's side of the conversation in the vehicle, but his tone tells me I won't like what's happening. He's muttered *Jesus* too many times for me to believe there's anything good to report. "Right, yeah. I'll ring you back."

"What is it?" My voice is tight with tension.

"Demid Kunznetsof was killed in a car bomb earlier today."

"Holy shit," I mutter and bang my fist against the steering wheel. "How are they a step ahead of us?"

"I reckon they're more than one, brother. We're playing catch-up on all sides." He stares out the passenger window. "Volkovs and Kunznetsofs were in bed together?"

"Enough." I wonder if his mind is heading where mine is.

"Who can you call to find out where Semyon and Hagen are?" Lorcan peers at me in the darkness. The streetlights flash across his serious face at regular intervals.

"I'm not asking the Volkovs for help."

"What choice do we have? The CIA aren't going to offer protection. I asked. Not part of your deal—or mine." He grimaces.

"Well, screw them. Maybe I won't fulfill my part of the deal." Bullshit tough talk. I will because I don't want Carys and Lucas to be hunted with me for the rest of my life.

The thought of slipping away, back to Cape Verde, *has* occurred to me. Take my woman and run. What would the consequences for my brother be if I did that? Would he end up suffering the CIA's wrath for not keeping me under control? The only time I've ever thrown him to the wolves was in the warehouse when he picked Kim over me. Never occurred to me then how hard I'd find a choice between him and Carys. His position was impossible, and I don't even begrudge him anymore for the non-life-threatening bullets he pumped into me.

"Here's the thing," he says. "Her sister's revenge on her mother, on whoever else she thinks has slighted her, will play out. You're not going to leave her threats unanswered, especially since she's making them against Carys and Lucas. Let's not pretend walking away is even an option."

I let out a frustrated grunt. "I can't go to Hagen. He tried to fuck me over in prison."

"Then approach Semyon."

"The old man is far more cunning than his son. If I ask him, he'll demand something I don't want to give in return."

"If you don't make the call, and she finds out later you could have saved her son and didn't..."

He doesn't need to tell me the lengths I'll go to for her. I've been living them from the minute she dragged my ass out of the warehouse.

She's forgiven me a lot, understands me better than anyone, and while she might not like what I have to sacrifice to keep Lucas safe, she'll never forgive me for letting him die. "Grab my phone. Call Sean in Boston. Our organization has been eaten up by the Volkovs. He'll know where to find Semyon."

"I can't talk to him." His tone is heavy with meaning. "He'll recognize my voice, and as far as the world knows, I'm dead."

I squeeze the steering wheel and then rub my face. "Right. Put him on speakerphone or Bluetooth or whatever."

He dials Sean's number on my phone from memory, and then we wait.

"Sean Hastings." His familiar pitch stretches across the car, yanking me back to another time and place. So long ago, and yet not. Months that've felt like years.

"It's Finn. I need to know where Semyon is right now."

"Finn? What the hell, man? You broke out of prison." Sean chuckles. "When I saw it on the news, I wasn't even surprised."

"No one can keep me down," I say. "Where's Semyon?"

"Why?" Sean shifts from amused to wary. "You gonna get me in trouble?"

This time I laugh. "Only if you tell him you told me. He's not gonna hear it from me."

There's a long pause. "You calling because Demid Kunznetsof is dead?"

"Does it matter?" I grit out, already tired of this conversation. The days when I could bark out an order and get a response on the spot with the word 'sir' tagged on are over. Should have enjoyed them more.

"I don't know if I should tell you, man. Things have been weird between you and Hagen for a while." He takes a deep breath. "Semyon's got like ten guys with him. You won't get past his guards."

"Just tell me where he is," I pitch my voice low. "I'm out now." I let the implication fill the phone line for a beat. "You wanna be counted as a friend or an enemy?"

"He's in Belfast at a hotel. A stopover on the way to Russia. He's going there to secure Demid's assets." The words tumble out of Sean without hesitation. "I'm the middle guy. I'm not worth your time."

Which is why he couldn't hold on to the organization once Lorcan and I were gone. Guys at the top have to do whatever it takes to stay there. Someone calls with a threat? *Come at me, fucker.* 'Course, that only applies when you're at the top. When you're scrambling for purchase like me, you have to spend your street cred wisely. Sean is a good investment. Going after Semyon is not. Wish I had a better option.

Sean's given me enough information to track the Volkov patriarch. I punch the hang-up button with my finger without bothering to say anything else.

"Think he'll call Semyon?" Lorcan asks with his eyebrows raised.

"The old Sean? The guy loyal to me? Not a chance. But he's not my man anymore." I sigh. "At least we got a bit of luck. Semyon is close."

"A narrow window." He opens a search engine on his phone. "We've got to find his hotel and get to him before he catches his next plane."

When we arrive at the bar where Carys, Jay, and Kim are waiting for us, Lorcan and I have carved out a plan. A desperate, risky ploy, but we don't have the time or resources for something more ironclad. If Sean called Semyon, he might already know we're coming. The request we're making has to be done in person, or he'll never listen to a word we have to say. Semyon will be our captive audience.

When I enter the pub, I scan every table and booth for Carys's blond head. Kim waves to Lorcan near the back, and the two of us walk in tandem to them. Jay glances up from his phone, and there's a haunted look in his eyes. I expect Carys to have the same expression, but when our gazes meet, she's full of determination.

"I'm not giving up. Or rolling over. There has to be a way," she says.

"There is," I admit. She throws herself into my arms, and I hold her close, breathing her in. She might not appreciate whatever Semyon asks of me in exchange for his protection, but I'll give him anything—anything—to keep her safe.

Lorcan slips into Carys's abandoned spot and starts relaying the plan to Kim and Jay in hushed tones. We have to move fast.

"Everyone is already on my private plane, headed in this direction." Carys glances over her shoulder at Kim. "Her idea, and I didn't have a better solution."

"It's good." I smooth her hair. "It's a start."

"Are you going to tell me?" She peers up at me.

"In the car," I say. "We gotta go."

Lorcan kisses Kim's temple before sliding out of the booth with Jay. They follow us to the vehicle we parked illegally right outside the pub.

We're no sooner buckled up with Carys wedged between Jay and Kim in the rear when Carys says, "I'm not going to like it, am I?"

"No." I steer toward the hotel. Lorcan called the high-end establishments close to the airport asking for Semyon Volkov's room. When a receptionist said, 'please hold while I connect you' Lorcan hung up.

"Who does this plan involve?" she asks.

"Semyon," Lorcan says, ripping off the proverbial Band-Aid. "We're asking Semyon for help."

Carys's gaze meets mine in the mirror, and her amber eyes are clouded with worry. Neither of us will say it, but we understand cornering Semyon is a Hail Mary.

Until the kids are safe, going after Jade like I want to isn't possible.

The hotel is more American in style than European. The lobby and bar areas are spacious and well lit. None of the elevators groan when a car approaches, which is good because Carys and I are stationed there, making out. Our task is to appear so into each other we can't keep our hands—and lips—to ourselves. Not hard. Well, something is hard, but it's not our roles in this deception. Christ, I can't wait until I can get her alone again.

Behind us at the front desk, Kim is introducing herself to the receptionist. A gift for Semyon Volkov. If there's one thing Semyon can't resist, it's a prostitute. So, we're sending him one as a 'welcome' gift from a rival organization in Russia. It's plausible, but we're counting on him to enjoy the ego stroke too much to confirm the present before welcoming Kim into his room.

Since he's met Kim before, Carys worked makeup magic to play up her more exotic features, and she borrowed a dress from Carys's suitcase—too small, too bright, and too tight, but just right for the mission. With any luck, he'll be focused on assets other than Kim's face.

When she pads over to the bank of elevators, she stumbles and giggles, pretending to be high or drunk. Semyon's guards who are accompanying her steady her to keep her from toppling over. Before the doors to the elevator close, I tug Carys into the far corner. Let's see how many ways I can make her moan. The highlight of my night.

"Get a room," one of the security guards mutters to us and averts his gaze.

"Working on it," I growl in response and slide my hand up Carys's skirt.

Never a woman to worry about an audience, she gasps and cries, "Oh, yes. Right here. Oh, God. Yes. Yes."

Her acting is fantastic since I'm nowhere close to pushing her button. I'm going to have to get a replay of this later—assuming we survive. The elevator dings, and Kim and the guards pile out. Carys and I slip out behind them, and I practically carry her down the hall, pretending to fumble for a keycard I don't have.

At the door to Semyon's room, there are two more men. We counted on more security outside the room. If he's got guys in there with him, we might be in trouble. These four, we can handle.

Kim staggers, crying out when she almost falls. Two of the guards are trying to heave her up, and the other two are watching. Lorcan and Jay are on them before they have a chance to react. All four are felled by the same drug we used on Pierre-Jacques earlier.

We hustle along the hall to the group. Kim digs a keycard out of the pocket of the guard closest to her and passes it to me. She's no fan of the Volkovs either.

To avoid being spotted, Kim and Lorcan disappear down the staircase to the waiting car, which leaves me, Jay, and Carys. I squeeze Carys's hand before I swipe the keycard and release her to take out my gun.

"Ah, is she here?" Semyon calls from within the spacious, neutrally decorated room. "What a nice—" The words die on his lips when he sees me, Carys, and Jay with guns pointed at him.

No guards inside his room. That's a win for us. I would've done the same, but it's careless and overconfident. He strides toward his phone, but it's closer to us. I lunge for it, getting it before he can signal for help. If he did bring ten guys, there's six other men somewhere in the hotel.

"I could yell." He reads my mind. "I've got other security on this floor."

"So have I." I bluff. "You don't think I came alone, do you? Want a bloodbath or a conversation? Your blood will be the first spilled." I smirk.

He eyes me, his reptilian gaze enough to send other people to their knees. There's no mercy in him, which is a thing we used to have in common. Right now, I'm wishing we still did. It's harder to negotiate when I actually give a shit about the outcome.

"When I heard you were out, I wondered if you'd come." He eases into the desk chair. "Didn't expect your visit quite this soon. I suppose I should have expected it somewhere other than America. Too risky for you there." He picks up the pen on the desk and rotates it over his fingers.

"You thought I'd come for you?" My gaze narrows. For the shit Hagen tried to pull in jail? That's between me and Hagen, and someday we'll talk about how stupid he was for trying to get me, of all people, to follow his orders.

Why would I go after him for his son's maneuver?

"What do you want?" Semyon raises his eyebrows.

I shake off my train of thought and zone in on what's important. "I need protection for people."

He taps his lip with his index finger and stares at Carys. "Your son?"

"And my family," Jay adds.

He narrows his gaze. "I'll negotiate with her—alone."

"That won't work." While I don't think he's dumb enough to try and hurt her, I'm not letting her float in water filled with chum. Semyon is a shark.

"Then I suppose my answer is *no* to your request for protection. You can leave."

"It's fine." Her hand rests on my forearm.

"Jay stays." I stare down the old man who reminds me too much of my father. "I'm not leaving her in here alone with you."

An answering smirk touches his lips. "Something I always liked about you Finny, boy. When your back's against the wall, you still come out swinging. Fine. He can stay."

The keycard from the door is in my rear pocket. If she screams or even raises her voice, I'm storming in the door, and a bullet will be lodged in Semyon's brain.

Carys and Jay are framed in the open door as it eases to a close behind me. What will Semyon ask in exchange, and will it be something we'll both be able to live with?

Chapter Thirty

Carys

The door clicks closed, and Semyon studies me for a beat. I'm surprised Finn folded to his request. Our backs must be pinned against the wall. Not that I doubted our weak position, but I hoped there might be another fraction of light somewhere else if this meeting didn't work. Apparently not. Hail Mary, here we come.

"How is your arm healing?" Semyon indicates my cast.

"Well enough." I hold up my broken wrist. "A few more weeks, and I can take it off."

"An unfortunate set of circumstances," he says. "A bomb and a gas leak coming together at exactly the wrong moment."

Jay shifts closer to me, but Semyon's words aren't a threat. Not yet at least. "The police don't think the two are related. Hard to believe."

"Coincidences in this business are rare." He rises and crosses to the minibar. "Would you like a drink?"

"Whiskey." I recognize my role in this conversation.

We both know what I want. He's trying to decide what he needs in return. Hope threatens to rise in me, but I tamp it down. Semyon could ask me for anything, maybe even something like Demid did, that I can't give. The possibilities are endless when a man already has so much influence. What can we offer when we have so little right now?

He pours the whiskey and passes it to me, but he doesn't give Jay something. A power play, but neither of us will complain. Jay is, after all, my employee, even if I treat him more like family.

"I'll take your family under my wing while you sort out your issues with the PLA in exchange for your silence and your unwavering protection in return." Semyon's gaze is glued to me.

I frown and draw my glass to my lips, considering his words. Jay relaxes beside me. I'm not so sure we're out of the woods with this request. Silence and unwavering protection can be big asks. "Who would I protect you from?"

"The one who is not in this room." Semyon releases a dark chuckle. "The loose cannon you seem to enjoy watching go off."

I eye him for a beat. "Do I get to understand why or how I'm meant to protect you?" I throw out my hand. "I'd be more effective if I understood what he could learn that would make him seek revenge."

"In prison, Hagen was applying pressure on Finn to kill a guy who owed us money and tried to turn evidence against us. The snitch didn't have shit on us, so too bad for him. But I needed a message sent—a *strong* reminder not to mess with me. The strongest man in the minimum-security prison delivering my justice, a man who never takes orders from anyone else? Having him would have given me unprecedented power inside."

"You wanted Finn to do your dirty work."

"Initially a death sentence for my former employee, and eventually much more. I could have made Finn a powerful player inside. But he didn't want to learn my games."

"As you said, he doesn't take orders from anyone."

"We tried to apply a little pressure—let him realize the risk in turning us down. Obviously, with so many life sentences, and Finn pleading guilty to them, I never expected him to get out."

"You planted the bomb in the hotel?" Jay tenses beside me, putting the pieces together much faster than me.

"So, you aren't just the muscle," Semyon says. "You've got a brain. Since your family is also at risk here, I expect the same deal from you I am making with Carys. Unwavering protection and silence. If he ever learns the truth you talk him down or pin him, but he does not come at me or my sons. Ever." He points his finger and his drink at the two of us. "My son was supposed to find the right person to do the job on Cape Verde. He failed, and you were injured more than we intended. A scare. A warning. A reminder to Finn he was on the inside, and we were on the outside."

"Except," I swirl the alcohol in my glass, "now he's on the outside too."

"While I have your family, it should be easy for you to keep him under control."

A brief spike of anger surges through me, and I wish Finn could be allowed to make this right. Tear them apart. Semyon and Hagen shouldn't have tried to take advantage of Finn's weakened position in prison. They should never have positioned a bomb that might have made my son an orphan.

"The bomb you set." I search his face for the truth. "The serial number on it was ours, from the warehouse theft in Russia."

"Are you asking if I stole from you?" He lifts his eyebrows.

Since he went there instead of to the connection to the PLA, I should be comforted. I don't want to rescue my family from the jaws of one shark only to thrust them into the mouth of another beast. "No, I'm asking if you're working with the PLA."

He chuckles. "I don't work well with others." He winks. "Hagen hired a local in Cape Verde who secured the bomb. My guess? The PLA sold off your items on the black market. Not a bad way to raise some capital."

I clear my throat and force my frustration aside. "He won't come after you." Do I have that much control over Finn's actions? If he was in this room, he might have put a bullet between Semyon's eyes already. "But," I say, "I need to tell him what happened. If I leave the culprit of the bomb a secret, he may discover the truth when I'm not around to stop him from doing something stupid." Even if his wrath is justified.

"I'm going to second Carys on this one. She can wait to tell him until our families are wherever you're going to stash them, so you feel protected. But she needs to inform him before he finds out on his own."

Semyon tips back his drink. "He threatened to saw off the limbs of anyone responsible for the Cape Verde bomb. While I'd like to believe he can't get to me, today proves otherwise, doesn't it?" He gives us both a long look. "You're confident you can control him?"

"Yes," Jay and I say at the same time. I'm tempted to smile. There's no way either of us are certain. We're desperate.

"This 'kill them all' strategy he employs is not one I'm keen to see in action. My family will retaliate, and it *will* be bloody."

"I understand." I slide my finished glass onto the table. "Do we have a deal?" I hold out my hand, and Semyon embraces it.

"Send them to Boston." He sets his drink on the nightstand. "My best compound is my home in Boston."

Jay is already taking out his phone to get in touch with the pilot. "I'll message Dominic the details," he says.

"I'll have men collect them from the airport." A hint of a smile touches Semyon's lips. "Good luck with the PLA."

I don't acknowledge his sinister well wishes, and we back out of the room with the deal done.

Outside the door, Finn has propped the four security guys up against the wall. He lifts his eyebrows in question, but I shake my head. Shift change for the guards will be happening any minute, so we need to get out of here. We hustle down the back stairs, and when we get to the bottom, Finn grabs my wrist. "What'd he ask for?"

"I'll tell you as soon as we're sure our family is safe." While we're still within striking distance, I can't be certain his temper won't get the best of him. "You're not going to like it," I admit. "But it could have been much worse."

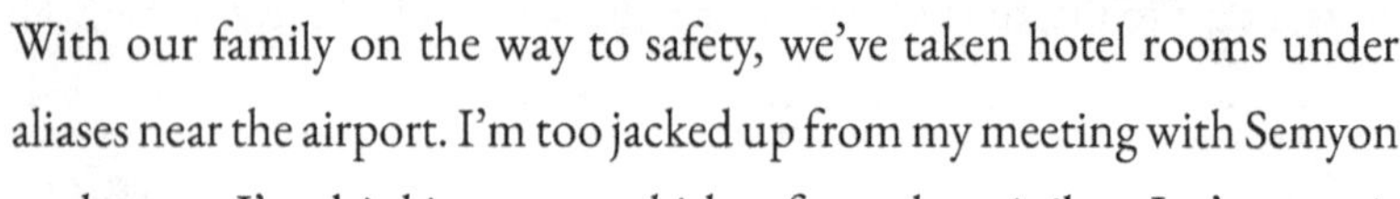

With our family on the way to safety, we've taken hotel rooms under aliases near the airport. I'm too jacked up from my meeting with Semyon to sleep, so I'm drinking more whiskey from the minibar. Jay's room is on one side of us, and on the other is Lorcan and Kim.

Their handler is pissed we abandoned the PLA compound when we seemed to be making progress. Kim and Lorcan assured them we got enough information to track and foil the PLA's plans. I don't know what Finn and Lorcan discovered, other than Pearl's identity, but there's been no concrete talk of disrupting the PLA's plots.

I'm in the en suite bathroom washing my face when Finn leans against the entrance clad only in his boxer briefs, arms crossed, and muscles bulging. In the mirror, I drink in the sight of him. We need to figure out and foil the PLA as our top priority now that we've secured protection for our family, but I can't help the pang of sadness when I realize Finn will be going back to jail when this is over. We'll have another three years of separation to battle through before we get to be together for the rest of our lives.

Given how much has been going on since I arrived in Ireland, we've had little quality time together when we didn't have to worry about someone listening in or danger dropping into our laps. Are we safe now? Hardly. But it's a relief not to have to watch our words. For conversations to be real and genuine rather than coded and, sometimes, riddled with false starts.

"What's that look for?" he asks.

"When I decided to break you out of jail, I did not see it going this way."

He glances at his feet and then meets my gaze in the mirror. "We took your sister's threat to your mother seriously months ago, but we turned up nothing. Too many aliases, I guess."

"She sent the confetti bomb—sent all the bomb threats." I pat myself dry and face him. "They're the ones who raided the house in Russia too." His jaw tightens a fraction. "Did you kill Eric?"

Finn searches my face for a beat, but whether he says the word or not, the truth is in his eyes. He's debating whether telling me will make the future harder or easier. Either way I know, so he might as well say it.

"Yes." He holds my gaze. "There was an opportunity, and I took it."

My heart thumps at his bluntness, at the danger in his words. He killed my ex-fiancé, the biological father of our son, and I'm not even fazed—the briefest twinge of anxiety at explaining the circumstances to

Lucas, but that's it. There must be something wrong with me, but I'm not going to question my sanity. As much as Finn might rage against others, he loves me with the same fiery intensity. Who wouldn't want to be loved like that?

"Was he—was he conscious? Jade mentioned she gave him a message for me."

"They tortured him. You wouldn't have wanted to see him. Did he have a note somewhere on him? Not that I found. Did they tell him something? Maybe. He wasn't in any shape to speak."

"She said if I knew what was coming, if I'd known all this time, I'd be terrified."

He straightens, tension oozing out of him. "She wants you afraid."

"She wants me beyond afraid. Terrorized. Said she watched the video of me trying to diffuse the confetti bomb in my office on repeat. She gets off on the power."

He rubs his face with both hands. "We should've looked harder when your mother told us Pearl was hell-bent on seeking revenge for being left behind."

"Not just for being left behind—for being left behind with a man who abused her."

Finn gives me a long look. "Assuming we can trust that motive."

"What do you mean?"

"She's slippery. Tells people what she thinks they want to hear. Turns and twists herself into whatever version suits the person she's speaking to. Did her father abuse her?" He shrugs. "I got a feeling it was more"—he taps his temple—"than physical."

His phone buzzes on the nightstand, and he leaves the door to check it. I follow him into the bedroom and run my hand along his back. His muscles flex under my fingers, and he turns to offer a quick kiss on my temple. "Lorcan and Kim think we should head south tomorrow."

"South?" I frown.

"One of the bombs the PLA secured was delivered to someone in Cork."

"Their PLA faction there?" Finn and Lorcan just gave them more manpower by taking over the McCaffrey organization in Cork. We were always flies in their web, and we've been luring more flies with us.

"Don't know." Finn sets down his phone. "Lorcan thinks we should go see Thomas in Dublin."

"Lorcan can't see him." We're walking a dangerous line with him by going south. At least up here, few people recognize the Donaghey brothers. Down there? Their misdeeds are legendary. "Even Kim they've met before in Boston."

Is she supposed to be dead too? I try to remember the news stories I read, but I can't recall those details. My primary focus was Finn. Every outlet reported Lorcan's death, but my FBI contact, the one who dragged him out, relayed the truth.

"You gonna tell me what Semyon wanted from you?"

I check the clock on the nightstand. Have they landed yet? I haven't heard from anyone to be sure they're safe. Until then, I can't take any chances. Would he listen to me? To reason? Likely. Not worth derailing everything else we need to accomplish right now. "Not yet," I say. "But I will."

He searches my face, and his gaze is intense. "Is whatever you agreed to do going to cause you any pain or hurt?"

"Not even a little."

He wraps his arms around me, drawing me into him. "Then the truth can wait."

When we get into bed, he gathers me close. My head rests on his chest and my casted hand on his stomach. He sighs into my hair.

"What are you thinking?" At one time, I would have cringed asking. Now it's natural—normal—to ask and to expect him to tell me the truth. There's no pretending between us anymore. We are who we are.

He tightens his hold, and his lips brush my hair. "I lay in that prison for months not letting myself remember what being with you felt like. *This* wasn't something I was ever going to get again."

Whereas I lay in my bed and tried to recall every detail of him. What it felt like to have his arms sliding around my waist, my head pillowed against his chest, and his breath stirring my hair. The easiest way for me to get to sleep was to wrap myself in a blanket of Finn memories and sensations. I never stopped hoping or believing we'd be together once again.

"I'm not a good man, and I'm not a peaceful man, but I'm almost both of those when I'm with you."

I glance up to make eye contact with him, and love swells in me. He's the man I'm meant to be with, and I'll love him until the day I die. "When this is all over, you can be whoever you want to be."

"I'll fight like hell to make sure I come home to you and Lucas in three years. They may think they have the lead, but I've been doing this long enough to realize I can steal their advantage and make it mine. We just have to figure out the right moves."

I mull over his words as sleep threatens to drag me under. When we understand our opponents, the right steps are easy to determine. Pearl Jade and Pierre-Jacques are so cloaked in false identities, how will we ever know enough in time to foil them? Impossible isn't a word we use, so I keep my thoughts to myself. Whether or not we can win, we'll go down fighting. Giving up isn't an option.

243

Chapter Thirty-One

Finn

The buzzing beside my bed wakes me. I squint at the clock on the side table and realize it's 5 a.m. already. The alarm isn't what's woken me up, though, it's Lorcan calling. I extract myself from Carys, who is groggy and curled against me, to answer.

"What's happening?" I ask as soon as I hit the green button.

"We've got company at the hotel. Not sure how many or where, but Kim gave the front desk people extra to let us know of anyone milling around."

"Shit," I mutter. "How do you want to play this?"

"Kim reckons we split up and meet in the car park. It's possible they've traced our piece-of-shit car, so we'll need to nick a vehicle."

Not a problem. Lorcan and I have hot-wired enough vehicles in our youth to stock a car dealership. Little trickier now with this digital crap. At the window, I peek out the curtains to the darkened cityscape. Carys dresses in silence behind me. She must have heard enough of the conversation to understand we must move fast. "Across the street, there's another carpark, not the one we used, so we should meet there. Toward the back, there's an older black SUV. Do you see it?" It's the farthest, oldest car in the lot. Here's hoping there's a full tank of gas.

"Aye," Lorcan agrees. "We're taking the south staircase. You, Carys, and Jay take the north. Jay knows. Car leaves in fifteen minutes whether or not we're all there."

"Yep." I hang up and start yanking on my clothes, slipping my phone into the front pocket of my jeans. When I see Carys zipping up her suitcase, I realize she's not going to be happy we're traveling light. "No suitcase. Stuff *essentials* in your purse. We'll have to use cash to buy on the run as we head south."

She unzips her bag and throws it open, grabbing various items and stuffing them into her oversized purse. She opens my backpack and grabs a few pairs of underwear for me. From the bathroom, she takes our toothbrushes. The reality is nothing we've got in this room is essential, but if it makes her feel more in control to pick a few things, I won't stop her.

For a beat, she stares at the open suitcase. "You rescued my clothes from the mansion only for me to abandon them here. Someone is going to inherit some really nice outfits."

I ignore her mournful tone because if we get out of this alive and free, she can afford to buy those items again. "No heels. You need shoes you can run in."

Carys scoffs. "I can run in heels."

"Fine then," I grit out. "Shoes that don't make noise. Happy?"

She grumbles as she sorts through her suitcase and pulls out a pair that look like slippers, but I'm not going to say anything else. As long as she can run in them with no noise, I'm not complaining. "Passports in your purse?" I ask.

"Yes." She snatches her phone off the nightstand. "Does Jay know?"

"Lorcan told him. We have to move quickly. If we're not at the SUV in fifteen minutes, they'll leave without us."

"We're really going to abandon each other?"

"Whatever the PLA has planned has to be stopped. If they're here looking for us, they think there's a chance we can prevent whatever they're doing. Doesn't seem like good news, but it is. At least some of us need to be alive and free to get the job done." It's easier to hide and maneuver ourselves to safety in smaller numbers. Five of us is conspicuous. Groups of one and two is less so.

With my hand on the door, I take a beat to figure out the best strategy for exiting the hotel. Stealthy or as though we've got nothing to hide? Do the people looking for us know who we are or are they fishing at each hotel near the airport? Have they tracked our car? Do they realize we're here?

I rearrange Noel's gun at the small of my back to ensure I can get it in an instant. Once I'm satisfied, I stare at Carys before giving her a quick kiss. "Stay behind me. Whatever I tell you to do—run, duck, hide—you do it? You got me?"

She meets my gaze and then offers me another quick kiss. "We stick together, but other than that, I'll follow your lead."

I peer into the hallway. Empty. Have Lorcan and Kim already gone? What about Jay? Can't worry about them. With her hand grasped in mine, we slip along the hall to the emergency exit, and I ease down the cement stairs, keeping my tread light, listening for anyone else in the stairwell.

At the bottom of the stairs, there's no window to see who might be on the other side of the door. "Gun?" I glance at her purse, and Carys roots inside until she finds her small handgun. Not the best weapon, but better than nothing. Opening this door and having her in immediate danger makes my stomach clench. But there's no way around it. I kiss her temple, shove her behind me, and crack open the door.

No talking. No footsteps. I peek out, and the street is deserted. Dragging her out behind me, I hustle across with my gun drawn.

"There!" a deep male voice behind us cries.

We're at the first row of cars in the parking lot, and we duck. Heavy footsteps pound the pavement behind us. I weave us through the vehicles, and while we can hear the two guys calling to each other, they don't seem to have a good sense of where we are amongst the parked cars. If I keep heading to the black SUV without losing them, I'll lead them right to us. A *pop-pop* goes off in the night, but I can't tell where the shots are coming from. None of them land near us, and then more gunfire follows. My instinct is to rise and engage, but I can't put Carys at risk. I tighten my grip on my gun and on her hand. I keep moving in and out of parked cars.

They're not chasing us anymore. I have to hope that means they've been taken out and not Lorcan, Kim, or Jay. When we get to the SUV, I dare to look for the others. We've got five minutes until go-time, and Carys and I are the first ones here.

I peer around the edge of the vehicle and several rows away, Lorcan and Kim are huddled behind different cars—one on each side of an aisle. She clutches her arm, and Lorcan's attention is divided between her and the man stalking them.

Where the hell is Jay?

I tug on the handle for the SUV, and by some miracle, the driver's door is unlocked. If we're going to get out of here, we need to kill the other scout or outrun him. "Get in the back seat," I instruct Carys, keeping my voice low. "Don't get up for anything until the vehicle is moving."

More shots are fired while I work on hot-wiring the SUV. When it roars to life, I hop in and roll down the driver's window, gun in hand. "Stay down, Carys," I say when I glimpse movement in the back. "Stay the fuck down."

I wheel the vehicle around and tear toward where Lorcan and Kim are pinned. When the guy following them pokes his head up over a car, I fire. The shot pings off the roof, and the guy ducks again. I screech to a stop in the aisle, and Lorcan and Kim open the doors and dive in, piling on top of Carys. The PLA scout pops up again, and I fire. This time he cries when I nail his shoulder. I'm rusty, but at least it's a direct hit.

I head for the exit, but ahead there are two bodies in the middle of the street. "Stay down," I growl toward the back because if one of those bodies is Jay, Carys isn't going to handle it well. I slow enough to realize one is Jay, and his chest is still rising and falling. He's alive. A blessing and a curse with the other scout on our ass.

I wheel up beside him and shout to Lorcan, "I need help."

He's out of the car and at my side, while Kim climbs into the front seat. Carys gasps at the sight of Jay and the pool of blood around him.

"Is he dead?" she cries.

We haul him into the back seat of the SUV, his head resting on Carys's lap, and Lorcan scoots in behind him, Jay's legs bent over his thighs. I slam my door, and we peel out of the airport toward the highway.

"He's alive," Carys marvels, taking in his unconscious form.

"For now," I mutter. "We need help and fast."

Chapter Thirty-Two

Carys

Jay is bleeding out on my lap. Panic surges, and I try to shove it deep enough for my mind to kick into gear. "The hospital?"

"Last resort," Finn says. "I'm a wanted fugitive as far as the world knows, and I'm not leaving you unguarded anywhere."

Lorcan takes off his shirt, muscles rippling, and passes it to me. "Apply pressure to the wound," he says. "A lot of pressure." He helps me search Jay until we find the entry point that is leaking blood.

I ball up Lorcan's shirt and press it against Jay. He groans with his lashes fluttering. *He can't die. He can't die.* My pulse pounds with the words.

Lorcan leans forward in his seat to check on Kim. "Are you all right?"

"A graze." She glances at him over her shoulder. "A little late getting off the shot."

"You killed the other one?" I ask.

"Yes," she grits out. "Got him before he could deliver the kill shot. There were four of them. Another one shot at us, nicking me, and one pursued us. I'm not sure where the other went."

I shudder at the thought of a PLA man standing over Jay, ready to finish him. Thank God, Kim and Lorcan arrived in time.

"Fucking cowards." Finn merges onto the highway.

Jay's breathing is labored even though he's still unconscious. "We have to do something. I can't—I can't sit here and watch him die," I cry.

Finn doesn't meet my gaze in the rearview mirror. Instead, he seeks Lorcan. "How bad is it?"

He eyes Jay sprawled out across us. "Bad enough. At the very least, he needs stitches. Maybe blood. Hard to say."

"He won't wake up." How can he only need stitches?

"They knocked him out, I reckon. Wound isn't in a place for too much worry. Blood loss is concerning." Lorcan goes over Jay's body, checking for any other injuries.

"If all he needs is stitches," Kim says from the front, "Carys, doesn't your father have a doctor friend outside Belfast?"

"Yes." The word escapes on an exhale.

How have I forgotten about John? I shift around to dig my phone out of my purse. Early, too early, to be calling an old family friend for a favor, but if we can't go to a hospital, John is the best bet. He used to have a clinic attached to his house. Does he still? I search my contacts for his number. We met with him a few times when my father wanted to expand Van de Berg Ammunitions with an office outside Belfast.

His voice is groggy when he answers. "Carys?"

"John, I'm so sorry for waking you at this early hour. We have a medical emergency, and the situation is too sensitive for a hospital. We're in Belfast. Can we come to you?"

There's a brief pause, and there's rustling in the background. "Of course. Do you need my address?"

"Yes. Can you text it to me?"

"No problem. I'll meet you in the clinic. Can you give me an idea of what I'm dealing with?"

"Gunshot wound. Possibly too much blood loss. We're not sure."

"I'll be ready," he says without hesitation.

We end the call and within a few seconds, an address pings to my phone. I hit the navigate button and offer my phone to Kim in the front to help Finn navigate.

"Take the next exit," she tells Finn.

Other than Kim reading out directions, we pass the few minutes in silence. Lorcan's shirt is darkening with blood, and I'm praying John has enough of everything we'll need at the clinic. Otherwise, I'll regret the choice to avoid a hospital for the rest of my life.

Finn wheels us along a long gravel drive with trees and bushes encroaching on the vehicle. Then the path opens, and we're at a modern building, with an older farmhouse in the distance to the left. The clinic looks newer. John must still run it. Thank God.

Finn and Lorcan maneuver Jay out of the back seat, and he moans at the swaying motion. John, a gray-haired, slim man in his sixties, meets us at the door and directs us to a back room. Finn and Lorcan lay Jay on the table, and John glances at us.

"Which of you would be best to assist?"

"Lorcan," Finn says.

"Can I—can I come in as long as I'm not in the way?" Whether or not this goes well, I need to be there. Jay would never leave me alone to fend for myself.

"As long as you can stay out of the way," John agrees.

As soon as I'm through the door, Lorcan and John are working in tandem as though Lorcan's dressed a thousand bullet wounds. Maybe he has. Finn sounded certain he was the best bet for help, and in the car, he looked to his brother as the authority on Jay's injury.

"Where am I?" Jay mumbles, and his lids flutter.

"A clinic," I say. "You were shot. Stay still."

"Shot?" he grumbles, trying to sit up.

John sticks a needle in Jay's arm, and he slips back into unconsciousness. At least he woke up for a moment. I hope that means he'll be fine once the bullet wound is taken care of.

Once they've dug out the bullet and dressed the wound, John runs a few other tests. He hems and haws, and then says, "The blood loss is worrying, but we're not in the danger zone. I don't have any of his blood type here. We'd have to go to the hospital for that."

"If he doesn't get it," Lorcan says, "he'll be weak and need a lot of rest, right? Special diet?"

A hint of a smile touches John's lips. "You've been down this road before?"

"A few times," he admits.

"Yes. With the amount of blood he's lost, he'll be weaker than normal for weeks. A modified diet can help get his hemoglobin levels up faster. Vitamin C is important."

Jay stirs on the bed.

"I gave him something for the pain, so he'll be unconscious a bit longer. He does have a head wound. A concussion is an almost certainty."

"Should we take him to the hospital?" I grip Jay's hand.

"I'll send you with a care package to prevent infection and keep him comfortable—including a sheet about concussions."

"Do you have any towels we can use to clean the SUV? Then I'll get Finn, and we'll load Jay back into the vehicle." Lorcan takes the cloth and spray from John's outstretched hand and ducks out of the examination room door.

"Spoken to your father lately?" John leans against a small desk housing a desktop computer.

A bitter laugh escapes me. "He doesn't seem to be taking my calls. Have you spoken to him?"

"He's busy with the European expansion project." He waves me off. "You understand what he's like—very singular when he's deep in the business trenches."

So singular he's avoided my calls—my desperate, desperate pleas—when I worried my son might die. "Yes, I do know him."

"Well, the grand opening of the building is supposed to be within the next week or so. After that, I'm sure he'll be back to normal. He was here for a visit the other week."

I want to tell him my father's selfish, self-interested behavior *is* normal, but after John helped us on short notice as a favor because of my father, voicing my anger might be petty. "I appreciate you opening your doors for us this morning."

"Of course. Of course. Your father and I have known each other a long time."

"You said he was here the other week?" Typical for him to be in the same country as me and for me not to know about it. If anything highlights how far apart we've grown, this conversation with John is driving home the alienation.

"A minivacation from the expansion and the problems with your mother." He lets out a deep sigh. "I'm sure you're aware. I don't need to tell you." He gives me a sympathetic smile.

Since my parents came to see me together a few weeks ago, I wondered whether they put their differences aside. In some ways, I'm glad they haven't. Whatever their marriage was built on to start has eroded into unhappiness. My mother might have found a measure of physical safety with my father, but she didn't find emotional support or security.

Finn and Lorcan come into the examination room and hoist Jay into their arms. Finn's gaze connects with mine. "He'll be okay," he says.

Tears spring to my eyes even though he's right. I trail my hand down Finn's back as they leave the room with Jay in their arms.

"Does your friend have another shirt? Being without one might make you conspicuous wherever you're headed next," John asks.

"We can buy one." They dove into the SUV without any bags, didn't they? All of us will need new clothes after the blood Jay shed. I'm afraid to look at my shirt and pants.

"Nonsense." John opens a cupboard and riffles through things, taking out a black T-shirt emblazoned with charity information. "The clinic did a run in the village a few years ago and printed too many shirts."

"Thank you." I hold it up to check the size. Looks about right.

"When you see your father, tell him I said hello."

"Sure." I won't. "Do you want—how can I pay you?"

"No need. You're Charles's daughter. He'd help one of my children if they ever found themselves in trouble."

Once again, the urge to correct him rises to my tongue, but I hold the words back. "We're building a hotel and casino in Cape Verde. If you ever want to come visit, let me know. Your stay will be on us."

He puts a hand on my shoulder and smiles. "Charles raised you well."

When I leave the office, Finn, Kim, Lorcan, and a semiconscious Jay are already in the car with Lorcan driving this time. Finn is in the rear with Jay, and my heart squeezes that he took the back to help monitor Jay's condition or maybe to rib Jay about getting shot. In any event, when I scoot in, Finn grabs my hand and gives it a quick squeeze.

"You all right?" He peers at me with his familiar intensity.

"If Jay's going to be fine, I'm fine too." I scan Jay's pained expression and dig around in the care package John gave us while Lorcan steers us along the long path again. I offer Jay pain pills, and he takes them gratefully.

Soon, he's asleep again. I stare out at the lightening sky, thinking about how so many people know my father in so many ways, none of them quite like me.

CHAPTER THIRTY-THREE

Finn

Jay's sleep is fitful beside me. I bet he's never been shot before. Knocks the shit out of anyone the first time. The blood loss doesn't help.

"It's too early to roll up to Thomas's house," I say to Lorcan when we enter the city limits two hours after we left Belfast.

"Jay needs a place to sleep." He catches my attention in the rearview mirror. "We've also got to figure out a strategy for approaching him for help. Jay's no good to us for the rest of this assignment."

Carys sucks in a sharp breath. "We're not *abandoning* him."

"We can try to send him to the Volkovs in Boston, or we can see if Thomas will protect him," I say while she stares at Jay with guilt written on her face.

"Could he get on a plane like this?" she asks.

"Not a commercial flight," Kim says.

Carys eases her fingers across her forehead and meets my gaze. "What do you think?"

"As long as we're sure we can trust Thomas when we talk to him, I vote we leave him there until he's better or we've knocked the PLA out."

She doesn't say anything else but goes back to looking out the window. I wish we were alone, so she'd let me into that head of hers. She's keeping too many thoughts rattling around, and I hate not knowing what they are. The expression on her face makes me think they can't be good.

Lorcan steers us toward the Byrne family estate despite the early-morning hour.

"What are we doing about the two of you?" Thomas knows my brother very well, and he met Kim during a business dinner when she worked for us.

They exchange an uneasy glance in the front seats. "Until we figure out what the PLA has planned, last night proved we need protection. They aren't going to let us do whatever we want while they execute their plan." He meets my gaze in the mirror. "What do you reckon Thomas will think about me not being dead?"

"He'll know we've cooked up some sort of scheme." Would he assume the FBI or CIA were involved? Why would the government declare Lorcan dead otherwise? "Not sure he'll believe there wasn't high-level intervention."

Kim's thumb brushes Lorcan's cheek, tenderness in her gaze. "The CIA doesn't want us to reveal ourselves. Holing up in a hotel for however long isn't a great option either." He covers her hand.

I stare out the window as we creep closer to the Byrne residence. Like many of the other mafia families, they once had a large estate far from the city borders with various smaller properties in the downtown core to move people or products. Now, their country property is nestled on the edge of the city, in danger of being consumed by urban sprawl.

Thomas commented on the developments when he came to Boston to visit and saw how our privacy was eaten by the expanding city limits. The Donagheys have a long history with the Byrne family, and if Lorcan reveals himself, we'll be counting on those connections not to sink us.

"I'll go in first. Everyone else wait in the vehicle. I'll find out about the PLA plan, and then I'll ask for protection while we go after them. I know we've got the CIA at our disposal once we've uncovered the details of the scheme, but until then, we might be wise to have more manpower," I say.

"You reckon Thomas will give us that?"

"Depends on why he turned down whatever they wanted from him in the first place."

"You think I'll be all right to reveal myself?"

I stare at him in the mirror, and he's not going to like my answer. "Only one way to find out."

Kim slides her hand along Lorcan's arm to grip his fingers.

She should be worried. I haven't got a clue what I'm walking into when I enter Thomas's estate, but I realize we need his help, and I'll do whatever I can to secure it.

"I want to come with you," Carys says when Lorcan drives into a parking lot about a half mile from the entrance to the Byrne complex.

My first instinct is to tell her no. She's covered in Jay's blood, and I don't know how Thomas is going to react to my request. Technically, I still owe him a favor from a few months ago. There's more of a tit-for-tat aspect to our relationship rather than my take-take-taking. I've got nothing to offer yet. Maybe a nice vacation in Cape Verde in the future, but there's no immediate gain for his help.

At my hesitation, she sets her jaw. "I'll rephrase that for you. I'm coming."

With a sigh, I climb out of the back seat and make sure Jay isn't going to topple over. Carys has kept him comfortable with various painkillers during the drive. He's barely been conscious long enough to hear how and why he was shot. I have a feeling he'll need the story repeated once the drugs wear off.

She slips out the other side behind me and links her hand with mine while we start down the street lined with residential row houses and tiny gardens out front.

"You've been quiet since Jay was hurt."

"Yeah." She clings to my arm. "I was terrified he was going to die. And then… and then, talking to John made me realize how far apart my father and I have drifted. I don't know anything about his life anymore. That should make me sad, shouldn't it? But—I don't know—I don't think it does."

I kiss her temple and remain silent. Her father is a shit, but her relationship with him has never been that simple.

"I'm forty-six. Shouldn't I be over this?"

I chuckle. "Over a shitty parent? Nah. That's not a thing. We carry that dysfunction with us. I'm damn sure going to try my best to be better to Lucas than my father was."

While we walk, she rises on her toes and kisses my cheek. "You're already a better father for wanting to be your best."

We're nearing the guarded entrance of Thomas's house, so I don't say anything in response, just squeeze her hand. We've got miles to go before I get to put my fatherhood prowess to the test again. I don't even know Lucas anymore, and the thought brings a brief pang of sadness before I push it down. I'm going to have a lot to make up to him and Carys when my sentence is done.

We approach the crew of guards, and one comes out of his guardhouse on the other side of the gate.

"We're here to see Thomas Byrne," I say.

The guy checks his watch and squints at us. "Mr. Byrne doesn't have any appointments this morning."

"Excellent." I offer a wolfish grin. "Means he'll have no trouble seeing us. Tell him Finn Donaghey and Carys Van de Berg are at the gate. He'll let us in." Will he at this early hour? I don't have a clue, but confidence breeds results.

The guard ducks into his hut and speaks on the phone for a few minutes. Other men shift, giving us furtive glances, flashing their concealed weapons. The camera on the top of the gate tilts in our direction, and I glance up, offering a wave. Thomas must be wondering what the hell is going on.

"We'll search you both for weapons." The guard returns to the small entry door off the larger one meant for cars.

Clearly Thomas doesn't trust this visit too much, but he's going to let us in anyway. The guards take the gun lodged in the small of my back and the one in Carys's purse. I haven't managed to accumulate any other weapons, but they are thorough. Thomas hires good people, which makes me more secure in asking him for protection.

We make the walk along the tree-lined drive to his estate built from some sort of stone. The house has a vague resemblance to a castle. I haven't been here in twenty years. Do his brothers still live on the estate as well? If I remember correctly, there were lots of cottages and outbuildings spread throughout the sprawling property.

At the front door, another guard searches us again while two German shepherds sit watching us. I have no doubt they attack on command or the first sign of trouble. Rather than annoyed, I'm pleased with the extra layers of protection until the guy's hands wander a little too close to Carys's more sensitive places, and she flinches.

"Hey," I say. "Watch where those hands are going on her."

The guard gives me a wry look, and the dogs growl at my tone. "Women are notorious for stashing shit where men are too timid to check. Next time she can come naked if she doesn't want my hands on her."

I'm about to respond with my fist to his face, dogs be damned, when Thomas chuckles in the doorway behind. Beating up security isn't the right tone to set.

When we step past the guard and dogs, Thomas, in his late forties with thick reddish-brown hair, offers his hand to shake. Carys doesn't loop herself around me like normal, but instead adopts the business persona I haven't seen much of since I got out. I suppose Van de Berg Ammunitions did have deals with the Byrne family. Habit, maybe, for her to become so cool and aloof.

"To what do I owe this shocking visit at 9 a.m. without a driver, or security, after a risky jailbreak and both of you covered in blood?" Thomas leads us through his hallway and into a narrow, but modernly decorated, sitting room. He gestures for us to sit on one of the couches. Carys takes one end and I take the other.

"The jailbreak was well planned." I smirk. "Nothing risky about it." No need to mention our morning escapades. Makes us appear weak.

"Except I heard the PLA hijacked Evander Williams's carefully crafted plans. Bit riskier then." Thomas's gaze pins me.

We're jumping right into it, then. Suits me fine. No need to pussyfoot around why we're here. "I wasn't so keen on being their puppet."

"Looks like you've evaded them. Though I heard Donal McCaffrey paid your price with his head. Why not return to Cape Verde? I hear rebuilding is in order."

I take a beat to consider his words. He's got his ear to the ground if he knows about the bomb in Cape Verde, Donal's missing head, and also the PLA kidnapping me. "They framed Carys for crimes she didn't commit, and they sent her a confetti bomb as a joke. As you can imagine, it's not a joke I consider amusing. I've got an axe to grind, and I intend to grind it right down their bony spines."

Thomas laughs, and genuine amusement lights his face. "I have no doubt you will."

"They were trying to get me to come here to talk to you." The smile falls from his lips at my words.

"Yes, they wanted to grind an axe into me as well. Wanted me to come work for them. Reorganize my men to help them. Take orders from PJ—Pearl Jade." He gazes at Carys. "No offense to you, but I'm not likely to take orders from a woman, particularly one so keen to use her body as manipulation."

Carys straightens and purses her lips. She won't like the comment about women not being capable of being in charge, but she won't like that her sister was using sex as a weapon either. Both are against Carys's personal beliefs.

It is interesting that Jade revealed herself to Thomas, and the PLA still wanted me to come down here to negotiate. She wanted me to discover her identity. "In Ireland? They wanted your help in Ireland?" The bombs they shipped went to so many places it's hard to believe their focus was solely here.

"No," Thomas says. "I've got connections, maybe what you'd call a small faction, in Shanghai and another in Russia."

"In Russia?" A frown mars Carys's forehead.

Have I told her about the bomb orders we found in Pierre-Jacques's office? Not yet. She won't be pleased to be one step behind.

"Volgograd." Thomas's smile is wolfish. "I'd planned to go after Demid, but someone else beat me to it. My money is on Semyon, but it could have been the PLA. Demid didn't want to play their games either. Perhaps he wasn't big enough to fend them off."

"A car bomb is hardly a fair fight," she says while one of Thomas's servants brings in a tray of tea and coffee.

"Does a fight need to be fair?" He pours himself a coffee. "Help yourself."

Carys and I fall on opposite sides of that line. I'm not going to highlight our difference by answering Thomas's rhetorical question. "So, you're not a fan of the PLA either?"

"Is anyone?" Thomas tips the cream into his coffee and stirs it with a spoon.

"I want your help to go after them." Might as well cut to the chase. "We'd like to stay here under your protection. I also have an injured man I need protection for."

Thomas sips his coffee and looks from me to Carys and back again. "That's no small thing. What can you offer me in return, other than money?"

She leans forward, getting her own coffee fixed. "What do you want?"

Thomas sets his coffee cup on the table and focuses on me. "Here are my two issues with helping you." He meets my gaze to be sure I'm listening. He crosses his arms. "For one, you killed your brother, and

I've heard you played a part in your father's murder. Maybe one of those I could live with—your father was an arsehole—but the other I can't. There's an honor code amongst families, and you violated it." He runs a hand down his face. "Then there's the matter of what you lost in killing your brother. You're not the strategy man. You're the muscle. We know it. Lorcan is the plan, and you're the execution. Nothing wrong with that, worked for you both quite well. But I'm not keen to throw my lot in with a man who can't win."

Carys tenses and glances at me. She's probably wondering the same thing I am. Is now when I admit Lorcan isn't dead? Doesn't change the fact that maybe a small part of me meant to kill him in the warehouse, or at the very least, was prepared for him to be severely injured in that confrontation. Thomas is right that impulsiveness can be my undoing.

"I'll regret what happened between my brother and me until the day I die." Maybe regret isn't the right word because the warehouse led me back to Carys, and I'm never going to be sorry about that. The complete truth won't do me any favors. "So, if my brother were still here, we'd be aces?"

Thomas eyes me. "Why would you put that question to me unless his death was a trick of some sort? Lorcan isn't dead?"

"I'll tell you everything, the whole sorry tale, if you'll agree to protect us and help us."

A hint of a smile twitches Thomas's lips. "I must admit, I'm a sucker for a spot of intrigue and fucking over the PLA. If you've got your brother stashed away somewhere, you've got my protection and my help."

"Then I guess we've got a deal." I extend my hand to Thomas to shake, and I pray that once Thomas realizes Lorcan and Kim work for the CIA, he doesn't put a bullet in our heads.

CHAPTER THIRTY-FOUR

CARYS

I drink my coffee and pour a second one while Finn gives Thomas the barest, most essential details of what's been happening over the last year and a bit. He listens to the story with an impassive face and calculating eyes. I can't tell with any certainty whether he'll welcome Lorcan and Kim into the house or he'll shoot us dead.

Finn finishes, and Thomas takes another sip of his coffee before sliding his cup onto the wooden table between us. "They turned him."

"Toward the PLA, yes," Finn corrects.

"But if they told him to come after me, for example, he would do it." Thomas scratches his stubbled chin.

"Doesn't work like that." I set down my drink too. "Since he's dead, he could only be slotted into positions where he wouldn't be recognized."

He pins me with his gaze. "You want me to believe he wouldn't come after me if they told him to? I'm not naïve, Carys. Once you sell your soul, you've got no control over what it's forced to do. Such is the bargain you strike."

I school my face to hide my annoyance. He has a bit of a dramatic flair like Finn. Makes sense they'd like each other.

"You're worried my brother will use this opportunity to amass intel on you and your family?" Finn asks.

"You'd be suspicious too. Murderous, probably." He gives a wry smile. "Just because it suits you now, let's not pretend."

"It's true." Finn leans forward to fill a cup with coffee. "I'm not sure I'd be brave enough to take the risk I'm asking you to assume."

He chuckles and then scoffs. "Brave. Stupid. Sometimes with you those are interchangeable."

He smirks and draws the mug of coffee to his lips. "Flattery usually gets me farther with you. I've got no problems calling you stupid if you want."

With a shake of his head, he stares from me to Finn and back to me again. "As the one not involved in some seriously dirty dealings, what's your gut instinct on Lorcan and Kim?"

I half expect Finn to tell Thomas my gut instincts are always wrong. Finn isn't going to contradict me—we're on the same team. Thomas wants to help us; he needs a little shove in the right direction. No one wants to believe they're stupid, even if it's dressed up as brave. "I've spent the last two weeks with Lorcan and Kim. They're very focused on taking down the PLA and keeping everyone on track. The CIA didn't want us to reveal their position to you, but we all believe you can be trusted."

The golden ticket. Trust. If he doesn't want to be called brave or stupid, everyone in this business likes to be trusted, even when they shouldn't be.

A hint of a smile tugs at Thomas's mouth. "Do you *trust* them?"

Not in every way. Kim's deception altered our friendship forever, but I trust them in every way that counts for this situation. "I do."

He releases a deep breath and taps his fingers on the arm of the chair. "My gut is telling me I can trust Lorcan. Kim? I don't know her, but if

Lorcan ripped his life up and threw it away for her, she's got a powerful hold on him."

Finn catches my eye and tips his head. What's he want me to say to that? It's true. He tossed away his life for her. "You know." I sense my way through a response since Finn has confidence I can win Thomas over. "When people love each other deeply, the influence goes both ways. Each will do whatever they can to avoid hurting the other. Kim won't want to disappoint Lorcan any more than Lorcan will want to disappoint Kim."

Wasn't that the way I also felt about Finn? He might love me with desperate intensity, but I loved him back just as hard. Kim and Lorcan took massive risks with and for each other to become undercover agents together. The trust has to be mutual.

"Very well." Thomas gives a decisive nod. "I like your logic. I'll see him in private before anyone is welcomed into the house. The family will need guarantees only he can deliver. As much as Kim might be Lorcan's leash, while you're in this house, he's hers." He waves a dismissive hand. "Send him to me alone and unarmed. If he returns to you, we've struck a deal." He ignores me to focus on Finn. "Trust goes both ways."

He drains his coffee and sets the cup on the table in front of us. He rises and offers his hand to Thomas, but he refuses to take it.

"We shake when I know we're square. Until I'm sure of your brother, no deal has been done."

Thomas makes us leave our weapons at the front door when we exit. Another test to see how much we want his help. Will we abandon the few weapons we have? Finn's jaw is tight when he realizes Thomas's intention.

We're through the gate and walking back to the SUV, and Finn's posture is still strung tight.

"Lorcan can convince him. He's going to say yes." He might not like Thomas's tactics, but surely he can appreciate them.

"All these head games," Finn grumbles. "I've known the guy for years."

"Which is exactly why he's playing them. He knows you, and he knows your brother. For you to leave without your weapon, for Lorcan to see him unguarded and unarmed—those are huge markers of trust."

He loops an arm around my shoulders and kisses my temple, dragging me closer to him as we walk. "I want to solve this PLA puzzle quickly, pin them, show them they can't fuck with our lives without consequence. At the same time, I want to drag this out, steal every moment. 'Cause when this is over, I go back to prison, and you go back to Cape Verde."

"Three years isn't forever." I gaze up at his frustrated expression.

We're approaching the SUV, and he brushes his lips across the top of my head. "The more time I get with you, the more I want. Nothing is ever gonna be enough."

My stomach drops to my toes at his words. No matter how often he gives me a peek into how much he loves me, no matter how deep in my bones his love is secured, hearing him say something like that—so gruff, so true, never gets old. We only get this lifetime together, and sometimes I wonder whether I'll be on my deathbed begging for more.

"Well," Lorcan calls out the window. "He didn't put a bullet in your head, so it couldn't have gone too badly."

Finn chuckles. "Still might put a bullet in yours, brother. He wants to see you."

CHAPTER THIRTY-FIVE

FINN

We've been welcomed into the Byrne house. Whatever Lorcan said or guaranteed Thomas, it was enough to get us entry. So far, no one has fired a shot or thrown a punch. Not a bad start to an uneasy alliance. Jay is tucked away in a private bedroom, and Thomas called his personal physician to double-check John and Lorcan's patch job. He sent a maid to a shop to purchase us an extra set of clothes. Not a full wardrobe like the PLA, but I'll take loyalty over outfits any day.

When Carys gets off a video chat with Lucas, and she's been able to reassure Lena and Sofia about Jay's condition with a straight face, I figure I might as well know what she promised Semyon. Depending on how things go with the PLA, we might end up in debt to Thomas and his family. Perched on the bed, fresh from our shower together, she looks relaxed and, dare I say it, happy.

I drop my towel and crawl across the bed toward her. She eyes me with amusement. "Again?"

Instead of tugging her under me like she expects, I sprawl out beside her and drag one of the pillows under my head. "I didn't want to talk about it in prison—because what would be the point?—but in three years when I'm out, what do you want?"

With the PLA listening in while we were in Northern Ireland, I didn't get a chance to discuss the future. But I don't want to do it at a cramped table in a room full of other people during visitation either. Maybe it'll help when I'm back there to have an understanding between us of where we're headed.

Confusion flashes across her face. "Well, I thought—I thought we both wanted the same thing. You, me, Lucas, Cape Verde. The hotel and casino."

"I guess." I scratch my head and force myself to maintain eye contact. This is not a conversation I ever expected to have with any woman, but I want Carys to have everything she's dreamed about—even if she has to wait three years to get it. "I guess I'm wondering whether, and this isn't me asking officially because I know better, whether you wanted a wedding with all the family stuff."

She bites her lip, and a slow smile tugs her lip from her teeth. God, she's sexy.

"Are you asking me to marry you?"

I roll onto my back and stare at the ceiling, chuckling. "Uh, no. 'Cause I know better than to ask a woman like you without a ring."

"With or without a ring, Finn Donaghey, my answer is the same." She traces figure eights on my chest.

"Don't keep me in suspense." I turn to gaze at her. "Is that what you'd want?"

"I don't *need* to marry you to feel like we'll be together forever, but yeah, I *want* to. I really, really want to."

I tap my temple and smirk. "Noted."

"I'd marry you right now if I could."

I raise my eyebrows. "Really? Without the dress and the decorations and the other girly shit?"

"Well…"

"Exactly." Whatever she wants, she'll get even if it's not for another three years. I climb off the bed and grab my towel from the floor, scrubbing my short hair to get rid of the excess water. "How's everyone doing in Boston?"

"They said the staff has been very good to them so far."

I eye her as I pluck my fresh clothes out of the pile on the dresser. The maid took our other things to wash. She made a tsking noise at the blood. "They should be. They're honored guests." Semyon doesn't have much honor though, and whatever Carys guaranteed him has been eating at me. "What'd you promise him to get that treatment?"

Carys fiddles with the neck of her robe and doesn't meet my gaze. "I told him I'd protect him and his family from you."

I laugh, and amusement coats my face as I tug my shirt over my head. "Oh, yeah?" Just like Semyon to ask for the impossible.

"He made Jay promise as well."

"Jay's in no shape to hold me back from anything." Despite my enjoyment in the request, I'm not going to like why she'll be keeping me in line. While I might mock her for trying, if she tells me I can't do something, I try to listen. She's got me by the balls, and I don't even mind all that much. "Why would Semyon and his family need you to protect them from me? I'm one guy. I don't have any of my crew."

She tilts her head, and her expression is exasperated. "You didn't threaten them with a crew. Apparently, you threatened to saw off their body parts."

That does ring a faint bell. "With a dull saw..." The piece of my memory slots into place, and I swallow. Rage rises in me swift and sure. Now I remember why I said that. "They bombed your hotel. I wouldn't do their dirty work in prison, so they came after you."

Carys meets my gaze, but she doesn't deny the leap I've made.

"Nah, nah, nah." I wag my finger and then button my jeans. "That doesn't go unanswered. Those fuckers can't threaten you and not get a reprisal from me. I don't work that way. I don't care what you promised them. When our family is out of their grasp, I'm making good on my threat."

"Finn." She climbs off the king-sized bed. "I promised. I gave my word."

"And I gave mine in the prison. I told their errand boy if Hagen or anyone in his family was trying to use you to get to me, I'd find a way to cut off their limbs. I don't make empty threats."

"We're no longer in a position of power. We aren't. Maybe someday we will be again. Though that's not exactly the life I want for us." She slides her hand down the side of my face. "I don't want to start wars or keep those fires burning. A family with you. That's what I want."

I meet her gaze and flex my jaw with repressed emotion. A family is good until one of my old contacts gets a little too bold. Leaving something like this unanswered is bad for business.

"All this anger, all this rage, we need to funnel it into destroying the PLA. If you do that, then in three years, we're free. We'll get the rest of our lives together. You, me, and Lucas. The Volkovs, every other mafia organization, and the danger'll be in our rear window. You can't keep courting it. Do you understand? If you keep inviting it, we'll never be free."

Her words land, but I don't want to let them sink in. Maybe I can't keep pursuing dangerous people and expect to keep us safe. Doesn't mean the instinct isn't there, threatening to burst out and ruin our lives. I could yell and seethe—pour these emotions across the room as proof of how much I love her, and of the lengths I'll go to keep her safe. There are no limits and no barriers. For her, I'd burn every last inch of the world to the ground.

"Love me, Finn," she whispers, as her hand cups my chin. "I need you to love me. Nothing else."

I yank her robe apart and tug her naked body flush to mine. With a murmured curse, I capture her lips. If this is what she wants, this is what she'll get. She tugs my shirt off, frantic with need, and she makes short work of my jeans. Her heavy robe hits the floor with a soft thud. I throw her onto the bed and follow her down, covering her body with mine.

She won't let me litter the room with my rage, so I'll sink it into her. My anger can fuel my worship. I'll show her I love her enough to listen, even if leaving a threat unanswered murders a piece of me.

Liam, Gus, Jack, Connor, and Thomas stand around the world map with me, Lorcan, Kim, and Carys. Though the family has vetted us, and our families go way back, tension is thick in the air. No matter what guarantees we give them, there's still a chance Lorcan or Kim could screw them over with the CIA. Hell, even I might turn them over if the CIA says they'll get rid of those last three pesky years in prison. Trouble is, I've got nothing to offer them on the Byrne brothers, and they're being extra cagey with the information they have on the PLA.

"We're not going to get anywhere," Lorcan growls. "If you can't be more open with what you know."

The men exchange uneasy glances.

"I've given you my word." He presses his hands into the table.

Thomas squints at Lorcan and then nods at his brothers.

"Shanghai and Russia were the two main places of discussion between us and the PLA." Thomas sticks pins in those areas.

"Was Russia Volgograd?" I grab another pin to narrow our focus.

"Aye," he admits. "We were going after Demid's assets."

Lorcan picks up different colored pins and sticks them in the cities where bombs were delivered.

Carys frowns and peers over the table. "These are places where Van de Berg Ammunitions has branches."

"Except Cork," I say. We already deduced as much about the other locations.

"Even Cork." Thomas gestures to his brother Connor. "What'd you tell me the other day?"

"Met Charles in Cork for lunch last week. He reckons the new build is on track." Connor clicks something on his phone and passes it to Lorcan.

I peer at the phone around Lorcan's shoulder and the banner across the top of Van de Berg Ammunitions webpage declares their expansion. The grand opening of their office building on the outskirts of Cork is in four days.

"Four days?" Carys stares at her phone and at probably the same image I'm seeing. "How did I miss this?"

Her father hasn't been returning her calls, so there's that. We've also tried very hard to separate ourselves from him. One stint in jail for Carys at her father's hands is more than enough. Most of the illegal activities she was accused of were deals Charles and Eric did, and yet she was poised to take the fall.

"Finn." Lorcan eyes me after passing Connor his phone. "Whaddya say we check in with Francois?"

Would they have told him not to speak to us? Roughly three hours to get there, and if Thomas will give us some extra men, we might learn something about the PLA's bigger plan.

Thomas folds his arms over his chest. "You got them the McCaffrey men."

He doesn't put the pieces together for me or Lorcan, but the implication is clear. If the PLA is planning to bomb or attack the grand opening of Van de Berg Ammunitions' building in Cork, we gave them the tools to do it. Beyond frustrating.

"I'd say we plan for some kind of strike on the building the day of the grand opening." I run a hand along the top of my head. "Are they setting off the other bombs on the same day? They could. Or maybe they want us to think they will."

"Divide our resources." Lorcan stares at the map.

"We have to tell the CIA." Kim is on the other side of him. "We've got locations and a rough time frame. We need to report this."

Thomas's jaw clenches. Like me, he'd rather deal with the PLA without intervention. Kim is right, though. We can't be everywhere. We might be able to cover Cork, but we haven't got a hope in hell of doing anything in Chicago, Switzerland, Shanghai, Volgograd, Mexico City, and Cape Verde. As much as I hate to admit it, their reach is bigger and better than ours. I'd have needed months to foil every threat.

Looks like we've got four days.

"Kimi, you meet with your handler and give them what we've got. Thomas, can you spare us a few men? Lorcan and I will pay Francois a less friendly visit."

"Should I warn my dad? Some of his employees?" Carys's phone is cradled in her hand.

"Not yet," Lorcan says. "Don't want anyone spooked from Van de Berg Ammunitions. If we've sussed out the PLA plan, we need them to move ahead."

"So, is going to see Francois wise?" She cocks her head at me and raises an eyebrow.

"Smash-and-grab." I shrug. "We'll kidnap Francois and mine him for information."

"Can we trust what he tells us?" Kim's hands are shoved into the pockets of her light jacket.

"Only one way to know for sure," I say. "The PLA is going to expect us to do something."

"Quick, decisive moves." Lorcan makes eye contact with each of us. "We've got four days. No time to question if we're right. We have to act like we are—like we can't be bested."

"Buckle up, buttercup. We're headed to Cork." I rub my hands together. We're taking the fight to them.

CHAPTER THIRTY-SIX

CARYS

Kim left to meet her handler somewhere secret. She didn't know when she'd be back. Lorcan and Finn, along with five of Thomas's men are leaving for Cork in a few minutes.

I pick up a few of the photographs littered around the guest bedroom assigned to us. Idyllic scenes of pastoral life in Ireland. The exact opposite of Thomas's reality. Almost enough to make me laugh.

"You stay on the Byrne property until I'm back." Finn shoves guns and ammunition into his pockets and any space to conceal it.

I give him a wry smile. "Where else would I go? Kim is gone. Jay is recovering. All I can do is wait."

"Yeah, well. Our best guess is an attack on Van de Berg Ammunitions in four days. The grudge she's got is personal. If we can secure Francois, we might get concrete details. A better way to disrupt her plans."

I still Finn's hands, and he meets my gaze. "We're going to figure it out."

"You're calmer than I expected." He smirks. "You got that much faith in me?"

"Yes." I tuck a stray strand of hair behind my ear. "But if we can't lock in on their plan, we call in the bomb threats and have the places evacuated."

"Last resort." He cups my cheek. "I only get my deal if we disrupt them or prevent their campaigns from succeeding."

"The people we love are safe, and we have each other to lean on while we put their plan together. We'll do it. Our team is better."

He gives me a quick peck and fingers a single bullet left on the dresser. "I don't worry about shit. No point. But I listen to my gut, and the last couple of days I can't get that Shakespeare quote out of my head. You know the one I'm talking about?"

"Nothing can be wrong..." The end eludes me, but it's a favorite from his not-quite English degree.

"If she is well." He links our fingers together and draws me into his chest. "I've been wondering whether I should've sent you to Boston too."

"Finn," I chastise. "We've talked about this. *I'm* safest with you."

"Here's the thing." He gazes down. "I realize that's bullshit, but I want it to be true. You'd never send Lucas to Boston if you truly believed having him *here* was the best place for him."

"It's not the same." I flounder for a better explanation because Finn isn't wrong. I wanted every moment I could get with him, especially knowing he'll be back in jail for another three years after this. Stupid? Maybe. So far, I haven't regretted my choice.

His lips brush my forehead. "Sure, it's not." He chuckles.

There's a knock on the bedroom door, and Lorcan calls Finn's name.

After another quick squeeze, he frames my face and kisses me deeply. "I love you." His voice is gruff, and a thrill dances along my spine at the words. He gives them to me, but not often, and every time I hear them, I marvel that they're true.

As long as we've got each other and Lucas, we can handle anything.

Jay's sleep is deep and even. He woke up, so I video called Sofia so she could see he is fine-ish with her own two eyes. Tears slid along her cheeks while she talked to him, but there is relief in her voice.

I check the time. They should be nearing Cork. Fingers crossed Francois is there and they can take him without any major problems. Finn said the farm wasn't well guarded. Hopefully, that hasn't changed.

My phone buzzes in my hand. *Dad* is displayed on the caller ID, so I send the call to voicemail. The call has no sooner clicked to voicemail than my phone rings again. I send it to voicemail again. He couldn't be bothered to take my calls when I needed him.

The third time it rings, I answer with an impatient bark. "What do you want?"

"Carys?" My father's voice is remote and far away. "I need you. I'm in trouble. I need you."

"Dad?" Even if he's been absent and self-absorbed as a father, my spike of panic is real. He's my dad. When he left us twisting in the wind over a place for Lucas to go, I told Finn I'd never do the same to him. If he's in trouble, I'll help him. "Where are you?"

"I'm in Ireland. Kilkenny. I need to see you."

John and Connor said he'd been in Ireland. He's still in the country? Why hasn't he been answering my calls? There's something weird about his voice too. It's him—definitely him—but his speech isn't smooth like normal. "Where are you?"

"The Fox's Burrow on Thornback Road. Leave now. I'll be waiting."

With a click, he's gone. I drop my phone on the bed and rub my face. Considering everything going on, I believe my father is in trouble. Is he dragging me into more danger with him?

Since Jay is sleeping, I leave his room to find Thomas. I could call Finn, but he's too far away chasing his own lead. I locate Thomas in the spacious, modern kitchen making himself a coffee.

He holds up his cup in offer.

I shake my head.

"You're looking a little pale. You worried about Finn?"

A slight smile quirks up my lips at the notion. "No. My father called and asked to meet me at the Fox's Burrow on Thornback Road outside Kilkenny. Can I take a few of your men with me?"

Thomas raises his eyebrows and sips his drink. "You can take more than a few, I reckon. Finn'd skin me alive if anything happened to ya." His expression turns pensive. "Unusual for your father to call you?"

"He hasn't been answering my calls for days. He says he's in trouble. But he has a history of dragging me into waist-deep shit when I was only at my ankles before."

"Maybe you should wait for Finn?"

"He said I should leave now. If he really needs help, he's my father." For better or worse, I can't abandon him when he needs me.

"Leave now," Thomas muses. "Strange that. How would he know where you are?"

A great question. The dots connect and form a different picture. A trap? "Maybe I'll need more than a few men. It was his voice on the phone. If he's in actual danger, I have to help him. If he died and I did nothing after he called me pleading..." I ease my fingers along my brow. Finn would tell me not to leave. "I'd never forgive myself."

Thomas drains his cup and sets it in the sink. "Come with me. I'm not sending you to Kilkenny without a plan of action and a substantial number of men. I know which side my bread is buttered."

The drive to Kilkenny is longer than I expected, and the whole time I stare out the window, clutching my phone in my hand. I half expect my father to call me to say he's left Kilkenny, and there's no need to come. Wishful thinking.

Three of Thomas's men are in my bulletproof car. Following us is another bulletproof car with four other men inside. Thomas suggested I text or call Finn to give him the details of the plan we cobbled together to meet my father. If I did that, he would have told me not to go, then raved at Thomas about my safety. Wouldn't have mattered how careful he was or how many security people he gave me, nothing would ever be enough.

These mixed-up emotions are another reason I didn't go to Boston. We would have spent too much energy worrying about each other. Out of sight, out of mind doesn't work for us. Everything is worse when Finn and I aren't together.

Having me ride to my father's rescue would grate on Finn. He thinks my father is a waste of air, and while there are days I agree with him, he's my parent. Not all my memories of him are bad. We had good times—particularly before my brother died. After that, my mom and dad as I knew them, closed up, and closed in. How much can I blame them for protecting their hearts? How traumatized would I be by the loss of Lucas? Would I ever recover? My miscarriages wrecked me. I can't imagine losing Lucas who is a child with his own personality, a child I've held in my arms through feedings, teething, and sleepless nights. All his potential—gone in a flash. The loss must cling to a person like tar.

"Thomas texted," the guy in the passenger seat says and glances over his shoulder. "He got confirmation the Fox's Burrow isn't in business anymore. You still want to go?"

I bite my cheek and consider my options. Seven guards. Bulletproof car. We went over various ambush scenarios with everyone. They're armed to the teeth.

If the building is abandoned, he could be a hostage. He could be hurt or injured.

Or he may not realize it's no longer a functioning bar. To some extent, that's like him. Pick an out-of-the-way spot that just so happens to be closed.

He could be dead.

Something about the voice on the phone didn't ring true to me, but I can't put my finger on the difference. Stilted—a smidge—not enough for most people to notice.

He needs me, and if I rail against him for not being there when I need him, I can't let him down now. He might be a shitty father, but he's still family.

"We're going." I give a decisive nod.

The men check their guns and their ammo, but that's the only indication I get about their level of comfort with my decision.

We approach an intersection in the middle of nowhere, and up ahead is a pub, the windows boarded-up with plywood, a single car sitting in the parking lot facing the road.

Relief sprouts in my stomach. He's here alone. My clueless father has picked a place that's no longer in business.

But when we get close enough for me to peer at the driver, I realize it's not my father, but by then it's too late. Other vehicles are streaming out of the rear parking lot, charging toward us. Gunfire bursts from the other cars, pinging off ours. My driver wheels us around and speeds along the road we've come from.

Leaving isn't the plan we cooked up with Thomas. "This wasn't one of the plans. What are you doing?" I yell over the bullets hitting the car.

"Thomas's orders. If it's an ambush, we secure you and get out." The guy is checking his mirrors, and a thin sheen of sweat coats his forehead.

He must have told them the final plan on the sly behind my back. Give the little woman what she wants, but not too much. Being pursued down this narrow highway isn't a winning strategy. My heart gallops in my chest. I shouldn't have come. If I make it out of this, I'm cutting my father out of my life for good. I can't keep doing this to myself because it's not just me anymore. *Lucas.* My gut clenches.

SUVs flank us on either side. Bullets hit the vehicle in sharp succession, and I flinch. When one of the SUVs inches ahead of us, I throw a quick glance at the driver who is sweating buckets now. Once the SUV is a full length in front of us, it wheels into our path.

The move is so sudden, so swift, I don't have time to think, and I brace for the impact.

CHAPTER THIRTY-SEVEN

FINN

Lorcan cruises along the highway toward Cork. His phone is in the cup holder, and mine is beside his. He's tense, but I don't know if it's because Kim went to their CIA handler without him or if he's worried about what we'll discover in Cork. While he might be an overthinker, he's not a worrier. Surprisingly, there is a difference.

"What're you worried about?" I ask when I can't take him flexing his hands on the steering wheel anymore.

"Our CIA handler is a prick." Lorcan glances at me. "Not that Kim can't handle him—she handles him better than me—but I don't like sending her alone."

She took me down several notches and hardly broke a sweat, so he's not going to get a lot of sympathy from me about her having to handle a CIA dickhead. "This what you two are doing for the rest of your lives? Working for shithead government agents?"

"Government says I have a debt to pay."

I like the way he phrases it. As though, like me, he doesn't buy into their bullshit. The FBI and CIA posture themselves as heroes, but I bet if someone dug deep enough, they'd come up with lots of people who weren't so heroic. Sometimes good and evil is arbitrary.

"I'm in it until Kim decides she's done," Lorcan amends.

"How badly would it fuck you over if I ducked out of the country once we foil the PLA plans?" I'm already out of jail, and I gave my word I'd take down the PLA in exchange. It would be so easy to vanish. Three more years of incarceration after solving their problem rubs me the wrong way, even if I might deserve it, even if I might deserve a lot more.

"Don't know." Lorcan eyes me. "I suspect they'd be a tad pissy with me."

"Only a tad?"

"They like to think they're the good guys." Lorcan flexes his hands. "Wouldn't bother me except it'd land Kim in the shit. She's already on some sort of probation for what she did for me. So, if you ran, brother, I'd hunt you and drag your arse to America."

I sigh. It's the answer I suspected, but I had to ask the question. No point in going back to jail if I didn't *have* to return.

"They're already none too pleased about Donal."

I wave him off. "Price of doing business. I made that clear when I signed on the dotted line. Nothing was off the table if it got me an inside track."

Lorcan makes a noncommittal sound and remains silent for a few minutes. "You're going to live in Cape Verde with Carys when you get out?"

"Assuming I'm alive." I rub a hand down my face. "They reduced my sentence to three years, so I suspect the odds of me surviving must be low. That's the plan, though. Cape Verde. Me, Lucas, and Carys. Set up a legit hotel and casino. Live the good life."

"You're going to be a father to her son?"

I stare out the window as the scenery passes. Why does his question bother me? We grew up with the same shitty father, but his experiences with Eamon Donaghey and mine aren't the same. The five-year age gap between us, the death of my mother at the request of his, and his mother's excruciating battle with cancer don't accumulate the same in us. We're damaged by the same events in different ways.

"Think I'll be any good at it?" I ask, not meeting his gaze.

Lorcan is slow to respond. "I reckon you'll be as good as you want to be."

I chuckle. "Not much of an answer."

"Means you'll set your own course and make your own fate. 'Tis not a bad thing." He glances at me.

"I never thought much about being a parent, or marriage, or any of that other shit. Once I—once I lost Carys the first time, none of it crossed my mind again."

"And now?" Lorcan gives me a steady look before focusing on the highway.

"Now it's all I think about—how do I get that life with her? Coats everything I say and do. My goals used to be how much money I could get, how much power could I accumulate, but now it's just her and Lucas. Except—it's not a 'just.' So much bigger than a *just*." I stare at him. "You want that with Kim?"

He rubs the back of his head. "Eventually, maybe. She's not sure about kids. We've got a lot to sort out once this version of our life is done. I reckon we can't live like this forever, but she's not ready to quit."

"Christ, you picked a complicated one, didn't you?" I chuckle. The women who came before Kim were brief flings, glossy, with little substance. Pretty women who serviced his dick but didn't touch his heart. Suppose we weren't so different in that regard.

He sighs. "And like you, I wouldn't change it for all the power and money in the world. 'Tis a tough thing to reconcile sometimes, though. How much a heart can love. How one person can so completely consume you."

He passes a car, and I gaze out the window, thinking about our history together. "We should have talked more."

Lorcan lets out a mirthless laugh. "Talked more?" He raises his fist. "We were men of action. What would be the point of talking?"

I smirk and shake my head. "Might have done both of us some good, maybe. When I'm out, and you and Kim have done your time with the CIA, you should come to Cape Verde for a beer... or two."

The GPS speaks through our phones, a reminder for Lorcan to take the next exit. He doesn't comment on my suggestion, but a comfortable silence lapses between us.

Lorcan turns down the long farm laneway, and wariness coils in me. The other vehicle full of Thomas's men follows behind us. Ahead, the charred remains of the farmhouse looms.

"Doesn't look good." Lorcan mutters. The SUV crawls along as the gravel cracks and pops under the tires.

"As long as the barn is still standing..." The sentence doesn't need to be finished because the barn behind the farmhouse becomes visible. A cement foundation and a pile of charred wood. We park well back from the destruction and remove our guns. We signal for everyone to stick close together as we approach the buildings, keeping an eye on any of the secondary structures for people or animals. Gone are Francois's gruff brother, the barking dogs, and the smattering of farm animals.

We designate people to search every structure, and then we stand at the edge of the burned barn. Lorcan steps in and wades through the debris while I try to make sense of the carnage.

"Do you think they're dead? Francois and his brother?"

"Aye." Lorcan points at a boot in the rubble. There's still a foot attached.

"The McCaffrey family seeking retribution?" The other option isn't comforting. "Or the PLA making an adjustment to their crew?"

"Could be either," he admits. "Francois is no use to us now. We could try to contact some lads at the pub. I doubt they're all dead. Could be an ambush or a waste of precious time." Frustration colors his voice.

"Let's see if anything useful survived, since we drove here." I take up the search with Lorcan, picking through debris, overturning beams, looking for discarded papers or anything the PLA might have forgotten.

When my phone buzzes in my pocket, I take it out to check the display.

Thomas.

I'm inclined to ignore him, but this trip looks like a bust. Maybe he's got better news, or he needs his men back. Best I don't send his call to voicemail.

"This has been a waste of time," I say by way to greeting. "I hope you've got better news."

There's the briefest hesitation, as though Thomas is holding his breath. "Carys's father called her asking for help. She insisted on going to him in Kilkenny. I sent her with seven guards and armored cars. They were supposed to check in once they'd made contact. I haven't heard from any of my men."

I stare out into the fields, his words dropping like boulders. My heart does a funny thing, as though it can't decide if it should stop in its tracks or start racing. "When was this?"

"Too long ago. I've got another group of men headed there, but you're as close to Kilkenny in Cork. My man will send you the GPS coordinates."

I hang up on him before a slew of curse words escapes. "Get in the cars," I yell out across everyone searching. Everyone stops in their tracks to stare at me. "Now!"

"What's happened?" Lorcan jogs beside me toward the car.

My phone beeps with the GPS coordinates, and my stomach clenches. "Carys has been ambushed in Kilkenny. Thomas called."

"Why was she in Kilkenny?"

"Excellent question." I clench my jaw so hard I can barely get the words out. "Charles called her."

"Fecking hell." Lorcan starts the car and whips it around to race down the driveway.

"If the PLA does anything to her," my voice cracks, "I'll hunt every single member to the ends of the earth." There'll be no redemption for me if anything has happened to her.

Chapter Thirty-Eight

Carys

My head pounds, and when I try to open my eyes, the bright lighting causes a groan to escape. I'm sitting up, and my neck is stiff, sore, not happy about propping up my head.

"She's waking up," a female voice cries.

Is that—is that my mother? Where am I?

"Mom?" I crack open an eye to squint in the direction I heard her speak. The woman across from me is my mother, but she's dirty. Makeup is smeared across her face, and her hair is in disarray. Do I look that awful? "Where are we?" Beside my mother, my father stares blankly, his mouth taped shut.

I glance around the white room. The tiny window to the right makes me think we're in a basement. The sky and the canopy of a mature tree are visible from where I sit.

"I don't know." My mom sniffles. "I got a phone call from your father a few days ago to meet him for dinner in Kilkenny. But the restaurant didn't exist, and when I got there—" She starts to cry, and her sobs drown out the last of her words.

No need to tell me the rest since the same thing happened to me.

"Why is Dad's mouth taped?" I peer at him. Although he's awake, he doesn't seem to be following my conversation with my mom. His stare is sightless.

"He's—" She hiccups. "He's drugged."

"How long has he been here?" His doctor friend, John, said he spoke to him a week or so ago, and didn't Connor say the same thing? I tried to get in touch with him for days with no luck. Has he been in this basement for a week? How has no one noticed or reported him missing?

Tears run unchecked down my mother's cheeks, and she shakes her head. "I don't know."

Her helplessness annoys me. I test whatever is holding my arms secure behind my metal chair. There's no give to the plastic, and they've placed it above my cast on one side, so I'm forced into a weird angle. My ankles are also restrained. My mother and father have thick plastic bands around their ankles, and I have to assume mine are the same. Not easy to bend, break, or saw. Not that I have tools or anything else to get me out of here. Am I in Ireland or somewhere else?

"When did I get here? What day it is?"

She shakes her head, but she consults what must be a clock behind me and reads off the time. I realize wherever they've taken me, assuming today is the same day, we haven't gone more than a couple hours. If I can keep a level head, despite its pounding, I might figure a way out of here.

The door at my rear clicks open, and the strike of heels on concrete makes me tense. It has to be Jade, here to gloat or threaten. Maybe both. She hasn't killed either of my parents. She took me alive. So, what does she want? Do I already know?

She's carrying a knife when she comes around me so I can see her. It's the same knife I saw Pierre-Jacques take out of his pocket many times.

Sharp and tiny. The kind meant for carving or covert stabbing. Death by a thousand cuts.

"You're awake." She smiles, but there's no greeting in her expression. "I thought maybe the high-speed chase took too much out of you. Thomas gave you more protection than I anticipated." She tilts her head, examining me. "In the end, it didn't matter." She slides the knife across my cheek, and I flinch. Blood trickles down from the cut.

My mother cries out, and Jade spins on her heel to address her. "Don't worry. It's not deep enough to scar." She turns back to me, her mouth twisted with calculation. "Not yet, anyway."

"It's fine, Mother." I maintain eye contact with Jade. "When Finn finds me, she'll regret every single drop of my blood she shed."

"Sassy even when confronted with your imminent death."

I feel the color drain from my face, but I can't do anything about the bolt of shock and despair racing through me at her words. Bluffing is all I've got. She wants fear, and I won't show her a wisp if I can help it.

"I must say." She taps the tip of the blade with her nail. "I was worried you were too much of a damsel in distress to handle being kidnapped. It's nice that you're trying not to be afraid. It'll be so much more satisfying when I break you."

"Leave her alone," my mother pleads. "Break me instead. Leave her alone."

Jade glances over her shoulder. "You're already broken. What's the fun in that?"

"Do your worst," I mutter. "I can guarantee for every torture you inflict on me, Finn will find a way to repay in kind."

She circles me, and her blade slides into my other cheek. This time, I don't wince. A paper cut. A sharp sting, but if I ignore the pain, it'll go away. From behind me, the chair screeches on the floor as she draws it around close to me and sits down.

"Since you keep bringing him up like he's some kind of savior, let's talk about Finn. Did you realize he killed my boyfriend?"

Do I want to participate in this conversation? If Finn does come for me, and we make it out of here, I might learn something important about her plan or her motives. "I did."

"I was in the pub the night you were stabbed. Sometimes I wonder if that episode is why I became fascinated with powerful men being absolutely terrified. Do you remember the expression on his face when he realized the knife was protruding out of your chest?" She crosses her legs and puts her chin in her palm.

I'm not giving her that memory or any other memory she tries to drag out of me where Finn is concerned.

"God, his face." Her sigh of satisfaction is chilling. "To see it morph to absolute, all-encompassing rage the minute the ambulance door closed was incredible. I'd have taken that rage from him. Sucked him dry. So hot. Don't you think? Out of control and yet in complete control. Does the thought make you slick with need too?"

"There's something wrong with you," I say. "Not just a screw loose. A whole floor in your brain has vanished."

She chuckles and swivels in her chair. "What do you think, Mum? Reckon you're the reason I'm missing important sensitivity chips? Though"—she rotates back to me—"I'm not sure I'm missing them so much as they've been hard-wired differently. Being raised by a psychopathic father can do that, I suppose." She stands, and the chair screeches across the floor. "Charles Van de Berg asked you to jump, Mother, and you said how high. Isn't that right?" She stares at me for a beat. "He was the one who made the illegal deals the FBI tried to pin on you, you know that, right?"

"And you gave the FBI the evidence to make *me* appear guilty."

She wags a finger. "A gamble, in a way. I wondered whether Charles could put aside his own self-interest for his child. Our mother couldn't. He failed too." She chuckles. "Which I'm sure you understand since, instead of turning himself into the FBI and admitting his dirty deeds, he resumed control of the company and started making more."

"I could have gone to prison for a very long time."

A frown mars her forehead. "Least of your worries right now, sister. You'll be dead in twenty-four hours when this building caves in on you. The perfect family my mother sought when she left my father will go up in smoke or drown in rubble. Maybe both. I'm looking forward to the carnage."

Perfect family. God, she's so deluded. As if I've had an idyllic life because I had two parents.

"My life has been far from perfect."

"Oh, you poor soul." She clasps her hands in front of her in fake compassion. "Please, tell me the injustice you've faced as a pretty, white, rich, blond woman."

I purse my lips. She's not getting my trauma to feed off. "I'm sorry your father wasn't a good man. I'm sorry you were abused. Seeking to hurt other people because you've been hurt doesn't make any of it better."

She laughs. "Funny—isn't that Finn's calling card? Fuck with me, and I'll fuck with you harder? I'm not sure how you said those words with a straight face. Highly amusing, though. I'll give you that." She laughs again. She slices another cut on each cheek. Had she put crosses on my cheeks? I don't have any desire to be a martyr.

"I need to figure out how to get Lucas here, and then I can wipe out the whole Van de Berg line. The legacy our mother tried to build without me will be gone."

Behind Jade, my mother's tears are soaking her shirt.

"You'll never get my son." It's false bravado. Will Semyon sell us out? Finn's taste for revenge is a powerful motivator to stay loyal.

"No matter." She waves her hand. "If I can't get him now, I can get him later. He won't be a guest of Semyon Volkov forever."

A chill races down my spine. She knows where he is. "Finn would never let you near Lucas."

She smirks. "After you're dead, Finn will either die trying to avenge you or he'll end up back in jail. I'm not worried about Finn Donaghey. He's no match for me."

I stare at her, our gazes locked. "Then you're even more of a fool than I thought."

Chapter Thirty-Nine

Finn

Three cars in total. Two are Thomas's, and the third must be a PLA junker. Lorcan, me, and Thomas's men are piecing together what we think happened based on tread marks on the ground and the crash sites. Except for the driver of the vehicle we suspect had Carys, the men were shot execution-style while inside their vehicles. None of them escaped.

Definitely an ambush.

My pulse pounds with frustration, outright anger, and dread. Was Carys hurt? There's a trickle of blood in the back seat. She's still got a broken wrist. Helplessness threatens to get a foothold. I've got no space for that useless emotion. I must get her back.

If she wasn't hurt, what does the PLA intend to do with her? Where have they got her? If they wanted her dead, they could have shot her here. They either want something from her, or there's a performance aspect to killing or injuring her. Jade likes to create fear.

She's got my attention, but I'm not afraid yet, just unbelievable angry. At least Carys is alive. We need to figure out Jade's plan before Carys suffers.

Lorcan's shoulder brushes mine. "I reckon we should go back to Thomas and regroup. Nothing on the driver of the PLA car or in the car itself."

"I told her not to leave. I told her. I warned her I had a bad feeling, and she still went."

"Aye," he agrees. "She shouldn't have gone, but Carys has a soft spot for her da', yeah?"

"Unfortunately," I grit out. Too much softness for too many people. Anger courses through me, and I shake out my arms, flexing and releasing my hands.

On Thomas's advice, one of the guards calls the cops to report the shootings. They're staying here to handle the questions and payoffs. Not how I'd normally suggest doing things, but my only concern right now is Carys. Where have they taken her? How can I get her back?

I'm not going to let myself dwell on any outcome that doesn't bring her to me alive and well. No matter what I have to do, where I have to go, or who I have to demolish, she'll be alive and unharmed by the end. That's the only satisfactory resolution, and I'm clinging to it. If I don't, I'll sink into inaction. Blame myself for not sending her to Boston when my gut told me it was time to let her go.

We climb into the SUV and head for Dublin. My heart is lodged in my throat. I'm not a crier, but these emotions are welling up in me at once. I should have made her go to Boston with Lucas. Selfish and stupid and careless. The whole ride, my thoughts race with possible scenarios—locations, tactics, outcomes. The whirlwind of possibilities doesn't help my mental state.

"How are you holding up?" Lorcan asks when we turn onto Thomas's street.

"How would you be holding up if this was Kim?"

"I'd be furious and petrified," Lorcan answers as though he's imagined this scenario so many times, he's lived it.

"Then I don't suppose I need to tell you."

"Ah, right." He gives me a pensive look. "See, I thought you said we should have talked more?" We're through Thomas's gates and at the front door. Lorcan shifts the SUV into park.

There's a hint of teasing in his voice, but I'm not in the mood for him to lessen my dark cloud. She's gone, and until she's back where she belongs, I'm not discussing my feelings. "We're men of action." I throw open the door. "Right now, I'm feeling murderous—all my feelings and actions rolled into one. How about that?"

When the guards try to lay their hands on me to check for weapons, I let out a string of curse words so loud and aggressive Thomas appears in the entry behind his men with his dogs.

"Leave them," he says.

The guard raises his hands in surrender, and I storm past him and the low growls of the German shepherds into the living room. There are no words for the depth of my anger. I told Thomas, and I sure as hell told Carys, to stay at the house. Her father could have called her on his deathbed, and I'd have tied her to a chair rather than let her go.

"You had to know it was a trap." I take the whiskey off the sideboard and pour myself a generous glass.

"Which is why I sent her in armored cars with seven of my best men. She's a grown woman, and she insisted. I'm not in the business of restraining women." Thomas's jaw is tight.

Kim appears in the doorway, and Lorcan loops his arm around her waist, kisses her temple. The sight of them together makes my chest squeeze as though in a vice.

"What'd the CIA say?" I ask, gulping my drink. "Do they have a beat on where Jade took Carys?"

"No." She leans into Lorcan. "We're working under the assumption, at this point, that the bombs will go off in sync the day of the grand opening."

"Logic has no place with Jade," I mutter. "She's just as likely to set them off tomorrow because she can. We've got no firm hour or date." I rub my face, and for the first time since Carys dragged me out of the warehouse, I don't have a clue how to fix this mess. Jay is recovering upstairs. The CIA knows nothing. The Volkovs already tried to hurt Carys and are repaying me with protection. Thomas doesn't know any more than me. "Thomas, have you got any favors you can call in? Any ears to the ground? Someone's gotta know something."

"I made some calls as soon as I realized she was ambushed. I didn't get anywhere."

"Your brothers?" Every option has to be exhausted.

"Their connections are my connections, I'm afraid." He grimaces.

I leave the room and take the stairs in twos to find Jay. He's sleeping, but I don't care. He'd want to be told. I touch his shoulder, and he wakes, his gaze unfocused for a moment.

"Finn?"

"Carys has been taken by the PLA. I need contact options and people to call. Someone who'll know something."

Jay tries to sit up and groans at the motion. He eases both hands over his face and doesn't say anything for so long I think I'm going to have to repeat my demand.

"Evander Williams. He's the most connected guy I ever met. If anyone knows anything, it'll be him. Or he'll know who to call to get information."

"Except he fucked up my escape," I scoff.

"Yeah, he did," Jay agrees. "So, maybe he'll be motivated to make it right. His contact info is in my phone." He nods to the device on his bedside table.

Ah, hell. What have I got to lose? We're out of legitimate leads. Might as well call the guy who set this whole shitshow in progress. I snatch Jay's phone off the nightstand. "I'll bring this back later."

I'm out of his room and sailing down the stairs before he can respond. We need a list of questions for Evander before I reach out. At the bottom, I freeze at the familiar and unwelcome face in the hallway.

"Thomas!" I holler, not acknowledging our intruder. Not that I would have considered him much of a threat before. I've still got my gun, and I drop Jay's phone into my pocket, and then take my gun from the small of my back to point at Daniel. "What are you doing here?"

Thomas peers around the edge of the stairs. "Don't shoot him or me." He steps out and shoves his hands into the pockets of his jeans. "Though I was sorely tempted not to let him in. He's been thoroughly searched. Twice. Made him strip too which is why he's in his boxers."

His lack of clothing registers. Not sure I'd have noticed if he'd been naked. "Where's Carys?"

"Can we sit? I haven't got much time." Daniel's hands are raised, but his usual dopey demeanor is absent, sly cunning in its place.

"Is this a trap, Thomas?"

"Unlikely. Says he's from the Directorate of Military Intelligence. Supersecret government agency. Not exactly a person welcome in my home."

"He's also one of Pierre-Jacques's men." I narrow my gaze and come down the stairs, my gun still trained on Daniel.

"I reckon that means the Irish are better than the Americans at planting spies." He winks at me.

I raise my eyebrows in disbelief. He's going to joke with me when Carys is missing? He must still be high. "I reckon that means I can shoot you and bury your body in the backyard and your government will pretend like it never happened."

Daniel pales. "Look, mate, I came here with information for ye. The Irish don't work with the CIA normally, but your reputation as a man who gets jobs done can't be denied."

I nudge him toward the living room where Lorcan and Kim are sitting next to each other on the couch. They both rise at the sight of Daniel. Apparently, Thomas was the only one in the greeting party.

"What's he doing here?" Lorcan steps in front of Kim blocking Daniel from getting much of a look.

"Military Intelligence for Ireland," I say. "He's got information for us."

"And not a lot of time." He keeps his hands up. "Jade's plan is to have the bombs go off around the world, starting with the one in Cork in a few hours. She's got Carys, Charles Van de Berg, and Opal Van de Berg somewhere in the building. The exact moment for the bomb is unknown."

"The CIA has information on the other bombs, and they'll put people in place to dismantle them," Kim says. "You don't have a firm timeline?"

"No, but they're at Van de Berg properties. She wants to annihilate the family. Wipe them clean off the planet."

My blood chills. *Lucas.* "Was a bomb sent to Boston recently?"

"You're worried about the wee lad? Last I heard, she hadn't been able to get to him. Semyon's throwing his full weight behind your family. Wouldn't budge on turning them over or giving her access to the kid."

Thank Christ for that. Semyon is such a weasel, I wouldn't have been surprised to hear I'd been outmaneuvered with favors or money.

Kim takes her phone out of her pocket, and I point my finger at her. "Until we've got Carys, they can't raid the other buildings. It'll tip off the PLA, and they might move her, or shorten the detonation on any of the bombs."

She hesitates and slides her phone into her coat. "Then I'll wait to reach out."

Daniel eases his raised hands. "The task force is raiding the building in Cork in three and a half hours. If traffic is good, you can make it there. They won't be keen to let you join, but they won't want you to screw anything up either."

"Saddle up, people." I stride toward the entrance. I haven't got time to fact-check Daniel's claims or to make more phone calls to ensure his lead isn't a decoy. He's different enough standing in front of us—coherent, thoughtful, specific—to make me believe he was playing a part in the mansion. I'll have to trust he's not running interference for the Irish intelligence. A bit of false information could send us far from the main event.

Bad for my deal with the CIA. Bad for Daniel when I hunt him and kill him for making it impossible for me to rescue Carys.

Everyone trails behind me, and when we get to the main entrance, Daniel's clothes are stacked in a neat pile. "If you're lying to me, I will leave no stone unturned to find you. The job I'll be getting done is removing your head from your shoulders."

"I'm not lying to you, mate. She's in Cork inside the new Van de Berg build, and in three and a half hours, Irish intelligence will be laying siege to it."

"Not if I get there first," I say. "Thomas, I need your men, and we need to be armed to the teeth."

Chapter Forty

Carys

Since I can't see the clock, I'm not sure how long I've been here. Jade came back to give my father another shot. She wouldn't say what drug, but it's knocked him out cold. A mercy or a punishment?

This time when the door swings open behind me, she's wheeling a cart. On it is a device with a timer, similar to the confetti bomb from months ago. If only I could be sure this one would spew out harmless pieces of paper. A sweat breaks out under my armpits at the four hours counting down. How is Finn going to find me with so little on the clock?

"I suppose four hours and twenty-four hours are easy to confuse." I raise my eyebrows.

She cackles and eases the bomb off the trolley. "Maybe this bomb won't go off in four hours and then I'll wheel in another one. Maybe I'll drop off bombs at random intervals, and you'll never be sure which will lead to your demise." She rubs her chin. "An explosion of fear over and over again doesn't sound so bad to me. How long would it take for you to become desensitized? Would you ever?"

"You're sick," I say.

"Please, Pearl." My mother is out of tears, but her tone is pleading. "We'll get you help. It's not too late for you to have a different life. We can get to know each other. We can have the mother-daughter bond you always wanted."

"I bet you wish you had a time machine." She smiles at our mother. "Would you still have left him—left me—if you knew you'd end up dying with your lying, cheating husband and your weak daughter?" She crouches in front of her. "Was your life really so much better without me?"

"I regretted leaving you every day."

She swivels to me. "Carys, did our mother seem sad every day of her life? Did she seem filled with regret over me, her lost daughter?"

No, but I'm not about to say that. How do we ever realize what goes on behind the faces people choose to show us? My father wanted her to pretend her first child and her first marriage didn't exist, so that's what she did. She survived, but I'm not sure she was ever free of her past. Do I agree with her choice? No. Do I think she should be murdered for it? No, again.

"My mother and I have never been that close," I lie. There was a time when we were, but that was so many years ago I barely remember those days. "Once I learned about you, I understood why. She must have felt such enormous guilt and remorse over you. The daughter she left behind."

Jade's jaw clenches. "Lies," she spits out. "You think I haven't pored over your lives? Tried to insert myself? Figure out how a mother could abandon a child with a man like my father? A man who beat me and manipulated me and warped me into this." She gestures to herself before rising to her full height. "But he didn't break me. I can't be broken."

I'm afraid she's far more broken than she realizes. The clock behind her keeps losing time, speeding us closer to some kind of ending. Is it a real bomb? Or has she planted another fake to enjoy our screams of frustration before it doesn't detonate?

"You rose out of the ashes." I try to mollify her. "There's no point in burying us. You survived. You're thriving. You're leading the PLA, one of the biggest worldwide organizations. Where is Pierre-Jacques, anyway?"

"He's out of the country on another errand." She titters. "Or maybe several errands. We've been very busy planting our seeds. They're ready to bloom."

"You don't need to take us down to prove your greatness."

A hint of a smile touches her lips. "The point, dear sister, is that I *can* do it. I was left with a monster of a man, and I learned to adapt. Every day, a different version of myself. Whatever meant I didn't get hurt. But there's power in that, too, isn't there? In being able to become the person someone *wants* you to be."

"There's a lot more happiness in being yourself," I murmur. "You're capable of redemption. We all are. You have to want it badly enough." Recovering ourselves comes at a different cost and manifests in unique ways, but we can seek it, embrace it.

Her sinister smile slips a little. "*This* is what I need. Once you're gone, I'll be happy. There'll be no more reminders about how much better my life could have been had my mother cared enough to take me. Had that man"—she points at my father—"not been a selfish bastard."

"Fine," she cries. "Fine. Punish me. Punish Charles. Just let Carys go. Don't make her pay for our mistakes."

"We all—" Jade is cut off by shouting somewhere outside the room. Her heels click on the floor as she goes to investigate.

Hope stirs in my chest, but it's too much to believe Finn has already found us. It's a skirmish among her men.

"Dissention in the ranks?" I ask. "Maybe you should go out and get them sorted."

The door opens, and Jade calls out, "What's going—" Bullets ping off metal, and she slams the door closed. Her heels click across the floor, and she slices through whatever is securing my ankles in one swift movement, nicking my skin in the process. She yanks me off my chair and hauls me into the far corner of the room with her, using me as a shield, facing the entrance. Her knife is pressed into my side.

Outside, the shooting and shouting goes on forever. Then I hear familiar voices—Lorcan and Kim. My ears strain for the voice I want to hear most, but if he's out there, he's not close enough yet.

"He came for me," I whisper. Whether or not he's spoken, they wouldn't be here without him. He's out there.

Jade chuckles in my ear. "And he'll get to watch you stabbed over and over again. You can bleed out in his arms. My knife will hit the right spots to make that happen."

"He'll kill you." I try to wriggle free, but the awkward angle of my arms makes it hard for me to move. She's also a lot stronger than she looks when she tugs me tight against her.

"I've got the remote to the bomb in my pocket," she croons. "None of us are walking out of here today."

"I'm leaving here, even if I have to crawl," I say. Can she sense how sweaty I am? How nerves have spilled out of me in the last few hours? I steel myself. Maybe I won't make it out of here. But I'm not giving her the gift of my fear. I'm not feeding her obsession.

She readjusts her grip on my arms, and I try to wrench myself free. Her nails dig into my skin, and the knife pricks my side.

"Careful, Carys, or you'll be dead before he arrives. I'm so looking forward to seeing his expression when he realizes he can't save you."

"I'm looking forward to seeing yours when you realize how terribly you've underestimated him." The shouts are outside the door, so loud they almost drown out my comment. The *rat-a-tat-tat* of gunfire rounds my mother's shoulders as she cries more silent tears. She thinks we're going to die. Not today, Mother. Not today.

The door flips open, but no one enters at first. "Carys?" Finn's voice, strong and sure, stops my heart.

"In here. She's got a knife. A detonator to the bomb in her pocket." The words leave me in a rush. She'd have to loosen her hold on my arms or on the knife she has digging into my side to stop me from talking. "My mother and father are tied to chairs. There's a bomb in here. I haven't seen a gun on Jade, but she's got a knife pressed to my side. A very sharp knife."

"Tell him whatever you want," she murmurs. "Nothing will save you. He can't save you."

Waves of hot and cold run through my body. Finn is here. Even if she stabs me, he'll get me to a hospital. He won't let me bleed out on the floor. She's no match for him. The words are a mantra in my head.

The door stays open, but no one enters. There's low, indistinguishable talking outside and the sound of more distant gunfire. Then, Finn steps in the entryway, and my heart kicks.

He's here. He came.

"Let her go." His voice is gruff. His gun is trained on her and me because she's using me as a cover "You're outnumbered. Outsmarted. There's no way out of this."

"I'll stab her over and over again before you even get a shot off." She presses harder with the knife, and it slips in before she slides it out. I give a muffled cry. "How does it feel? To know she can't be saved?"

Finn chuckles. "Feels like you don't know me very well." He shifts to his right and fires low. Jade's left leg collapses, and she digs the knife into me again before releasing me. She tries to brace herself against the corner.

She struggles to grab me, but he lunges, bringing me to his side. The knife, still lodged in my side, burns. How deep did it go? She makes eye contact with him and smirks. "Doesn't matter. This is the tip of the iceberg. So many Van de Berg employees will greet me on the other side. They'll never realize I was the cause of their demise. You can't stop what we've set in motion."

Finn answers her smirk with one of his own. "I would say 'watch me' but you'll be dead. Whatever you hoped to accomplish, I want you to understand you failed."

She stares at the spot where the knife is still embedded in me, and a slow smile spreads. "See you on the other side."

When Finn's gun goes off, I squash my face into his chest. A second shot follows, and there's a loud thump as Jade's body hits the concrete floor.

A sob rises from my toes, the fear I wouldn't let myself experience rushes up and out, and he holds me tight. He takes my tears and my pain and my fright. I glance at Jade's lifeless body, unable to believe she's dead, that this is over.

"I've got you," he whispers into my ear. "I've got you."

Lorcan and Kim rush around the room, releasing my mother and father. Kim crouches near the bomb, checking the connections and wires.

"The bomb might be a decoy. Doesn't look like anything I've dismantled before. I've phoned it in. We need to get out of here," Kim calls over her shoulder. "Thomas's men are covering us. There're still a few live ones out there."

Finn lifts me into his arms and carries me out of the building, past the dead PLA agents, past some of Thomas's men who are also dead. Sporadic gunfire goes off around us. He climbs the stairs from the basement to the main floor, and I burrow into his chest, relishing his closeness. My side aches from the knife.

"She stabbed me," I murmur to Finn. "In my side, at least twice." Tiredness is seeping in.

"She's losing blood, Finn. A lot of it," Kim shouts from behind us. "Get her to the hospital. Lorcan and I will wait here for backup."

"I need a driver." He catches one of Thomas's men. "You. Drive us to the hospital."

At the SUV, he slides me into the back seat and follows me. The man he flagged as the driver wheels us out of the parking lot and speeds along the highway.

"It is a lot of blood?" I try to lift my head, but I'm woozy. "I think the knife is still in there."

"No, no." Finn brushes a hand over my hair. "You'll be fine. Just fine."

The tension in his voice makes me realize maybe I won't be, but I don't have the energy to argue. Instead, my cheek settles against his leg, and my eyes drift closed.

Chapter Forty-One

Finn

Carys is pale against the white sheets in the hospital room. She lost a lot of blood, but they were able to stitch her up and give her a transfusion. Thank God, she's going to be okay.

When she passed out in the car, I thought I screwed up again by holding her too long and letting Jade talk when I should have been ending her. I should have rushed Carys out of there and straight to the hospital. Now I'm sitting here, staring at her as she sleeps off the pain medication they gave her. At least she doesn't have to stay here overnight. As soon as she's awake and not too groggy, we can go.

Kim stands in the doorway, her arms folded across her chest. "I negotiated a day and a bit for you. You'll have to turn yourself into the local police, not tomorrow morning but the next morning at nine a.m."

"Didn't I save the world?"

She rolls her eyes. "*We* did, yeah. They caught Pierre-Jacques in Chicago with a crew. He'll never see the light of day. The other bombs were found and dismantled in the locations we pinpointed, including the one in Cork. The bomb with Carys was a decoy. The real device was in the next room. Who knows what Jade intended to do? In the Chicago office alone, hundreds of lives were saved. Probably a few thousand overall with the detonation times."

"I saved the day, and they're still going to put me away?" I eye her, annoyed, even though it's not her fault.

"You did the crimes, now you serve the time."

"I get tomorrow night too?"

"It was the best I could do. I realized you'd want to be sure Carys was fine before you went back."

"I need to check in with Semyon." I rise from my seat.

"Jay called the Volkovs." Lorcan appears at Kim's side. "He's organized Carys's plane. Everyone will be at Thomas's house tomorrow night for one last hurrah."

My chest tightens at the realization I'll get to see Lucas before I return to jail for another three years. Bittersweet. At least everyone will be there for what I want to do for Carys.

I stare at Kim for a beat, debating whether I can or should bridge the gap. "Once I get Carys settled at Thomas's house. Can you run an errand with me?"

Kim raises her eyebrows. "Just me?"

"Yeah," I say. "I promise it's nothing bad. I want to do something for Carys, and I'd appreciate some guidance." What do I know about girly shit?

Kim and Lorcan exchange a glance, and he gives a nod of approval. "Okay," she says. "I can do that."

Every ring looks the same. We're on our third jewelry shop in Dublin, and Kim hasn't seen one yet that she thinks Carys will like. Part of me expected her to pick the first decent-looking one, so she didn't have to be alone with me. While I wouldn't call her talkative, she's been very thorough in her examination of any ring she's considered suitable. I don't have a clue, so it's comforting she has an idea of Carys's taste.

"Not sure if Lorcan mentioned it," I say as we wander down another row of rings, peering into the cases. "I suggested he come to Cape Verde for a beer or two when you're both done working."

Kim stills beside me. "A beer or two?"

"Or however many you want. Carys and I will have a hotel and casino to run. Lots of jobs if either of you wants to semiretire on the island."

"You've got another three years before you need to worry about that." Her tone is acidic.

Normally, I'd bite back, but I understand her conflicted response to me. "I realize that. I appreciate the extra time out you negotiated." We pause by one of the glass cases, and Kim searches my face.

"I don't think I'll ever be able to forgive you for what you did to my family. To my brother. Sometimes I wish I was the type to sweep it aside, but I can't."

"I'm not the type to brush it aside either," I say. "I'm actually impressed you didn't drive a knife into my back during this assignment."

Her dark eyes turn sad. "I could never do that to Lorcan. Despite everything, he loves you. And while I can't forgive you, in the last couple of weeks, I've seen the reasons why he loves you—why Carys loves you. You're not all bad, Finn Donaghey. Maybe someday you'll even be good."

"I'm working on it." I smirk. "I'm not going to be the father to Lucas that my father was to me. I'm going to raise him better. I'm going to be better. I can guarantee that."

"I won't stand in the way of you having a relationship with Lorcan, or from him having the chance to be an uncle to your son. So, if he wants to come for that beer, then we'll be there." She turns to peer into the case and then points to a ring. "There," she says. "That one."

I stare at the diamond she's selected, and though I don't understand cuts or settings, a calmness settles over me. I can imagine this ring on Carys's hand. "I'll take it," I say to the saleslady when she wanders over.

"Would you like it sized?" the saleswoman asks. "We can have it ready for you in an hour."

I grimace, but Kim holds up a hand. "I've got this. I went jewelry shopping with her enough to know her ring finger. She used to try on and buy a lot of jewelry." The woman gives Kim a slip of paper, and Kim scribbles down a size.

An hour later, I've got my future secured in my pocket.

As soon as Lena and Sofia arrived and finished fussing over Carys and Jay, I enlisted their help in decorating the gazebo overlooking a small pond on Thomas's property. They sent runners to get these tiny lights, flowers, and rose petals. I'm not too proud to admit when I need help. Romance is not my thing, but I've got to create a moment that'll last Carys for the next three years of small tables and stolen conversations. Maybe I can't give her everything she wants right now, but I can give her the promise something better is coming our way.

"He remembers you." Carys strokes my arm while I feed Lucas his bottle.

"He won't be drinking a bottle next time I see him, will he?" He's making little contented noises in my arms while he sucks back the formula.

"Since you're going back to minimum-security"—she tries to catch my gaze—"I can bring Lucas for visits. I can arrange for you to see each other. It'll make the transition easier in three years."

"Will he remember seeing me in there?" While I don't want to hide my past from Lucas as he grows up, he doesn't need the full weight of the decisions I made—the bad things I've done.

"I don't know," Carys admits. "He'll be almost four when you get out. So, he might. But I think it's more important for you two to have a connection than whether he remembers you were once in jail."

I take a deep breath and give her what she wants because maybe it's what I want too. "Yeah," I say. "He can come. If you think it's a good idea."

She kisses my cheek and snuggles into me, looping her hands around my bicep. "The next three years won't be easy," she says. "But I'm sure they'll be worth it."

The lights are strung, the petals are flipping in the breeze, and there are giant vases of flowers at the entrance to the gazebo. I told Carys I had last-minute calls to make before I have to turn myself in tomorrow morning. She didn't even question it. Kim and Carys are walking around the property, and Kim agreed to end their walk at the pathway that leads to the gazebo. I check my watch. She should be here soon.

Are most men nervous when they propose? It's not something I ever thought much about. I'm not nervous about the marriage, and I'm not worried she won't say yes. Mostly, I'm worried I haven't gone big enough, extravagant enough in my proposal. I don't want to let her down.

There's a shuffling noise along the path, and then Kim says in a loud voice. "Why don't you go check out the gazebo? I have to reply to this message from Lorcan."

"Oh." Carys's voice drifts on the wind. "Sure. Thomas said it's a lovely lookout over the pond."

Kim chuckles. "I'm sure it is."

Carys comes around the corner, and even in the dim lighting from the strands strewn around, her expression is everything I could have hoped for.

"Finn," she breathes out and takes the two steps up to the wooden platform where I'm standing. "Did you do this?"

My lips tip into an almost-smile. "I'd love to take the credit. I am this amazing, but I had help."

"Wow," she murmurs taking in the petals, the lights, the view of the pond, the bouquets of flowers. "This is incredible."

Relief rushes through me. As long as she likes the presentation, the rest is easy. I have to speak from the heart which used to be impossible but doesn't feel so difficult anymore. "We've got a tough few years ahead of us, but I wanted to give you a really good memory to hold on to. Something concrete to look forward to in three years." I draw the ring box out of my pocket.

Carys frames my face, and there are tears in her eyes. She kisses me hard. "Yes," she says against my lips.

I chuckle. "Haven't even asked you yet. I've got this whole sentimental speech planned. You don't want to hear it?"

She stares up at me, and I've never loved anyone more. "Carys Van de Berg, you've had my heart for probably more years than you realize. I worshiped you from afar as a kid, loved you fiercely when I was still too much of a boy, and now as a man, I can't imagine my life without you in it. So, I'm not even going to try." I go down on one knee and open the ring box. "Will you marry me?"

She wraps her arms around my neck and sits on my bended knee. "Yeah," she says. "I can't wait to be your wife." She kisses me.

"I can't wait to see what you can cook up with three years to plan."

"You'll be horrified." She traces my face with her index finger.

"And I'll love every minute of it." I take the ring out of the box and slip it onto her finger. As soon as it's secure, a sense of peace blankets me. The next three years might be hard, might even feel impossible some days, but prison isn't where we end. We've got a future together.

Epilogue

Carys

Three Years Later

My stomach flutters. It's the same sensation I have each time I walk into the minimum-security prison to visit Finn except I'm not walking in; he's walking out. My plane is fueled and ready to take us home to Cape Verde. Today is the start of the rest of our lives together. No more fingertip holds and longing glances across a tiny table. Tomorrow, we're getting married, and I'll officially be his wife. Though he's been referring to me as his wife since the night he proposed.

Every time I heard him call me his spouse to a guard or another inmate waiting for the phone, a thrill raced down my spine. Finn Donaghey as a happily married man. Who would have called this outcome a few years ago? None of us, I bet.

When the metal gate retracts, he wanders out and squints against the sun. His hands are thrust in his pockets. My palms are slick with nerves, and I slide them along the sides of my skirt. Why am I nervous?

He comes to a stop inches from me and searches my face. Then his hands slide along my cheekbones and into my hair. A sigh escapes me at the contact, at being close enough to catch a whiff of his familiar scent. He slants his mouth over mine and kisses me like I am the sweetest thing he's ever tasted. He devours me, and I cling to him. One of his hands leaves my face to cup my ass, tugging me flush against him so I have no doubt where this embrace is headed.

I roam his body, delighting in everything that's still the same. "I missed you," I whisper when we break apart.

He smooths my hair and stares deep into my eyes. "I can't wait to marry you."

"The plane is ready to go." I tug him toward the car. "Let's get you home."

He chuckles. "First, I might want to get you out of these clothes." His finger runs along the hemline of my shirt.

"It's just you, me, and the pilot." I slide into the back seat, and Finn follows.

I buckle myself into the middle spot, so we're cuddled together. He traces everywhere on my body his hand can reach without removing clothes. Will we make it to the plane before we're tearing off our clothes?

"Lorcan and Kim are in Cape Verde?" His voice is husky.

"Yeah." I run a finger along his arm. "They're in between assignments. Kim says the last one they did might have been the last. Lorcan ended up in the hospital. Scared her, I think."

I haven't told Finn the truth about tomorrow's ceremony. I've been teasing him with details for months—all made-up, escalating in their extravagance. So, for him to come out of jail and say he can't wait to marry me knowing I've planned a spectacle, well, that's love.

"I remember." He nuzzles my neck. "How far is the airport?"

I chuckle and kiss him. He shifts and deepens the kiss, and it's all I can do not to unbuckle my seat belt and climb onto his lap. So surreal to have him close. I want to cling to him so tight he never slips away again.

"The hotel and casino are doing well?" His tongue flicks against my earlobe.

"Yes." I'm breathless. His lips capture mine, and I'm lost again.

The driver in front clears his throat. "We're here."

We break our embrace and grin at each other. Finn kisses my forehead and tugs me out the door behind him. We climb the stairs to the plane, almost drunk with desire. Are we ripping each other's clothes off or savoring every moment?

Three years.

At the top of the stairs, the pilot greets us. "I'll need you to stay in your seats until we reach cruising altitude. I'll make an announcement when that happens."

Finn and I lock gazes and then settle into the chairs farthest from the cockpit. The door to the pilot is locked, and he'll be too busy flying the plane to interrupt us. I hesitate for a second.

"It's a long flight," Finn says. "And I've got three years to make up for with you." He winks. "You can catch me up on all the chatter before we reach cruising altitude. After that, the only talking I want is 'yes, yes; more, more; give it to me.'" There's a wicked glint in his eyes.

"Deal," I breathe out, and my body is ready to go in an instant.

His fingers dance along the edge of my skirt. "How are Jay, Sofia, and the girls?"

We taxi down the runway. "Everyone is settled and happy. Lena," my voice hitches when his finger slides up my skirt. "Lena has a new boyfriend."

"She's making up for all that lost time with Charles." His breath stirs the hair by my ear, and I shiver.

We're forced back against our seats as the plane rises into the air.

"You've kept your parents cut off?" There's warning in his voice, but I don't mind.

"Yes," I say. "I learned my lesson more than once. Nothing good comes from having them in my life." They tried to reach out once Finn was back in prison, but I made it clear our relationship was done forever.

He nods and squeezes my thigh. "Does Lena or Sofia have Lucas?"

"They're probably fighting over him right now. He's a well-loved little boy." A smile rises. "He's going to be so excited to see you."

"The visitations were a good idea. I'm not a stranger walking back into his life." He kisses my cheek.

"We have now reached our cruising altitude. You are free to move about the cabin unless we hit some unexpected turbulence."

Finn unsnaps my seat belt and his own. "Is the cabin door sound-proof?"

I laugh. "I don't know."

"We're gonna find out." He gives me a wicked grin, and then his lips descend on mine.

The last twenty-four hours since Finn got out have been a whirlwind in the best possible way. I've had three years to plan our wedding, and I started with grand plans, but I realized I didn't need something big and extravagant anymore. At one time, maybe I would have wanted a big venue, hundreds of people, a thousand bouquets of flowers, with decorations on overload.

Instead, we're getting married barefoot, on the beach, with only our family present.

At noon, Finn sips his coffee on the couch and eyes me. "Shouldn't you be doing something with your hair and applying makeup? Putting on a dress? Organizing the parade or whatever you told me you were doing?"

I laugh at his parade comment and gesture to my relaxed waves and everyday makeup. "I can't get married like this?"

"You can, but the five hundred people you invited might be expecting the full Carys experience." Finn smirks.

That's right. At my last visit I told him I found whittling down the invites impossible, so I expanded the guest list. My lips twitch with amusement.

"Daddy, can I please have a drink?" Lucas wanders over to the couch with his plastic cup.

Lucas has called Finn his father since he started speaking, but there's something about hearing it in this house that causes my body to glow with warmth. Since Finn arrived yesterday, Lucas hasn't been far from his side.

"Sure thing, buddy." He sets down his coffee, ruffles Lucas's hair, and goes to the fridge.

"You're probably right." I stretch. "I should start getting ready. I wouldn't want to disappoint anyone."

"What am I supposed to wear? Is it in a closet or something?" He pours the milk into a cup and passes it to our son. Such a simple thing, but my heart constricts for the thousandth time since he's arrived.

"Everything you need is in the spare room. Lorcan can show you when he gets back."

"What's he doing?" Finn asks, and he lifts Lucas into his arms at his request. He carries him over to the couch and perches him on his knee. The two of them sip their drinks and stare at me.

"Had to pick up a guest." I head for the bedroom. "Should be back soon." He went to collect the justice of the peace to marry us. Kim meets me in the hallway, a dress bag over her arm.

"Go-time?" she asks.

I grin. "I'm getting married," I squeal and escort her into the master bedroom.

There we spend the next hour getting ready. Kim is the lowest-maintenance woman I know, but since I've hired a photographer, I've cajoled her into wearing some makeup. All of us will remember this moment forever.

There's a knock on the door, and I peek out. Lena passes through two bouquets for Kim and me.

"So, you're just going to walk out there and get married?" Kim's skepticism is clear.

"Yep. I decided I didn't need all the pomp and circumstance. The right man, the right place, and the right people. Lorcan has probably told Finn by now that it's a low-key affair, right?"

"Oh," Kim says. "I'm sure. I'm also sure he's not going to believe him."

I check my appearance in the mirror again. He likes my hair down, so I haven't bothered to put it up, and instead it hangs in loose waves around my shoulders. My dress is my one extravagance. It's a custom-designed masterpiece that fits me to perfection. "I guess he's in for a pleasant surprise then."

"This is really what you wanted?" Kim smooths down her gown, which is the one we bought in the nearest city a week ago off the rack.

One of the perks of looking like a supermodel is the ability to throw on almost anything and have it fit.

I whirl around the center of the room and take a deep breath. "Three years to plan, and in the end, all I wanted was this beach, this man, and our son."

"I'm glad you're so happy," she says.

Our friendship has come a long way in three years. Lorcan and Kim have stayed here between assignments several times, and Lucas calls them aunt and uncle. Family doesn't have to share blood.

"All right." I check the clock on the nightstand. "Let's do this."

Kim throws open the bedroom door and leads the way to the beach. There, a trellis sits in the sand strung with flowers. Underneath and beside it stand all the people I love: Finn, Lorcan, Jay, Sofia, Rosa, Luciana, Lena, and Lucas. They're all here to witness our happily ever after.

A photographer snaps photos, but I can't tear my gaze from my husband. Legal or not, he's been mine for a long time. Today we're making it official and forever.

When I get to Finn, there's a sheen of tears in his icy gaze. "I never thought I'd get this." His voice is thick. "I never really believed I'd get this."

Ignoring everyone else, I cup his chin and give him a quick kiss. "We made it," I say. "I'm never letting you go."

Instead of starting the ceremony, he tugs me tight against him and whispers, "I love you, Carys. Forever."

Want more? You can read bonus chapters here: https://bookh ip.com/NCSMMST

Bellerive Royals Series – Interconnected standalones

Fake Crown

Scarred Crown

Heavy Crown

Fallen Crown

Tucker Billionaires – Interconnected standalones

Temporary Love
Fierce Love
Colliding Love
Reckless Love

New Adult Sports

Saving Us

Fake Crown

Donaghey Brothers Series – Romantic suspense

Retribution

Resurrection

Redemption

Little Falls Series – Small Town Romance

Rival Hearts

Mending Hearts

Healing Hearts

Guarded Hearts

First Date Challenge – loosely linked to the same world – for maximum enjoyment, read after Book 2

Adult Contemporary Romance

When Stars Fall

Miss Matched

About Wendy Million/W. Million

Wendy Million is a high school teacher whose award winning contemporary romances about strong women and troubled men have captivated her loyal readers.

Writing as Wendy Million, she is the author of the romantic suspense series *The Donaghey Brothers,* as well as the contemporary second chance romances, *When Stars Fall*, and *Miss Matched*.

Writing as W. Million, she's the author of the *Bellerive Royals* series, the *Little Falls* series, and the *Tucker Billionaires* series.

When not writing, Wendy enjoys spending time in or around the water. She lives in Ontario, Canada with two beautiful daughters, two cute pooches, and one handsome husband (who is grateful she doesn't need two of those).

Acknowledgements

Thank you to Shanoff Designs for the awesome new covers for this series. She was incredibly patient as we worked toward the final version.

Thank you to my husband, Jay, and my daughters, Hannah and Autumn. I would not be able to do this without your love and support.

Thank you to everyone who contacted me after they read Retribution or Resurrection. There's nothing better than sharing this world with you. Your excitement is a gift.

A special thank you to my beta readers and alpha readers who made sure my plot held together: Rositza Bratovanova, Carmen Insfran, H.H, Jabulile Tshabalala, Mariannareti, Renee Womack, Sherylin Barrientos, Nicole Bontaine, Yvette Davids, and Tamara Smith. Thanks to superfan Sammy who has loved this series from the start.

Thank you to all my first reviewers from Resurrection: Rositza Bratovanova, Wairimu Kibathi, Carmen Insfran, Jennifer Thompson, Ashley Haltom, Liana Reads, Samantha Grubey, Meka Rascoe, Phyllis Jones Pisanelli, Misty Donohue. Michelle Sauve, Taryn Reder, Sumaiyah M, Celeste Williams, Karen Sampson-Venzon, Stephanie Kazowz, Sherylin Barrientos, 2user38, Juliann Nordstrom, and Camilla Gunzel. Each one of you has given me such an incredible gift by offering encouragement, criticism, and passion for my stories when I've needed it most. I'm here because you stuck with me and made me feel like my work had value.

Thank you, Cole Lepley, my writing bestie, and biggest Finn cheerleader. I wrote this book during a global pandemic, and without you nudging me for the next set of chapters, it probably would have taken me a lot longer to write. Thanks for going on this writing journey with me.

www.ingramcontent.com/pod-product-compliance
Lightning Source LLC
Chambersburg PA
CBHW021022310726
48969CB00006B/1508